THE WINTERING

STORM

Stephen Bowkett was born and brought up in a mining valley in South Wales. He taught English at secondary school in Leicestershire for many years before becoming a full-time writer, and a qualified hypnotherapist. He has published over thirty books, mainly science fiction and fantasy, for both adults and children. He also writes poetry, plays and educational non-fiction.

Storm is the second part of The Wintering, a major trilogy. You can learn more about the world of The Wintering, and check out Steve's other books, by visiting his website:

www.sbowkett.freeserve.co.uk

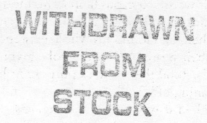

Also by Stephen Bowkett

Dreamcastle

Dreamcatcher

Ice
(Book 1 of The Wintering trilogy)

THE WINTERING

STORM

STEPHEN
BOWKETT

Dolphin Paperbacks

JF

6204946.

First published in Great Britain in 2002
as a Dolphin paperback
by Orion Children's Books
a division of the Orion Publishing Group Ltd
Orion House
5 Upper St Martin's Lane
London WC2H 9EA

A catalogue record for this book
is available from the British Library

Typeset at The Spartan Press Ltd, Lymington, Hants

Printed in Great Britain by
The Guernsey Press Co. Ltd, Guernsey, C.I.

ISBN 1 85881 874 5

A dream came to me
at deep midnight
when humankind
kept their beds
– the dream of dreams!
I shall declare it.

From 'The Dream of the Rood',
The Earliest English Poems, trans.
Michael Alexander

Contents

1

A New Day

The day had no beginning and would have no end, because time no longer carried any meaning in Kell's mind. Everything existed in the present moment and nothing was good or bad – it just *was*.

Kell found himself lying on a hard surface in a white room. The place smelt strange; not of the natural world. And he could hear sounds nearby, odd hummings, the tinkling of metal and glass, murmuring voices . . .

A man with a kind face and bronze-coloured skin came over to Kell and smiled. Kell thought he had seen the man before. When? Why? He had no idea.

'How are you today?'

'I don't know.'

'Do you feel well today?'

'I think so.'

Now the man was bending close, attending to something in Kell's eyes. Kell thought that the man wasn't really interested in anything he said, but when he nodded as he answered, the man made a sound of irritation and gripped Kell's head harshly at the sides and held him still. Kell quietened instantly, because another idea came to him just then; a memory of pain if the man or any of his helpers were not happy . . .

'We have something different for you today,' the man was saying. He tapped Kell's forehead briskly with a stiff forefinger. Kell's eyes focused and his whole attention hung on the meaning of the man's words . . .

Except the man was no longer there and Kell was dreaming again and he could see Shamra – Shamra! His heart clenched with the strength of his love for her – and then he quailed in horror as a silver dog-like creature sprang forward, cuffed her to the ground, and mounted upon her chest, dipping its muzzle to her throat.

'No! No! Let her be!'

'Stop it then,' said the man's voice very close. Kell's hand curled around the familiar smoothness of his knife's jewelled handle and he felt the power rising in him; the red power, the blood heat.

Miraculously he was able to leap up from the table. The strange room had gone and he was outside amongst trees and rocks and hills.

Kell yelled at the beast; it was an inarticulate sound of rage. The creature took a moment to look away from its prey, and there was blood on its face and the same hot light in its eyes as in Kell's.

Kell snatched up a stone and hurled it. His arm had known what to do, and the missile flew well and found its mark, striking the animal square in the jaw. It yelped, howled, flowed back over itself and then was running with the same liquid grace into the trees.

Kell immediately gave chase, caught on the hook of his hatred. Nearby, Shamra faded back into the nothingness from which she had been conjured. And the man with the smiling face and the glossy bronze skin leaned intently over a screen and read its messages of light, and every now and then reached forward to make some small alteration to the texture of the running boy's dream. How far could the child be pushed to ignore all that he had ever been taught in favour of his basic instincts? And could the wulf be similarly programmed? These answers had yet to be revealed, but already much had been learned and Helcyrian was bound to be pleased.

The beast – the *eargnewulf*, the miserable one – was nothing more than a silvery blur in the gloom of the tree shadows. Kell did not know this place, but some deep part of him understood the nature of the land and how he could best survive here. He slowed and calmed himself, reined in his surging breath, took stock of what was around him . . .

An ancient forest but not a healthy one; it was deprived of good light. The thin soil was stony and its nourishment had leached away long ago. It was no more than a shallow mantle, beneath which would lie porous rock riddled with tunnels and caverns, mineral-hoards and metals. Kell swept up all of these impressions too quickly for him to wonder upon them or trouble over where they had come from. Now he became aware of the smells of the breeze, laced with meanings that flickered so fleetingly by: but all of them, all of them, calling.

Kell was wary of what was happening. He had experienced this strange longing in his head once before. It was a dangerous moment. He calmed himself and smiled because he knew that the eargnewulf had been trying to sing to his thoughts and tempt him to his death.

But the wulf was just as frightened as Kell and just as much a stranger here. Like the boy it was using its instincts to read the stones and the trees; and those impressions had become caught up in its song and clouded it over.

Kell knew that his quarry was up in the rocks a little behind him to the left. It was going to higher ground for better vantage and . . . something else, too subtle to know about yet. But anyway, the creature was tired and afraid and lost and alone . . .

Kell moved quickly and blended in with the trees, tacking across the cut of the breeze to keep his scent away from the wulf. He heard the clatter of pebbles as it moved from its spying-place – and there it was ahead, struggling over rocks, scrabbling with some desperation now to reach the network of tunnels higher up in the hill. Its siren song was in ruins and now the advantage lay in Kell's hands.

The wulf disappeared in shadow, became a brief ghost as Kell's eyes adjusted, then truly vanished as it found the cave mouth and darted inside.

Kell reached the threshold a few moments later and remembered his own wisdom: he let his breath settle and began to listen to the small sounds inside the cave. And in that second the little frightened one swept out of the shadows and struck at Kell's knife with its paw. But the boy also moved by instinct; equally raw in youth, tight as a bowstring in his need to survive. The arm lifted to take the force of the blow and then snapped outwards, slicing the blade across the wulf's flank. The creature yowped and tumbled back in a tangle of gangling limbs, kicking dust in an effort to run.

Kell saw the red slash of blood on its fur and felt the death-thrill lift in him like an ecstasy. He changed his hold on the knife to a stabbing grip and plunged forward, following the bloodscent and the swirls in the sand where the animal had fled on into the dimness – on and on until there was a confusion of marks and a speckling of blood drops on the crumbled rocks to the right –

Too late he looked up into the eyes of the wulf, which leapt lithely from a crag along the line of its gaze and used the shock of surprise as much as the weight of its body to drive Kell backwards and down. Kell flailed out. His fist struck rock and the pain was a sickening bolt through his bones.

Seek to slay Fenrir and you only make him stronger!

The boast was hot with arrogance, though with little experience to give it any depth. And it infuriated Kell, so that the creature's snapping teeth and red jaws and the hardness of its muscles beneath the sleek silver fur lost their power to intimidate and drove him further into a fury.

And that strength feeds back to me, so I make an end of you!

Kell flexed his body as his left hand reached up to clamp round the muzzle of the wulf. He rolled over, pinning the animal beneath him; pushed back the head so the creature's white neck was exposed and the pace of its life was a swift pulsing rhythm in the skin. He brought the knife ready, envisioned the act . . .

And something stayed his hand, something beyond reason or rage, so that the words of the bronze-skinned man became discordant in the clutter of his mind, making no sense to him now.

Beneath him the young animal settled, though not in the passivity of surrender. It was listening.

And now Kell heard it too, a rattle of stones beyond the glare of the cave mouth; crunching gravels; a heavy tread.

Then a massive paw cuffed Kell aside with easy authority. The little space where the younglings had fought filled with a heavy musk, and Kell found himself looking up into the terrifying white-hot glare and fearsome jaws of a fullgrown buck wulf.

Be still.

The command was clear, but Kell's fright was endless. Pointlessly he started to struggle and scream. The wulf pressed him down with a limb that felt like an immovable rod of steel. The other forepaw snicked out a spray of claws and loomed towards his eyes.

There followed a confusion of thoughts and feelings and intense pain in his eyes that came and went and returned again more horribly. Trees and rocks, creatures of every kind, people's faces, events and hours and days swirled by and hurtled at the lens. Reality washed over him and left him helpless like a baby; wallowing, washed up on the floor of a dry cave with these proud and powerful animals standing over him.

You are free of the weorthan. Get up! Follow us!

The instructions boomed in Kell's head. They came from the same huge creature that had pinned him down, the pack leader. But there was no limb holding him now, only his own weakness and relief.

'Thank you – thank you –' He laughed at the inadequacy

of his words, and the fact that wulfen made little of human speech. But his intention must have been clear, for the pack leader whisked him up and swung him round so that Kell was clinging to the animal's neck even as he struggled to swing his leg over the undulating power of its back. And they ran deeper into the darkness of the cave.

Behind them the air was filled with an angry sizzling. The wulf leader leapt over a boulder greater than its own height, despite being encumbered by the weight of the boy. The instant was burned in ragged shadows on the rock wall, and Kell realised that others had come into the tunnels, enemies of them both.

Stay still!

In another moment Kell was joined by Littlewulf; the pack leader had grabbed him by the scruff of his neck and flung him to safety with an effortless flick of the head. Wulf and human regarded each other warily, though the hostility was gone out of them now. Littlewulf sniffed at Kell, and Kell sniffed inquisitively in response . . .

Near the cave mouth the heat-weapon flared again, and there was a shriek and the sense of injury among the pack. The dazzle of daylight became partially blocked by bulky silhouettes, armoured warriors who must have followed Kell and the young wulf here. Probably they had not expected an ambush, for their shock was like exploding colours, like a sudden sour taste.

And even as Kell watched the six or so wulfen do battle with the soldiers, he found himself intrigued, and honoured to be included in their thoughts, for surely that was what was happening to him now. It was a strange experience, like being in another land filled with unfamiliar sights, yet with an underlying certainty of welcome, all carried on the animals' song in his brain. That song was calling now, but like an undercurrent to the scalding passion of the battle. The iron-clad men were slow and disorientated. They had expected to find two younglings fighting, not the formidable force of wild creatures stronger than themselves and driven by a fearsome intent.

The lead wulf rose up from the darkness and his claws lashed out – shreek shreek – and scored bright streaks in the dulled grey metal of the warrior's chestplate. Then its head tilted and the awful jaws were clamped around the man's neck, tightening, tightening.

The soldier gave a gurgling gasp and sagged at the knees, bent backwards and crumpled. In a spasm he clenched at the heat-gun and an arc of flame roared up and back across the rock ceiling and gushed out of the entrance into the faces of the men who followed.

Meanwhile, a second wulf darted forward and made a snarling lunge at the leg of another stumbling warrior. Kell saw a chunk taken clean out. The man screamed and dropped forward. His attacker came in from the side and slammed him against a jut of rock; held him there while the jaws made an end of him swiftly and with brief pain, which is the dignified way.

Then the wulfen pack were running, just a few steps ahead of a tide of fire which surged and billowed like brilliant vapour into the tunnel. One wulf, engulfed, crashed heavily to the floor, and turned, and all aflame launched itself back at the advancing men.

Kell experienced the brilliance of its sacrifice which overwhelmed even its agony; though out of compassion the one-mind of the other pack animals reached out and ended its life even as the burning weight of flesh found its mark.

Down! Down this way!

The command cracked out clear and Littlewulf and Kell reacted together. The tunnel split and split again into a puzzle of ancient fissures. And the younglings simply followed the brilliant certainty of the pack leader as he made sense of the blackness and led them away from the danger. Far behind came angry shoutings and the harsh rush of the soldiers' weaponry; rocks exploded and the distance was filled with the fading sounds of pointless firings.

This way – here!

The dry earth sloped away like a throat into the ground. Kell, disconcerted by the steep angle, ran far too fast and overbalanced. He fell forwards on to his stomach and slid a little way, winded. Littlewulf beside him helped him up. The pack leader slowed, and warned him now to take extra care.

Kell soon knew why: the angle of the passageway became more acute, hard smooth rock replacing the soft powdery sand. Perhaps an old watercourse, long dried out. Kell felt the pack leader's caution and heard the scrape of his claws on stone. In his head there was an impression of openness – an underground chamber – and an unbidden knowledge of ledges and falls and the route through to their final freedom.

Just ahead of him there was a whisper and the lead wulf was gone. He had sprung into the darkness and landed lightly on a lip of rock a few body-heights down and one span out. Kell drew back and felt his breath lock in his chest . . .

But the wulf's eyes were his now, too. All that went before, the whole gift of the pack's shared mind, had prepared him for this brief ordeal. Wulfen sight had evolved beneath a million moons, and darkness was not a barrier to them. Wondrously, just for a moment or two, Kell was looking up at himself; and then at his body rushing down the glossy curtain of tawny stone, and being snatched easily by the buck wulf's jaws and held until his breathing had slowed and his exhilaration was only a flickering flame.

The others followed like elegant grey ghosts, one after another with equal ease. Littlewulf came up beside his new friend, this young slow-eyes whose passion was still greater than his knowledge, and loped beside him and was warmed by their feelings of friendship. He began to look forward again to the endless expanse of the forests and the hills –

But his leader stopped the thoughts with a stern command,

8

and suddenly the entire party was quiet and still, held by a fine anticipation.

Something else was coming. A new dread.

Making a small and almost dismissive grunt, the lead wulf sent Kell and Littlewulf along the way, to a narrow vertical crack in the rock that marked the final phase of their escape.

I smell the open sky!

The idea came to Kell as an excitement rather than in words. He responded with a smile and a glow of pleasure, and allowed his wulfling companion to lead him through the narrow cleft to a point where they could wait in safety for the rest . . .

Machinery was clanging clumsily through the tunnels. The pack leader, whose wulfen name was Magula, held back and watched it coming. There was greater danger in this, but only by his own direct experience could he know the nature of the threat and use it to help him survive in the future.

So he crouched low behind cover with his eyes like winter stars, drinking in the last drop of light. And presently he saw them, two globes spinning erratically into view; their senses confused by the proximity of rock and perhaps by the presence of magnetic minerals in the hill. However it was, their progress was anything but elegant. One struck a jutting tooth of jagged stone and wobbled away into open space, over-compensating a second later by swirling back too far, hitting the sidewall again, losing control and lodging fast in a gap. The other hovered lower to check on the plight of its companion . . .

The tension changed. Magula could almost hear the clicking of reactions deep inside the machines; the bitter stink of metal contacts; the first blue kindling of explosives –

He whirled about and with a brief sharp bark sent his kin hurrying through the narrow rifts, squeezing among a choke of boulders to the final double-dogleg of a tunnel, drenched by streamwater, that would bring them into the light.

Then behind them the whole hill trembled and a huge

pressure-wave of hot air and rock splinters and chemical smokes erupted out. In unison the wulfen ducked and hunkered down – but at Magula's command they ran on, while all around them dust ghosts swirled and the reek was unbearable and the noise of stone sundered and sundered again rang through the caverns in a series of thunderous detonations.

Kell, scorched and stinging from a hundred fresh cuts, dragged himself gasping along the last exhausting stretch into the sunlight, which at that moment was as much a pain as a pleasure. Behind him the last wulfen rescuer came leaping out between the mossy lips of a gap in a little cliff hidden on a forest-cloaked hillside. Then for many heartbeats they waited with patience to see if anything human or otherwise should follow, to be assured of their safety, at least for a time.

Kell sat with strangeness all around him, but felt no tension. The struggle underground had taken all of his strength for the present: if a sparrow had attacked him he could not have beaten it off. These animals, the wulfen, were many times more powerful than he was and their motives in letting him live were unclear. Yet he felt welcomed and comfortable among them, and while they went about licking their wounds and keeping watch, they let him alone to recover.

And that recovery happened for the most part *within*.

The old life came back first; the life of Perth; little things like Gifu's chidings and earthy wisdoms and the deep-rooted love he had felt for Kell despite his troublesomeness: the way they had sat on a grassy slope and watched what they thought was the whole world laid out before them: then the daylong ploughings and the warm solid bulk of the moxen . . . stupid moxen, that needed to be instructed by glass and metal inside their heads . . . as people needed to be, until a few found otherwise, like Kano whose outrage knew no bounds; and tortured Feoh who had given up her beauty the better to see and to hate; and Shamra whose face Kell tried to recall now: Shamra who had loved him so, enough to follow him past the edge of the world —

Elsewhere is nowhere Kell. Elsewhere is nowhere!

'No!' Kell forced his attention outwards to the mass of dark green pines and the steep-sided valley beyond, and past that to the misty pinnacles of the mountains.

Else-where is now-here?

Littlewulf had padded up close and sat on his haunches, head tilted sideways, watching this odd slow-eyes do battle with himself. Such an unusual chaotic fathomless fascinating breed.

Kell smiled and Littlewulf was puzzled even further.

'Yes, yes that's right. In fact, everywhere is now-here! I am Kell.'

I am Fenrir, the clear thought came back. And then the wulfling confessed freely that he didn't understand Kell's ideas at all. And equally clumsily Kell assured him that this did not matter in the least.

Later, once the sun had dropped behind them over the shoulder of the hills, and the chill and the blue sky were deepening, Magula joined Kell's newfound wulfen friend, and shortly afterwards the rest of the pack circled in and a certain air of solemnity crept over the group. One wulf, a pack elder whose silver pelt was streaked with black, came and faced Kell who was shivering now and hungry and starting to be frightened.

A wave of reassurance was offered first. It had Feoh's power behind it but was purely wulfen, alien and wild. Kell dipped his head in recognition of the gesture. He smiled thanks and his teeth chattered. He could not have spoken clearly if he'd wanted to: but words were pointless here anyway, for certainly the pack made use of the same one-mindedness Kell had found in the Shore Folk, and in the other wulfen gang that had ambushed them far in the forest . . .

Again the reassurance, followed by the wulf elder's name – Tir – the giving of which was a valuable gift.

Although all wulfen are joined, and fruit of the same bush, we are very different in the way life has taken us forward. Tir explained that over generations some packs had slipped back towards the wildness of instinct, while others – like this one – found that the addition of reflective thought and what came to Kell's mind as 'future mapping' made more powerful tools for survival.

Therefore we have associated ourselves with humankin, who have those same qualities though in a different direction; prowling in and around and beneath the enclave of Thule where you were held prisoner, which is also known as the Broken Place, so that we can learn more. Soon that may have to change because of the Tarazad's ambitions. But for a thousand cycles of the moon we have become more familiar with the wisdoms of men.

Tir looked to the pack leader, whose golden eyes held an intensity even in this quiet time. And something passed between the two wulfen that was kept from Kell, though a few moments later another wulf, a big buck animal with a torn left ear, dragged some kill into the clearing in front of Kell's feet. It was a pale-furred deer (*heorot* was how Tir mind-sounded it to Kell) with small spiked horns just beginning to back-curve, and large black eyes that were elegant and beautiful even with the life gone out of them.

Torn-left-ear backed off, turned away briefly, and reappeared with Kell's knife. Incredibly he had thought to snatch it up in the heat of the earlier battle and bring it with him.

The intention was clear: Kell was hungry and cold and here was the means to solve that problem. He picked up the knife – and like a mischievous child the memory of Munin's hot stews came so strongly that Kell smelt them and his mouth immediately moistened.

Then he set to work, skinning the deer as best he could, guided by Torn-left-ear's promptings. The old sage had on many occasions watched the trappers perform this act, and he had learned what their hands knew. So Kell's attempt was not a total disaster, and once he had scraped the globules of fat and membranous tissue from the underside, he had what for tonight would be a blanket, but which with a little ingenuity would make a passable – if smelly – cloak.

Now sleep was rising in him faster than the dark. But Kell was acutely aware that these animals had saved his life. They were not base creatures, but proud and intelligent beings with a culture rooted in the mountains and the glacial ravines. He had come into their domain, and a certain etiquette needed to be observed.

They guided him patiently, allowing him to know what to do short of telling him outright. Wielding the knife again Kell cut a lean chunk of meat for himself from the heorot's flank. This he put aside for now. Then he went about carving further morsels; for Torn-left-ear who had provided the food, for Tir who had been the first bridge between wulfen and boy; for Fenrir out of friendship and for Magula the pack leader, with the greatest respect and trepidation, since it was by Magula's wish that Kell continued to live. What remained of the deer was left to the rest of the pack, some dozen wulfen in all, who stuck strictly to the law of the generations: the elders took meat first, down to the yearlings finally, who gnawed at the bones with little growlings of pleasure and mock ferocity. And as each wulf accepted the gift of food, its name arrived in Kell's mind bright as a flower, as treasured as the most cherished possession.

And so Kell's life changed as the meal went on. He became *gefera*, companion to the wulfen pack because he had stayed his hand and spared the life of young Fenrir, *haewenwulf!* – green in his ways. Now he would walk their path, and learn their nature and offer whatever wisdoms he could. They, in return, would sustain and keep him for as long as he desired. That was their pledge and it was as hot and strong and precious as their very heartsblood.

Once the sky had lost its last blue the stars came out in a

13

blaze, together with a thin moon that hung between the peaks like a delicate shaving of ice. Tir called it the Claw-of-the-circle moon, indicating its shape and position in its spin about the Earth. This was something that Kell did not entirely understand, and although his interest was tempered by weariness, he framed one or two polite questions and assured the elderwulf he would want to know more when his energies were restored. Apart from being fascinated himself of course, Skjebne would be eager for all of the knowledge that Kell was able to glean . . .

Sudden stinging tears came to Kell's eyes as he recalled his mentor's face and the full force of his love, and the doubt that was attached to his fate. How cruel that he didn't even know if Skjebne were still alive!

We are not done with Thule by any means, Tir reassured. *Our pryings may discover if your companion has survived.*

Kell's anguish had sprayed out a welter of memories and notions and speculations that even so did not amount to a single coherent impression. Tir did his best to keep up, while Fenrir sat nearby and laid his ears back in a simple sympathy which was all he could think of to give.

Our belief is that no one dies until all the lives he has touched have themselves ended . . . That came from Magula, mind-sent with such clarity and command that all of the pack as well as Kell paid immediate attention. The wulf himself was perched on a black rock looking out over the mountain vasts. He was absorbed in the sky and the landscape of scents that shimmered in the cold night air across the valley. But some part of him always stayed with his kin, close as a prayer, keen as the sharpest of fangs. Such was Magula, the *maegenwulf*, the strength of the pack.

He turned his head and gazed back at the boy, and all Kell saw were the two glowing discs of his eyes and a sharp yet subtle silhouette marked out by an absence of stars. Magula's mind burned in Kell's mind and showed him how to go through the labyrinthine way – not with regret and dread-at-what–never–might–be, but with great courage and great endeavour, which was the very essence of life truly lived.

And Kell took the counsel as he had earlier eaten the heorot's sweet flesh, and was nourished.

Presently, as Kell's thoughts ran on more placidly, slower now like a lowland stream, one by one the younger wulfen settled to their sleep. The fullgrown followed, save for Magula and Tir and two others who sat guard, their senses open to the night.

A burden shared is no longer a burden, Tir said. *Our way will take us back to Thule with certainty –*

And before the moon reaches its full fruiting, added Magula, having come to that decision by what Kell's deeper thoughts were telling him.

Even Tir seemed surprised by this, though Magula made light of it. He leaped silently down from his rock and moved through the pack, a warming strengthening presence.

You know how the Tarazad swarm among their ruins. My concern is that soon they will move out beyond the mountain fastness, in which case we must be ready to run before them, away from this land which they despoil. If it is to be so, there are certain preparations to make. We must discover their intentions as early as we can . . .

Tir nodded and made a brief yowl of agreement, but he recognised fear, however cleverly it was concealed: the taint of it was on Magula now, which Tir found deeply disturbing.

Nearby, the guardwulfen and Kell who was slipping into his slumber knew nothing of it. And presently Magula returned to his vantage point and watched the vanishing of the moon and soon after the rising of the star patterns that marked the imminence of the lean months. He smelt his bloodkin's suspicion, but hid his deception until Tir's probing mind withdrew and the elder wulf started to doze.

Kell was a leaf in the forest. He had blown from the tree at the time of the Fall, and the wind had taken him to a place of dark stone, where he had been drawn deep under among the

15

corrupted things. There followed a period of darkness and an ignorance of what lay within it – though also a horror that would stay with him forever.

Now the world was stirring and the cycles of change heaved him up through the soil to this new day. Kell opened his eyes and was washed by the cool clean brilliance of the infinite morning.

2

Wulfensong

Kell did not understand the wulfen word for the particular kind of rain which was falling that day: to him it was a thin, chilly drenching drizzle, relentless. But Fenrir, explaining slowly and carefully and with a sense of great duty to his new charge, added what the pack felt more deeply. This was peaceful rain that carried in it apple scents and the aroma of loam, settled life, an understanding that the great busyness of the fall-time was done. For many creatures the next arc of the circle was the deathsleep of hibernation through the hard-long-dark, but that time was not quite yet. First, this short spell of soft wet days was unfolding. The hunger of the forest predators was satisfied and their minds had not yet fully turned to face the coming snows. They too, or most of them, were quiescent and benign.

That was the message of this rain. Each whispering drop said the wierds were benevolent.

Nevertheless, Kell shivered as an icy trickle slid down his neck and spread through the material of his tunic. It was made of roughweave cotton and it itched and it smelt. One of the pack, scavenging, had dragged it back from somewhere – Kell did not enquire too closely over its origins. Probably it had belonged to an earth-digger from one of the outlying settlements. These outskirt communities which riddled the hills around Thule were often troubled by predators. In this case the man had lost his shirt but kept his life. Kell thought this was a good gain.

And the tunic itself was not so bad. Prickly, yes, and baggy over the shoulders, but with the underlayer that had been his clothing in Thule, and with the heorot pelt draped over all, he was warm and dry enough and had little real cause for complaint.

Now he tried to ease his position as he crouched among the delicate young birches on the hill overlooking the track. Sodden grass squeaked underfoot and beside him Fenrir made a harsh-breath sound and Magula's mental caution cracked through Kell's mind and turned him dizzy.

They do not see us, but they can easily know we are here!

Kell blushed, reprimanded, and settled back and endured the stiffness of his posture.

Since he had been accepted into the pack, half a moon cycle had passed and days had grown noticeably colder. Other wulfen moved among the mountains now: at least two groups that were *wildedeor*, wild and blood-led like the ones Kell's party had once encountered; and another with all of the mental capabilities of Magula's kin, but somehow more distant and guarded. Magula spoke tentatively of this pack's 'darker meditations', but it meant nothing to Kell, and in any case he knew in a factless way that the pack leader did not want to dwell on such things.

All of this movement, as wulfen and other creatures came down off the heights for winter, necessitated much prowling and sniffing out of territories and intentions. Kill was plentiful, so the hunters had no need to invade each other's land, but the ones who were wildedeor might plague the fringe towns and stir up the Tarazad and the other peoples who came to Thule for their huge diversity of reasons . . .

Like the three *wyrda* mercenaries who walked along the muddy trackway now with their fearsome steel-plated boars that feared nothing and who waddled their great bulky bodies so haughtily. Kell felt the trepidation among some of the wulfen, which Magula tried to quell unsuccessfully.

They are leaving, said Tir: the thought in Kell's head as light and blue as cornflower, and tinged with surprise.

It appeared to be true, for each of the men carried his heavy leather backpack and a full kit of wargear. Two wore their helmets while the third had his hooked to his belt. Thus, Kell was easily able to see the bright red crop of hair which was the distinguishing mark of the mercenary clan. And so seeing he remembered his meeting with Zauraq an unmeasurable time ago, and the curious flying device that had accompanied the warrior –

Startled by recollection, Kell frantically searched across the grey bleak overcast of the sky and almost missed it, drifting as it was among a flock of circling ravens.

He sent out an alarm-thought and pointed with a small motion of his hand: the wyrda men were almost directly below on the track, at their closest approach, and any small noise or movement could alert them.

We know of it, Tir told him. *Or rather of them, for the wyrda possess many of these globes. They are mysterious. They seem to have no mind, but a definite purpose.*

Are they weapons? Kell was thinking of the gleams that had exploded in the tunnels under Thule.

Weapons. Eyes. We don't know. Sweorian, Kell – calm yourself.

And now Kell could hear the clink of the warriors' armaments and the brief harsh bursts of their conversation, and the solid tread and grunt of the boars as they swaggered by their masters. And he had no doubt that the wulfen could smell the creatures too, and powerfully at that.

The pack hunched down among the trees, in the long wet grass, and went very quiet. Tir, who was adept at this, swept through the soldiers' minds like a fleeting shadow. One of the boars looked up the slope and made a bad-tempered half growl. His eyes, shaded by metal blinkers, glowed like the coals in a hearth-fire, endlessly angry. But he decided he had detected nothing, and looked away again and trudged on through the mud.

When the company was out of sight around the body of the hill, and as the flying globe lost itself in the haze, the wulfen pack stirred and moved back deeper into the trees to trade their impressions and decide on next-action.

There was a disturbance about them, Tir declared with stout certainty. *There was — an apprehension.*

Kell experienced Magula's agreement as a sudden hot glow.

But what could trouble the wyrda? Although Thule is a tainted place and often barbaric, it is rich like a spring river, and there is always much work for the wyrda warriors to do.

Perhaps the Tarazad wanted to reap their dreams . . . Fenrir's small shy mindvoice spoke out among the musings of the fullgrown. His alert thin face glanced from one of his kind to another, and finally to Kell.

That's what was happening to us. I remember the glass, Kell. It was the glass that made us do things — you know how the longings and the rages and the fear poured from it! Maybe the glass could take from us too —

'And feed it back,' Kell said. He remembered Fenrir's bloody muzzle at Shamra's white throat, and how it had been only a clever deception.

But they couldn't trick me! I wouldn't bow to them!

However it was, that day is done with. Magula glanced at the sky. *But I sense a deep truth in what you have both said — the wisdom of innocents! And perhaps that is the intention of the Tarazad plan; to discover how much of our nature comes up through the blood, and how far it can be rewoven.*

What has this got to do with us? Tir's thought had a rough texture to it. *All of us here are safe, Fenrir is rescued and Kell adds a valuable strength. We suspect that there is danger in Thule, so let us leave it behind! The mountains can hide us forever.*

The Tarazad race is expanding, Magula pointed out. *They have attracted merchants and others here through the temptation of their mineral hoards — and there is the seduction of the weorthan crystal itself. They have learned a great deal about the world. And now they are ready to swarm.*

We can stay ahead of them! If we are cornered, we fight with nobility!

Tir's opinion had great force but little substance. It was clear even to Kell that the elderwulf didn't believe it himself. But what else could possibly be done?

We watch, Magula replied to Kell's unspoken question. *We learn, we survive. And when needs must, then we decide.*

So it was settled, and yesterday was gone and tomorrow was another new day.

The moon grew, darkness by darkness, towards its fuller and more sensuous light and the weather changed as the wulfen knew that it must. The constant gentle rains vanished for a short while; then the wind shifted and brought a crueller cold, and the clouds returned with the vanguard of the snows.

The wulfen pack kept to the forests, as low into the valley as they dared. But the exodus from Thule continued; the tradeways remained busy, and Tarazad patrols began to sweep through the passes and along the valley tracks, indicating that the wyrda's apparent concerns were well founded.

Now there was a greater pressure on Magula to act. Twice in as many days the pack was spotted by Tarazad soldiers from the Broken Place, and on the second occasion some spinning weapon came skimming through the trees and flew apart with a sharp crack and filled the air with iron splinters. One of them pricked the memory of Birca's death in Kell's mind, and in that second he knew without doubt that the All Mother was out in the world; they had not left her buried in Perth.

On the eighth day after the pack had seen the wyrda, they came upon the bodies of two wulfenkin, slain at the roadside. One was a yearling whose eyes, open in death, were dark incurious mirrors. The other, a female fullgrown, had been slashed the full length of her abdomen, probably in midleap as she had fought to defend the youngster. There were other signs, subtle things to do with the earth and the grass and scents left in nearby bushes; but their meanings were private to Magula and his breed, and so Kell withdrew while the dead bodies were buried and the song of farewell echoed through the trees.

It is Tarazad work, Fenrir told Kell a little later at Magula's request. This was a mark of respect to the boy. *They are becoming more active farther afield.*

'I hate them,' Kell said simply, though Fenrir had understood the loathing even before the words had been spoken.

Magula and Tir have had further disagreements. Tir still says we should leave while our chances are high. But Magula, for some reason, feels the need to stay near Thule and . . . no . . . he — he wants to go back there, for reasons he keeps to himself.

That's hardly fair! If he's a proper ruler of the pack then he should explain . . .

Then Kell shut up, realising he had transgressed. Naively he had assumed that the one-mindedness he found among the wulfen — and which he had first experienced through Faras and the Shore Folk — meant that all of the pack had equal weight in making decisions. Now it became clear that Magula's word on any matter was final: and while the elder-wise-wulfen like Tir might offer their opinions and feelings on any matter, in the end even they had to bow to the pack leader's greater authority.

Kell apologised with deep sincerity; not in words, not even in the mind pictures he was more easily able to offer up now, but by experiencing the feeling itself: Fenrir detected it immediately and, Kell knew for sure, so did Magula himself.

Fenrir's reply was difficult for Kell to understand, like a knotted cord he needed to unpick . . . any wulfen ruler, not just Magula, became so by his or her capacity to join with the Godwulf (that was how Kell perceived the idea). This was the All Being, the collective experience of every wulf that had lived and moved on. The Godwulf had its feet in the first red rage of the breed, going back as many seasons as there were snowflakes in a sudden blizzard; and its song echoed beyond the sky; and its eyes looked towards the final destiny of the kin; and its heart was mindful of every living wulf. The

Godwulf was everywhere, in the air and earth, in the water and in the fires at the core of the world. And its immense wisdom could be drawn up through the blood, most ably by the pack leader, but also by the youngest whelps who in their innocence sensed him as the simple deep joy of being alive.

Magula says it is time for him to commune again with the Godwulf, Fenrir went on. *He wants to be sure of his decisions. These are auspicious days. Your presence is part of this. That is why the pack brought you with me from Thule.*

I still don't really understand what Magula wants there.

Neither does he, I think. There is something terrible in the city . . . It is of the Tarazad's making, but it goes far beyond them . . .

And here Kell felt the restraints come down as Magula's protectiveness asserted itself. Human suspicion told him that Fenrir was involved, and Kell himself and all the things Kell had brought with him to the pack. But there were no further explanations, and the younglings had to be content with that.

Now preparations needed to be made and the wulves moved with greater purpose. Two days' journey from where they had spotted the wyrda lay a wide valley surrounded by soft-curving hills and an outer barrier of mountains. It was a place little visited by any creatures, for it was sacred ground used only for the purpose that Magula intended.

He led his kin over the high lonely fells and down through mist-drenched forest and a thick lower woodland of flat-leaved trees. The mountain shield kept the air warmer here in the valley; it was a haven that held winter at bay a little while longer. There was no trace of snow or ice, just the ever-present delicate mists wreathed with playful and constantly changing light, and the vegetation filled to bursting with saps and juices. Corvus flocks swooped and circled above, detected only by the rough dry abrasion of their calls. There were no other wulfen here just now; only the assembly of ordinary valley-dwelling creatures. And the auroks.

Fenrir's mental impression of one of them made Kell gasp.

23

Then came his friend's admission that he had never actually seen one, but that Tir had told of his single encounter long ago: and of course they were featured in the wulfensongs.

What Kell envisioned was a massive, shaggy red-brown pelted creature, twice the size of a mox with great broad horns and a haunting, hollow mournful cry that echoed through the night. They were herd animals, but now those herds were small and well scattered.

This is the only place where we have ever found one, Fenrir said. *Though another pack came across auroks living in the farnorth, in a valley shackled round with ice. The wulfensweor said they counted no more in the herd than the number of claws I possess . . .*

How can they help Magula to speak with the Godwulf—

And the answer came to Kell's mind in such a burst of ferocity and blood that he was sickened before he could stop himself.

The ritual began that night with a fasting that went on for five more days, until the moon was full-lit and round and hung over the valley like the luminescent globes that Kell remembered from his past life in Perth. The wulfen grew keen and sharp in their hunger. The slow-eyes was expected to participate, and he did so; and came to hear the little heartbeats of the rivervoles down by the water when he washed. He heard them, he smelt their blood, he imagined their warm, vigorous flesh in his mouth and tasted the gush of liquids and salts and their life-giving nourishment. He dreamt of them and found his whole existence pointed like an arrow to their hearts. When he woke ravenous on the sixth day he understood the wulfen's purpose in being here, and the final meaning of life.

Then it was time. On Magula's call the pack returned to the woods. They slipped among the trees with a soft pattering and left no signs. After a while they came upon a broad track carved in the land, at the sides of which the bark of the trees had been scooped away by teeth like broad-bladed shovels.

This is where the auroks come down from their dwelling grounds to the river, Fenrir told Kell. He was gathering this wisdom from Tir, who explained through a sense of duty towards the pack younglings.

Kell was astonished again at the size and power of the beasts. This trail, smashed through mature forest, had been made by muscle and bone: even with a machine as solid as an ice wain fitted with special tools, the task would have been dangerous and difficult. Yet here the way was clear, and all traces of the oaks and sycamores that had stood in the path of the auroks had vanished; eaten, crushed, trampled to bare earth.

Magula sauntered forward while the others held back. He leaped on top of a storm-felled trunk and lifted his nose and conversed with the wind. Then, more confidently, he leaped down and explored a portion of the trackway, sniffing vigorously to unravel the traces the *deorfifel* had left. Kell caught the notion of two suns-and-moons since the aurok herd had passed by: they had cleansed themselves and drunk their fill and would not be expected back for several days.

In that case, Tir said, *we go now to the hallowed ground and sing our song of summoning* . . .

And then? wondered Kell.

We wait.

So it was that way. High in the hills was a place of huge stones scattered across a broad shelf of flat grassed land. Fenrir said that all wulfen were born with the knowledge of its location. The ice had riven and sculpted the under-rock in such a way that the prevailing winds howled around the contours of the stones like the ghostly voices of a million wulfen ancestors. And, Kell saw with an involuntary shiver, wulf skulls had been placed in crannies and cracks in the boulders, where they were regarded with reverence by the living wulfen eyes that looked upon them now. Similarly, in a central spot, colossal aurok bones were piled up like the framework of some mighty hearth hall, and here again within lay wulfen skeletons and scraps of pelt from those that had come this way before.

The overall impression, and one that would stay with Kell always, was of mystery and power beyond the imagination of humankin; something forever alien to him. This unique yet simple place was essentially wulfen ground, drenched in the animals' musk, witness to the breed's ultimate passion and purpose; earth, rock, sky, blood, bone and a fearsome determination to survive.

Kell let his mind settle. He felt exhausted by his learning. Tir took charge of all of the pack's younglings – three males, two bitchwulf and Kell – and led them to a platform overlooking the arena. The fullgrown dispersed themselves to take cover behind boulders. Only Magula stayed in plain view on open ground . . .

Then the doleful note of the wind altered. Threads of meaning began to weave through the air and into the mind. Kell's throat clenched at the sheer depth of hope and longing and tenacity captured in the sound. The wulfen were singing – gently, yet so fervently and with such enchantment that no living being could resist their temptation for long.

Nor was Kell kept waiting. Within a short span, far off, came a sonorous answering call; a complex cry that was a roaring anger, an infinite sadness, a strident challenge to battle – all of these things. The note lifted and the air shivered like crystal, and the noise fell away and ended in a rumbling bellow.

Twice more like a fury, like a lament, the trumpeting reply echoed across the valley, each time louder, closer, more dangerously real.

Then Kell smelt a musk of such deep pungency that it stung his eyes and made them water. He snatched his hands to his face and rubbed at the irritation. And when he took them away and blinked the world back, he saw that the aurok had arrived.

It was immense, a fullgrown bull with lowslung shoulders

and a black boss of bone above its eyes where the horns met; and each horn was far longer than Kell was tall. Its weight and power seemed gathered at the front end, while its ridged back sloped down to a long whiplike tail, and its flanks and underbelly were lean and muscular, and its hindlimbs rather shorter than the fore.

The beast roared again, a withering blast of noise falling back to a low gravelly grumble. It had noticed the little predator standing there amidst the glamour of the wulfen-song; something solid that it could gore and trample to get the seductive magics out of its mind.

Without preamble the aurok dipped its head and rushed forward, its vast strength propelling it swiftly at the small silverfur who twisted and skittered aside just in time. Dust and stones flew in a spraying arc as the aurok swept round to face its tormentor and come on again, again, a third time – and now one terrifying horn clipped the wulf and sent it sprawling. The aurok used its advantage instinctively and tried to pin the animal under the span of its horn since just a small pressure would snap its spine and be done with it.

But the enemy was clever or desperate or lucky, or all three. It managed to wriggle free and whirl itself round and out of reach as the aurok scoured the earth with its horns. And, as the huge bull lunged forward again, Magula flicked out a paw catlike and raked his claws across his adversary's eye.

The aurok, *ealdbeorn*, old-as-the-stones, lifted its great head in a thunderous roar of agony, blinded by blood and pain and the tormenting melody of the silverfur song. In that moment Magula saw the victory path: he risked being instantly crushed by leaping between the stomping hooves of the beast, keeping half his attention on the shifting mass of the vast animal, and half on the looming underbelly above and the particular spot he was looking for . . .

As the aurok staggered about, barging into stones, kicking

up dust, Kell lost sight of the pack leader. A fear flashed across his mind and was immediately calmed by Tir.

Magula has won. This is the end for the great-horn.

'But how –'

The rest of his question, and any reply Tir might have given, was lost in the noise of the aurok's sudden rising wail of endless pain. Magula could still not be seen, but now there was blood, copious sprays and goutings that the beast trod down into a thick red mud. Kell heard a drumming sound, and across his mind's eye there swept a vision of limitless plains and a haze of dust: for before the Ice there were warm nights and sparkling constellations; and the herd was as plentiful as the stars amidst eternal peace and contentment –

It was the noble bull aurok's deathsong, drawn from a breed-memory even older than the glaciers.

The animal's legs suddenly lost their strength and it dropped. Its proud span of horn was now too great a burden to bear, flopping sideways so that its head was propped on a single horntip. The heavy bellowing breath grew quieter, weaker; its eyes clouded; a thin dribble of blood trickled out from its mouth, and its black tongue lolled in death.

Yet still the animal moved, the head tilting on the pivot of the horn, its chest heaving, heaving – until with a crackling of bones and a splitting of the skin Magula reappeared and struggled with all of his strength to drag the creature's heart from where he had come upon it within the cavern of its ribs.

The wulf and his prize flopped out into the dirt, steaming. All of his strength had been spent, but even so he found the will from somewhere to lift his blood-drenched body to its full height and point his muzzle upward and howl the news of his conquest to the heavens.

Under the old light of the waning moon, Magula feasted first from the raw heart of the slain aurok. Tir followed, then the other pack elders, and so down through the hierarchy to the younglings and finally to Kell. The boy understood the depth and importance of the ritual and kept his revulsion and nausea under tight control. He concentrated only on the scale of Magula's achievement; the reaffirmation of the great balance of all that existed. But the heart meat itself, crimson-black, rich and salty, was not at all unpalatable. Kell unexpectedly rediscovered his hunger, and to Fenrir's great pride and pleasure lifted the trophy to his mouth again and again and ate his fill.

After that the whole pack apart from the guardwulfen slept. When the dawn came and fresh cold light spilled over the battleground, the fullgrown began the long task of stripping the carcass of its meat: a little more would be eaten now, and the rest taken up chunk by chunk above the snowline to be stored for whenever it was needed again by any wulfen pack that might come this way. Then the huge skeleton would be left to the scavengers, the feral forest cats, the corvus flocks, the rats and the insects, who would pick the bones clean.

And some time after the hard-long-dark, Tir explained to Kell and the other younglings so they would know for the future, *we must return here and add the aurok's bones to the pile . . . and the skull will be missing*, Tir added, picking up Kell's question. *The bull's herd-fellows will by then have removed it to a place that is a secret known only to the aurok breed. For that is their way of acknowledging the price that life must always pay.*

By the point of midday the wulfen had finished their work and the pack retreated to the woods leaving only Magula behind. This was to be the time of his communion with the Godwulf, for which he had undergone his trial.

But what does the Godwulf look like? Kell wanted to know. *And is it vengeful like the All Mother? And why must Magula speak with it alone . . . ?*

Tir silenced him with a bark and a glare, for these things were forbidden to the slow-eyes. And Kell felt properly chastised until Fenrir took him aside and explained that the elder wulf's mood grew out of envy.

*There has always been some rivalry between Tir and Magula,
who was Faedera's favoured one – Faedera was the last pack leader.
He died in a rockfall five seasons ago. Both had the qualities of
leadership, but the balance fell Magula's way.*

And if Magula had died fighting the Aurok today?

Then out of respect Tir would have led the pack forward.

Fenrir went on to answer Kell's other questions, and took
time to sing him parts of certain sagas, which formed the
wulfenhoard, the wealth and inheritance of the breed.

Kell could have listened all day to these soaring tales of
adventure, for the world grew in the telling. But by the late
afternoon's red light Magula came into the clearing. He had
washed himself in some nearby stream, and had regained
much of his lost strength. Yet his eyes were dulled and an air
of sombreness surrounded him.

The eyes of the whole pack turned his way, but Magula
looked only at Kell.

*The Godwulf has spoken with me and I was taken into his spirit.
I have died and seen the world for what it is, and I have returned to
tell you this . . . Kell, you are the stone around which the river of
our wierd flows. I had known as much. But I thought ours was the
power and the protection. This is not so. It is you who carry us along
in your becoming, so it was no random circumstance that you spared
Fenrir's life – as you must do again, and very soon.*

'I don't understand this,' Kell said in words, troubled by
Magula's deep seriousness and this sudden weight of respon-
sibility. He tried to calm himself and repeated the concern in
his mind.

*Nor do I, nor any of us, in any detail. But I know that you must
go back into Thule with a wulfen guide and find our nemesis – the
one that legend calls the Luparo. The Wulf Slaughterer.*

3

Wyrda Craeftum

A million stars and a waning moon the colour of hearth-coals provided enough light to see by. Kell stumbled along beside the sure-footed Fenrir feeling clumsy and sluggish and stunned by Magula's revelations. He was not sure he could carry the burden of the wulfen pack's future; but never once did he consider turning away from the task. Whatever it was that needed to be done, so Kell was prepared to face the endeavour and die in the trying.

They moved out of the trees into a sudden cutting wind laced with sleet from incoming clouds: away from the protection of the hills that circled the aurok graveyard the air was freezing cold. Kell felt a sense of huge open space and a brief confusion – he thought there were stars underneath him! Then Fenrir bit at his heorot pelt and pulled him back, and Kell realised they had come out on a high promontary overlooking Thule. The stars were ligetu lamps and firetar brands, some of them moving as wains travelled back and forth along the bleak streets on the outskirts of the city. Further away, the sprinkling of lights stopped abruptly, cut off by an arc of darkness that swept the width of the valley. Tir explained that this was what remained of the shattered shell that had once been the enclave of Thule, and one reason why it was known everywhere and to all thinking creatures as the Broken Place.

Will I have to go that far in?

Not even the Godwulf has an answer to that, Magula said. *All I was told was that we ride on the river of circumstance. It has been decided that Tir and Wyldewulf will accompany you as best they can. Your only concern is to learn of the Luparo and bring back what you discover. Beyond that, all our futures are uncertain.*

But what is the Luparo and how will I know if I find it?

Magula turned from the brink of the crag and moved close up to Kell so that the boy could feel the heat from the beast on his face.

We will rest tonight and you will dream. It will be my dream, Kell; one that before me belonged to Faedera; and it came through him from a line of ancestors too long to imagine. Luparo is the first and last foe. I will show you all that my soul understands of the Slaughterer, but mind-to-mind so that my kin do not lose heart through the terror of it.

Then the pack leader swung away and would say nothing more.

After surveying the land, the wulfen went into the forest to a place where the rocks had sheared ages ago: there was a little rubble-strewn dell faced on two sides by a mossy green cliff and clumps of bracken. Beyond that the trees formed a thick wall of darkness above which the wind boomed like the ocean all through the night.

Here is a way into the tunnels and caverns beneath Thule. Tir showed Kell the well-concealed entrance to a dripping cave among a tumble of boulders: and with it came the impression of an easy route down to the city. *We have many such ways. Despite the efforts of the Tarazad, they will never uncover them all.*

Kell appreciated the elderwulf's attempt to reassure him, and gave thanks. He resisted the temptation to think ahead and anticipate what tomorrow could bring. Instead, he made a show of stretching and saying how tired he was. He sensed the pack settling around him in a dell; found a cleft for himself between a clump of boulders that kept out the wind; dragged his pelt up around himself and turned his mind inwards –

To a desolate moorland tufted with tough wiregrass and grey sandstones crumbled by the wind, which make a ceaseless moan between the horizons. The low sky, laden with cloud, is the same drear colour as the rocks. There are no trees, no hiding-places, and immediately Kell feels exposed and therefore vulnerable –

And he understands why. He is in the realm of Magula's dreams, experiencing what all wulfen fear; open ground, being seen from afar. Being hunted.

No sooner has the unease come clearly than Kell realises it is already too late.

He whirls round with his heart thumping. (Be calm! Be calm!) And there, moving quickly up the hill, is the monstrous form of the Luparo. It is not one man, but a host of writhing forms all circling around the central warrior, who is huge and solidly built and armoured in metal plate and heavy chainmails. His helmet of dully shining steel bears two fearsome horns: a slit with the shape of a Y gives the Slaughterer vision, and Kell a glimpse of cruel blue eyes and a strong jaw grimly set. A long grey cloak swings aside in the wind, and there clipped to one hip is a curved slicing-sword; and to the other a massive double-bladed axe with sharp spearpoints at both ends. There are other spikes projecting from the warrior's elbows and shoulders and knees, and from the knuckles of his mail and leather gauntlets. He is unstoppable in his power and in his mission to slay.

The glare of the Luparo's eyes find Kell out – wulfensweor, wulf cousin – vulnerable in the open. Black serpents twine up about the Slaughterer's head and hiss viciously at the doomed youngling. A mist of ghost shapes billow from the whole moving mass and come drifting closer like smoke across the hill.

Even in his fear Kell wonders over the nature of the Luparo. It is every dread thing; armour to break a wulf's fangs, finely honed blades to cut into his flesh, the weight of metal to crush his bones; and a human form that the wulfen had feared since the earliest times. Nothing can be more terrifying to the swift silverfur kin that had become Kell's friends and protectors.

As he must protect them, if only he understood how. Something is struggling at the back of his mind, an old knowing . . . But there is no time now to dwell upon it, for the smoke phantoms are blowing about him, losing him in their fog. The broad silhouette of the Luparo has become vague and uncertain – but Kell hears clearly enough the clinking of chain, and then the whoosh-whoosh as the Slaughterer spins his terrible axe in a circle over his head.

Kell's heart leaps up in a panic and he is gripped by ancient fears. This is the final torment of the wulfen, to be prey themselves. Some little clear corner of his reason tells him there is an answer, if only he knew where to grasp, if only it lay within reach.

But the Luparo is moving steadily closer, and now he is dappled with blood. A wulf's head hangs from the Slaughterer's belt and a wulfen skull decorates each spiked shoulder. Kell feels the terror intensify and knows he is going to drown in it. He darts this way and that, to the side, back, forwards —

Into the whirling orbit of the blade. With an easy snick and a jolt that hardly means anything, Kell loses a limb. He watches it spinning away and land in the grass and lie twitching before the shock hits him like a wash of dazzling light.

He drops to his knees and sees that his blood is gushing copiously over the ground. And it is fringed with a silvery light, bright and shimmering, like a glowing border around everything. All his life's energy is spilling away.

A great weariness comes over him, and all Kell wants to do is to lie down and for it to be over.

The Luparo, standing above him, is waiting. And somehow Kell knows that if he bows his head now and simply accepts his death, he will be tainted with the Slaughterer's contempt. He is dead anyway, but the way of it is what matters, for that is the way of his living.

So with a vast effort he drags himself up to his feet and climbs the high cliff of his pain and weakness, lifts his knife from its sheath with his one remaining hand and looks direct into the Luparo's tragic eyes.

He never sees the blow coming. But suddenly there is an enormous concussion and the world lifts and turns over and over. The light of everything intensifies and bleaches out Kell's thoughts and even the knowledge of who he has been. Then there is simply nothing, a darkness, in which he sleeps until morning.

He felt different, without knowing how he had changed.

Fenrir sniffed at him curiously – and quite impertinently, Kell thought – while Tir avoided him entirely for a while. The only clue he was given came when Magula took him briefly aside and touched his imagination with a fleeting memory of his dreams.

Some part of you will always know, and so you will be forever joined with the wulfen and understand the nature of our blood. Whatever you do, even after you have left us and gone your own way, will be right action. All we ask now is that you do this last thing and go back into Thule. It is the Godwulf's will.

Kell nodded solemnly. *I'll do what you want Magula, wulfenealdor. Not just because of the Godwulf, but because you are my friends.*

So the task began at once, which was the wulfen way. While the remainder of the pack rested in the hidden dell, Magula went with Kell and Tir and Wyldewulf – the one who roams wild places – into the guts of the hills. They followed the path of the water as it percolated down through the rocks as a trickle, a stream, a roaring river that surged into Thule. Presently the water-carved walls of the tunnel gave way to a conduit of ancient brick, and that passageway soon divided and divided again into many smaller forks.

From one came the pounding of heavy machinery. Kell surmised that vast pumps would be drawing the water up into reservoirs where it would be used for cleansing and to slake the city's thirst.

We go this way, Magula said. They struck left, away from the noisy torrent of the river's natural flow, to quieter waters that slopped and gurgled against the stone ledge where they walked. At intervals they came across openings in the brick tunnels, some with upsloping walkways, others revealing steep flights of steps.

We have searched through some of them, came Wyldewulf's distinctive mindvoice, resonant and rich. *Many led to the level of the streets. A number of them go downwards deep, deep into the mountain. One or two . . .*

35

And here the wulf's explanation faltered and his impressions became confused and a little apprehensive.

There are places under Thule that feel like forbidden ground, Magula said, adding an impression – perhaps an involuntary one – of weorthan magic and the horrors that it could bring.

We have no reason to go there. Our route is here, just a little way along.

And so it proved to be. The tunnel split into three parts. One of them, a gently spiralling upslope, was the way that Magula chose. And soon they left behind the unpleasant stinks of stale water and felt fresher air on their faces. Distant sounds of busy thoroughfares echoed down through a watery light. Kell blinked painfully after the long darkness.

They came to a series of terraces, a jumble of walls and a few dwellings that seemed to be empty. A narrow flight of steps led up to ground level.

We will let you go on alone from here – but we will always be close, Magula reassured the boy. *And we will never fail to come to you if you are in trouble.*

Kell understood that his companions would not wish to walk by daylight in the city, among their humankin enemies. And while there would be many dogs straying the streets amongst whom they could mingle, some keen eyes could easily tell these apart from the sleeker, prouder wulfen race.

But though Kell saw the sense of Magula's plan, he felt nervous as he came around the concealing wall into full view, and took stock of his surroundings.

This part of Thule – the broad band between the central Tarazad stronghold and the outlying mining towns – was where the city's commerce was conducted. Here people came from all quarters to ply their trade, to hear the gossip, and perhaps to explore the promised wonders of weorthan glass. Kell remembered how powerful its attraction had been from when he had travelled here with . . . with Alderamin, and his other friends looking for Shamra!

He smiled as the merchant's name returned to him so

easily: perhaps now that he was free of the weorthan's influence this would happen more often. Yet he must not allow himself to get lost in recollection, for Thule was a dark and dangerous place despite its colour and bustle.

Kell saw many traders along the street both ways. Some bartered openly, others merged with the crowds and sold their wares in greater secrecy. There were moxen trains and mwl-drawn barrows, stalls such as those Kell remembered from Odal, mechanical wains draped with goods, and stores housed in the stone and metal buildings that defined the street itself. To Kell's right, the road struck straight and true, opening to a wide plaza in the distance, beyond which open ground stretched to the first foothills. To the left the street curved into the gloom, for high above the tallest towers the fractured shell of the enclave swept over like a black wing. And in that portion of the city the lamps and torches burned eternally, for the heart of Thule forever lay in darkness.

For a while Kell felt safer with the wall at his back, but gradually he grew bolder in realising that no one was paying him the slightest attention. He was simply a foundling, a stray like thousands of others, like the animal discards that nosed among the rubbish. And camouflaged by the fact that he was nothing in these people's minds, he moved out into the roadway on a search that had no direction.

For the rest of the day he wandered, shuffling along as though dispirited, as he had seen other beggars do. Occasionally he stopped to eavesdrop gossip, and a few times he asked innocent sounding questions about the wulfen who plagued the city, and wasn't their nemesis near – Luparo, the Slaughterer? . . .

But mostly he kept his back bent, his eyes lowered and his ears open. Nobody approached him, save once when an irritable fruit-seller threw rotten brandyplums in his direction because she thought he was thieving.

He moved away, drifting on a whim, until the sun had set behind the dome of the city and the sky to the eastward glowed with broad-spreading veils of orange light. Tired now and truly disheartened, Kell let hopelessness wash through him – and was surprised to find Magula close in his thoughts.

Go to the place where the water outlets from the street. There is a lane between two tall buildings. Meet us there . . .

Kell followed that route, slipping around the side of a meat stall and the pile of stinking bones that lay behind it, into a gloomier cut-through that led in its turn to a culvert whose arches had collapsed here and there to emit the busy gurgle of running water and a multitude of unpleasant aromas.

Kell stopped – he knew he'd been seen – and turned to find Magula sitting in the shadows, radiating contrition.

We must apologise to you Kell. We thought the entire city would be buzzing with news of the Luparo. Perhaps after all I misunderstood: perhaps the image that came to my mind is only a symbol of the Tarazad's intentions. Perhaps it is nothing at all . . .

Or maybe his presence is well hidden, Kell replied. Magula's indecision felt wrong to him. He guessed that Tir had used persuasive arguments to make the pack leader reconsider his plan. *The Godwulf would not deceive you on to the wrong road . . .*

Your faith casts my doubt in a mean light – and I thank you for it, Kell. We have spoken together, Tir and Wyldewulf and I, and ask you to stay until morning. Thule is as busy by night as by day. Continue your search, if you would. And use these as your currency –

Kell looked down and saw a small moxleather bag between Magula's paws. He stooped to pick it up and caught the merest flash of an impression of Wyldewulf's swift and subtle thievery in separating the pouch from its owner.

Weorthan crystals, Wyldewulf confirmed as Kell hefted the bag in his hand. *Good quality. Powerful dreams.*

With a certain heartsickness Kell delved inside and plucked out the first piece of glass he touched. Immediately there was a pressure on him to give himself up to the vision: an insistent buzzing in his head; a warm and languorous relaxing . . .

In a vast arena, watched by thousands of people, Kell slid his sword from the dead heart of the rockbear he had just slain. There was a massive roaring that lifted on a rising note. The crowd stood as one and cheered and threw coins and jewels and favours at Kell as the pride and glory swelled inside him. He was *bealdor*, war-leader, the greatest warrior in the world!

Magula casually cuffed the crystal out of Kell's palm and the night reformed around him. Kell found he was shaking, and not from the cold.

The weorthan is seductive and you are still unsynnig, the innocent one.

Magula retrieved the gem and dropped it back into the bag. *And the merchants are clever, for they give you the illusion in morsels; you are never fully fed and the hunger is always inside you, and you always want more.*

Use these fragments to find word of Luparo, Tir advised. *That is their only worth.*

And Kell understood the wisdom of it, and his own weakness especially when his energies were low. He thanked his friends, tucked the pouch into the front of his tunic and went on his way.

As Magula had said, the city never settled and Kell found that the crowds had barely abated. Indeed, they seemed to swell as gangs of miners came down from the hills to spend their earnings forgetting their day's drudgery. All along the highways, as the stallholders packed up their stocks, taverns and communal hearth halls flung their doors open; and there was music and revelling, and the rich smell of roasting meat that wafted out into the chill night air.

Kell's mouth watered. He had been well nourished within the pack, but his diet had necessarily been of raw flesh; so now the aroma of cooked moxen steaks and the glimpse of a crispy brown hog turning on a spit tempted him beyond endurance and drew him into the hall.

Even as his imagination created the image of him tearing

39

into a chunk of the hot roast, Kell's eyes flicked this way and that to check for dangers. The place was packed with earth-diggers, and here and there, quietly observing, stood Tarazad soldiers in pairs or trios, masked and helmeted and unfathomable. But many children also moved about the place: some were plain beggars who received a clouting and some harsh words for their trouble; others seemed to have various trivialities to barter or sell.

Kell took his cue from their bravado and went over to a meat seller, amusingly a tall lean man who crunched on a lantern-apple in between serving his customers. A young girl with the same gaunt features and slightly dour look was busy beside him cutting slabloaf and slicing the joint.

Kell waited until the couple of burly miners who jostled in ahead of him had been served, then he smiled at the vendor with as much friendliness as he could muster.

'*Hwaet*. I would like to barter some food from you, *frea*, if it would please you to serve me . . .'

The man looked at him oddly and Kell wondered if he had been too deferential – for his language and look did not match. During these past moons he had grown used to wulfen words, which they in turn had found and moulded out of what they heard from the Thulian peoples. 'Frea' was 'master', as Kell might have addressed a tutor in Perth: 'Hwaet' was a call for attention, a politeness rather than a command. He ran over the sentence again in his mind, and was satisfied with it. He made a small respectful bow.

'If it pleases you . . .'

'I don't want your lousy pelt or your labour.' The man's voice was high-pitched and unfriendly. Even so, he glanced down at the hot iron platter his daughter was loading with food, broddled his fingers in the rich oil in which it lay, and tossed Kell a knuckle.

Kell caught the scrap automatically and tried not to show his annoyance. He felt insulted.

'I am not exchanging compliments for gristle, frea. I have

something to trade – weorthan,' he added in response to the meat seller's slightly tilted eyebrow. As he spoke, he reached inside his clothing and pulled out a small lump of the glass. By the better light inside the hearth hall, Kell could see that the crystal was rounded and dull, much used he supposed, having passed through many hands and many minds on its journey.

'What does it show?'

Kell could already feel the attraction of the jewel working on his mind, a subtler and more powerful enticement than the smell of the hot meat. He struggled with it, resisted it and shrugged indifferently.

'Does your curiosity amount to a meal?'

After a moment the seller grinned and showed his big square teeth. He made a gesture to his daughter, a rapid twist of the fingers that Kell hardly noticed, but which told her how large a portion to give, and of what quality. And as she crammed two flats of slabloaf with hog flesh, Kell handed the weorthan fragment over.

The girl pushed the bread into Kell's hands. The meat seller wrapped his fist around the weorthan and his eyes glazed over, then closed. A sly smile appeared, broadened, and he chuckled in a low and lecherous way. Meanwhile, Kell was stuffing the slightly salty doughy bread and savoury meat into his mouth, grinning to himself at the man's simple pleasure.

A customer came and was served by the girl. As he went he made some comment Kell failed to hear, but it had a sarcastic edge. Kell looked as he walked away and saw two Tarazad guards sauntering by, their blank black-leather-masked faces gazing his way –

'. . . the ending of the tale,' the meat seller said.

'What?' Kell's attention snapped back and the man was fully aware now and apparently displeased.

'This is but a portion. Where is the rest of the story?'

Kell went pale with misgiving. This was something he

hadn't thought about, and guessed that neither had Wylde-wulf.

'Well – yes – I have it here . . .'

He rummaged in the little bag tucked down inside his tunic, pulled out a cluster of weorthan lumps and saw nothing to distinguish between them.

The meat seller was growing impatient. Two more customers had arrived, but the daughter was distracted by the prospect of a quarrel.

'Any honest *ciepemann* would know his wares.' The seller's manner had become sly now, mean and manipulative. Kell began to sweat from the heat of the stall and his own uneasy circumstances. He shook his head and held out the meagre offering of crystals.

'Frea, I seem to have lost the conclusion of the tale you wanted . . . But please help yourself to another . . .'

Perhaps the angry seller would have grabbed them all, or smacked them out of the boy's hand, or called the Tarazad guards over. Kell never found out, for at that moment he grew aware of someone behind him and a second later a huge heavy hand clamped down on his shoulder.

He instinctively ducked and tried to writhe away, but the grip was firm. He twisted round ready to spit curses, while his hand slid to his hip for his knife. But then all resistance vanished as he stared with horror upon the fierce eyes and flame-red hair of a mercenary warrior, one of the Wyrda Craeftum.

The man was a giant, bigger even than the Tarazad soldiers who went on their way now, convinced perhaps that the little liar-thief would get his just punishment. The wyrda smelt of woodfire smoke and sweat and an odd tangy spice that was not unpleasant save that at this moment Kell found everything disagreeable. He hung helplessly from the man's bough of an arm while the rest of his weorthan hoard was taken from him. The wyrda made a tutting sound, dropped the pouch of crystals and ground them under his heel. He tossed a gold coin, a *sceatt*, to the meat seller, whose grin had come back with a vengeance. And then Kell's ordeal was completed; something nudged at his side and a brutal stench engulfed him. He swung round and a wet snout snuffled at his hand, arm, face –

The wyrda had a companion, considerably more savage; a great black bulky armoured boar.

'Stay still and Heorrenda will not bite your hand off. And you beware also –' The warrior pointed a grimy finger at the still smirking meat seller. 'For you are cooking his kin!'

The sneer vanished in a blink.

Then Kell found himself being hauled through the crowds, dangling as though weightless in the clamp of the mercenary's fist. Some onlookers laughed, others seemed shocked, a few jeered, but all moved aside as the warrior walked by, out of the stifling hall into the now freezing misty midnight.

'Please . . . please . . .' was all Kell could think of to say. His thoughts whirled but came to nothing. Beside them the terrible ironclad Heorrenda swung his head to and fro as though it was balanced on a pivot: he would see Kell's wulfen friends coming before the warrior did; and he would smell them long before he saw them.

The wyrda reached a street corner and turned briskly into an alley.

'Please –'

'Stay still *lytling*, and be thankful I spotted you before the Tarazad *drengs* plucked you off for their play. By Skjebne's bald pate, Kell of Perth, you can't be left for a minute!'

Kell's breath caught in his throat and his panickings ceased. The warrior plonked him smartly on the ground, threw back his head and let out a loud and satisfied guffaw. And after those few seconds of utter shock, and then profound relief and overwhelming happiness, Kell felt his eyes prickling hot with joy to see his friend.

43

'I never thought –' he said, embarrassing himself with a sob. 'I never thought I would see you again, Hora . . .'

They sat in a quiet place, on a patch of wild ground where scattered fires burned brightly and stands of close-growing cuprum bushes gave shelter from the wind. Such havens were common in Thule, Hora had said, intended for those who felt easier under the stars than beneath smothering roof-beams.

They sat together, four of them: Kell, Hora, his wyrda brother Fwthark and the man's *eofor*, the fearsome Heor-renda. And even as they talked and Kell's mind spun dizzily with all that had happened, he relished the warm, lazy comfortable feeling of being in his old companion's company again.

There was so much to say – and listen to. Kell's curiosity leaped ahead and a hundred questions clamoured to be asked.

'First tell me how you came to be wandering free in Thule, bargaining weorthan dreams for your supper!' Hora's pleasure at finding Kell alive was tempered with stern disapproval, which was a measure of his concern.

'No Hora, first you tell me how you came to have joined with the Wyrda Craeftum and changed yourself so much in a span of just two seasons . . .'

Something in Hora's eyes altered. The warrior leaned forward and looked intently at the boy. 'Yes,' he whispered, 'yes, you are almost out of your child years now. I hadn't noticed – Kell, I don't know how you have made this mistake. But I have been here searching for two summers now, since we first came to Thule with Alderamin the merchant. And you have been missing for *five* seasons; as the valley people say, for one year and a half.'

It felt like grief, like something that had been torn away from him and lost. Five seasons! What had happened to him during that time? And where were his other friends now? And how could he have forgotten so completely?

Quickly, and having to go back and retell some parts when speed overtook sense, Kell recounted his fragmentary memories of being imprisoned in Thule; of the experiments carried out by the bronze-faced man who yet had shown him such kindness and helped him through his time of confusion and fear; then of his battle with Fenrir and how he had joined with the wulfen and been accepted into the pack.

'You might grimace at me, Hora, but I am not making it up! I have not got this story from the weorthan glass!'

Furious with indignation Kell let his thoughts soar free, and Heorrenda began to growl, a menacing rumble of a growl from deep in the cask of his chest. He stirred, then stood with a clatter of armour and a gabble of guttural syllables directed at Hora.

'By the Rad!' Fwthark jolted and scrambled for his sword as Wyldewulf came loping, grey and silent as the fog itself, out of the darkness and into the reach of the firelight. Wyldewulf, chosen because he was the largest and looked most impressive; while Tir hung back in the shadows and Magula, the most dangerous, stayed out of sight entirely.

Hora laughed softly and laid a calming hand on Fwthark's shoulder, nodding with pride at how far the lytling had come.

'Be at peace,' Fwthark said. 'Heorrenda – *gesittan!*'

'The boy knows what he is doing,' Hora said. 'He is mind-joined to these creatures, and that is amazing in itself. Even more so that they accepted you, Kell, despite the fact you spared the wulfling Fenrir's life. Since the wulfen, for all you have seen of their kindness and intelligence, kill with unprecedented savagery when one of their number is threatened . . .'

And then Hora's look became distant and self-involved. He had spent too much of his life mind-chained – and the All Mother's shackles were barbarous! – and now wanted nothing more than to think for himself and learn from his own true experience. But his thoughts were not so closed that he failed to appreciate what was happening there now . . . the wulfen were trying to talk to him, responding to his surprise over Kell's survival. He was aware of the bright blades of many wulf lives, threading back into a wild ancestry; and the smell of the land, and the interconnectedness of all. He was aware of the love (or something like love) that these animals felt for the trees and the stones – and their intense hatred of the Tarazad for their minings and disembowellments of the earth. Of the weorthan itself and its links with human depravity, they had little understanding or care . . .

And all of this happened within the space of a few heartbeats, and when it was over and the wulfenlight faded from his head, Hora returned to the moment and nodded, glancing at the tall proud silver-grey animal before him with a new and profound respect.

'These are auspicious times,' Kell said, echoing Magula's earlier words. He told of the pack leader's heroic battle with the bull aurok and his meeting with the Godwulf, and how they had come here to learn more of the Luparo, for the existence of the breed depended on that knowledge.

Hora glanced at Fwthark, who shook his head and shrugged.

'We have not heard of this warrior, demon – whatever the Slaughterer may be. My concern has been to find you, Kell, before my business with the wyrda moves me on. But learn this. The Shahini Tarazad are growing increasingly ambitious in their plans. Their hearts have always harboured an outward urge – Perth was an egg, Thule is a hive. Yet the Tarazad, though individually of sluggish mentality, are collectively intelligent. And the core of that cleverness lies with their ruler, a woman whose name is Helcyrian.

'Now the wyrda, Followers of the Fate, with skill gifted by Wierd, have been here in Thule since the breaking of the enclave. The brethren come and go, but our presence is constant. We know that the way of the Tarazad is bound up with the use of weorthan. We saw it in Perth, in a different form. You have already felt the power of the crystal scraps – and my feeling is that your forgotten days here, as it was with Fenrir, was a time when you were joined with the glass. For the Tarazad, and ultimately Helcyrian, are dreamweavers first and foremost. I think that the minions of Helcyrian looked into your head and, like a trinketbox, put things in and took things out. In leaving Perth, you did not escape from its evil.

'And that,' Hora continued, 'is part of our purpose here now. Our way is the Sigel Rad, the Sun's Path. Our belief is that by following the Rad we will arrive in the end in Midgarth, the home of the true gods. And the search may take us anywhere, even into death. But for now it keeps us in Thule, not allies of the Tarazad but not direct enemies either. We simply stay here to learn, earning sceatt as we may.'

'And you have learned that the Tarazad plan to extend their influence?' Kell said, prompted by a bright impulse from Magula.

'Yes . . . but there's much more to it which involves us all in ways we haven't fathomed yet. I consulted seers and oracles to get to the root of it, but all they show me are scenes of fire and devastation which might be happening anywhere and at any time. *Pohst*! but I have wasted some coinage on their ramblings!'

Hora tutted and grinned and then went about the little ritual of packing a *claeg* pipe with dried threads of a dark, sweet-smelling leaf. Then he sat and puffed awhile, and the pipe was passed to Fwthark, and to Kell who took the merest breath of smoke; and the mood grew mellow and the talk flowed like the tides, and the fog gathered in for the night.

Kell opened his eyes on a frosty, hazy, startlingly beautiful morning. Mist hung like veils of white sylk in the motionless air, luminous and opalescent as the sun lifted clear of the hills and spilled its light out into the valley.

Nearby the campfire had smouldered to a bed of grey ash. Hora and Fwthark snored and grunted under their blankets;

Heorrenda, as still as stone and glazed with frost, watched Kell's waking with a contemplative eye.

Of Wyldewulf and the other wulfen there was no sign, but Kell knew that they were close and sure guardians. He took a stick and stirred the fire into life, and heated up the t'cha that was left from the evening before – making a great clattering of beakers and pots to rouse the slumbering men.

Fwthark woke first and coughed and hawked and swallowed water to clear the taste of the *wyrtgemang* leaf from his mouth. Quiet where Hora was outgoing, he simply nodded to Kell and poured out some still tepid t'cha for himself, then shook Hora to consciousness.

By the light of day, the appearance of the wyrda men was more shocking than ever. Apart from their vivid red hair, as Hora stripped off his tunic to wash, Kell saw that his back and chest were covered with coloured designs; strange hieroglyphs and a writing unknown to him.

Hora explained that these patterns went back to the dawn of the wyrda, to the beginnings of the Ice.

'And they are copied exactly whenever a man is initiated into the craft. I simply bear the sacred marks leaving others – the academics and the thinkers – to decipher them in time. Indeed, Skjebne has made some progress in this –'

'Skjebne!' Kell's heart leaped. 'Is he well then – is he here?'

'He is back at Edgetown, under Alderamin's care. After the night of the Ice Demon there was great hurt, Kell, and much sadness . . . I had meant to speak of it last night, but . . .'

The big man finished his drying and came and sat cross-legged beside the smiling boy. 'Skjebne is well,' Hora said. 'And he talks of you often. Nothing would please him more than to see you again. Perhaps you would think of it now, of making the journey there –'

'Won't you come?'

'I visit from time to time, taking Skjebne items of interest for his studies. In turn, he tries to gather meanings from the hallowed marks. I have a few things for him now that

48

Fwthark and I have, ah, happened across. Take them for me Kell, I ask you to do this; and I will join you there shortly.'

So it was agreed, at least in Kell's mind, though he had yet to persuade Magula to help. Hora gave Kell a small shouldersack to carry to Skjebne, together with the multiblade that had been a gift from Alderamin – a weapon that responded to the warrior's whim to give him a sword or a spear or a lance. Kell accepted it with gratitude and pledged its safekeeping.

Later in the day, the two wyrda men, with Heorrenda swaggering ahead, escorted Kell to the very fringes of Thule, and there let him travel on alone along the winding track over the mountains.

The boy had said he conversed with the wulves – and presently Hora's keen vision caught sight of a shadow joining Kell as he walked. Then the shadow became two, and four, and twenty; the entire pack placing themselves in his trust.

4

The Hard-Long-Dark

Things had changed since Kell had last seen Edgetown – five seasons ago, if Hora spoke truly. Now a tall stockade of stout oak trunks surrounded the little cluster of homes and workshops: the bridge had been strengthened and similarly defended, and sentinels stood their watch at strategic points around the perimeter. Even the pasture where the goats and cattle overwintered was protected by cleverly wrought link fencing topped with bladed wire. Kell felt a brief unhappiness at the sight, since the ramparts and guards surely reflected a change in the hearts of the people.

The boy came from the east, with the waning sun full in his face. Somewhere nearby, out of sight of all slow-eyes, the wulfen pack moved through the trees, pacing Kell's approach. Some distance from the town he came across a tall granite lith, a markstone where he was expected to wait until questioned by the guardians of the way. He remembered there were similar points around Thule, and recalled how he and his friends had met Zauraq on their journey to the Broken Place at such a spot, and how that had been his first glimpse of one of the Wyrda Craeftum.

Patiently, though his mood of sadness was deepening, he waited for the meeting-party to come to him. And presently four men, two on horses and two footguards, strode up smartly and demanded to know his business.

Kell gave his name and told of his journey from Thule. 'Hora, who is a friend of Alderamin and the folk of Edgetown, has sent me to deliver some items. He also lent me his multiblade, which was a gift from Alderamin himself.'

Kell indicated the weapon that he had earlier laid at his feet. The foremost guard, a stocky man with the hard muscular arms of a metalworker, picked up the device and turned it this way and that, but hadn't the daring to touch the controls. He was not stupid, and understood that the mind of such a weapon gradually becomes attuned to that of its owner: by passing the multiblade to the boy, Hora of the Craeftum had offered Kell his trust and the full control of the device. If it had been otherwise, the youth would not have survived his journey, for the blade would have carried out its true master's will at a distance.

So now the guard, who said his name was Waere, offered the weapon back to the newcomer, together with a smile which was intended to convey his respect, but which also carried a little envy.

'I will take you to Alderamin now. He has been waiting for news from Hora for the last half-moon. He will be very pleased to see you . . .'

'. . . Yes, yes Alderamin, and I'm happy to see you too!'

Kell could scarcely breathe, clamped as he was to the merchant's chest by his great bear hug of a greeting. All around the hearth hall fifty people or more grinned broadly to see Kell's discomfort, until at last Alderamin released him and he slumped down red-faced and gasping. The ruler of Edgetown jammed his hands on his hips, threw back his head and gave out a deep bass bellow of laughter.

'Well, well . . . Kell of Perth – no, Kell of the Wider World! You are alive!'

'Just. Your pleasure at seeing old friends is a dangerous thing!'

Alderamin guffawed again and clapped his heavy hand on Kell's shoulder.

'You've not lost your humour, boy – though your

youngling looks are vanishing quickly. Soon you will be a man and a remarkable warrior, or perhaps an explorer. Or, if you are lucky, a merchant like me!'

Kell smiled up into Alderamin's florid face and shining eyes and felt a wave of fondness for the man.

'If I am luckier, I will have your humour and generosity of feeling.'

And Alderamin's beaming smile mellowed and his laughing subsided. He nodded reflectively. 'I think you are to be a diplomat, Kell, and a good one; for your words are as open as your thoughts, and that is a valuable gift in a world of deceptions.'

Alderamin might have said more, and Kell thought he was tempted to do so. But the merchant made an effort to swing his mood another way. 'Yet before we talk of the future, let us catch up on the past. You have been missing for many months, Kell, and we feared you dead. One reason why Hora stayed on at Thule was to find out the truth of your fate –'

'As he has explained to me. But what about my other friends? Skjebne and . . .'

And by the sudden look that Alderamin could not keep from his face, Kell realised he must face some terrible news.

'Don't be fearful for Skjebne, since he is a brief walk from here and you will see him shortly . . . and I will tell you what I know of your other companions from Perth. But there is one, Kell, whose injuries after the night of the Ice Demon were too severe, and they overwhelmed him . . .'

'Kano?'

'Come with me now, and we will honour him.'

Alderamin led Kell out into the reddening afternoon light. The sun hung just above the nearer trees and the air was starting to chill. The merchant shrugged off his warm cloak and draped it over Kell's shoulders. Together they went away from the hearth hall and the ever-busy workshops to quiet ground set among maples and large gloomy baccata trees. Kell had not known of this place from his previous visit. As land it was just land, but Alderamin and his kin had brought it to peace and a great sense of reverence.

'Here we remember our dead.' Alderamin pointed ahead. 'For each one who has gone, a monument remains. I have a team of masons now whose only work is to prepare the stones that mark the passing of our people, since to forget is to make us less human.'

So they moved among the memorials, and presently came to the one where Alderamin stopped and knelt; and Kell did the same without being bidden.

A flat slab of rock had been set in the earth. It was carved with many signs, a few of which Kell guessed marked out Kano's name. A cluster of Alderamin's story stones had been placed at the head of the slab. The merchant picked one up now and rolled it in his hands and gazed for a few quiet moments at the messages it bore.

'These are some of the chapters of his life. Hora helped me to know them. One day you will be able to read them for yourself, and add to them from the time you spent with Kano.'

Kell bowed his head and pledged to himself then that he would come to know the meaning of the marks, and to make marks of his own: for this was a wonderful thing, to leave a life not written on water, but in stone. And that would be another adventure, but something for a different time.

For now, there were just memories and the terrible pain of loss that Kell knew he must endure. Presently Alderamin left him to his thoughts, and to the tears that needed to be cried.

'Goodbye Kano.' Kell laid his hands on the cold slab and trembled with his grief. The man who had brought him up out of the ground from Perth had returned there, woven back under.

Kell only hoped that this time he would find peace.

'. . . And Feoh keeps in touch with us day by day, though sometimes, like a phantasm, we realise that she has passed through our minds without understanding quite what she intends us to know . . .'

They were crossing the main courtyard of Edgetown adjacent to the wide caravanserai where the freight-wains still came from far and wide to unload their goods, and where they departed with the jewels so skillfully wrought by Alderamin's craftsmen. But now the high wooden walls of the town cast broad shadows across the open space as the last of the sunlight broke through the trees: and the night guardians were coming out to light the firetar brands along the ramparts and to begin their cold vigils. Many people had left their dwellings to catch sight of Kell, the sith – the one who travels. They were curious, for there was mystery attached to him now: here was a boy who had been lost in Thule, a place of danger and dark glamour, but now miraculously had found his way home. What stories he would have to tell! What terrors he must have seen!

Alderamin glared sternly at any who approached too closely, but that didn't stop the crowds from growing larger, so that the darkening quadrant rang and echoed with their murmurings. And if Kell had been truthful, he would have admitted his own wish to see a face that had affected him so powerfully when he was last here . . .

'. . . her journey is a strange one, Kell, that much I know. She took the remaining mechanical wain and went back to Thule, but soon moved on from there, far away to the east. In searching for Shamra, Feoh has come to learn of a remarkable alliance known as the Sustren. They are, by her account, goddess worshippers who keep their links with the All Mother of Perth. Feoh's dread is that the All Mother's influence extends far beyond the boundaries of your enclave, through the Sustren clan . . .'

'Yes, I have feared that also,' Kell said. He had started guiltily at the mention of Shamra, when at that moment he had been thinking of another.

Alderamin's news and gossip might have gone on – and no

doubt would do later in the night, when the wine juggons were opened. But now they reached a stout door safeguarded by a single warrior armed with an axe whose edges glimmered with a fierce blue light.

Alderamin smiled at Kell's show of puzzlement and wonder.

'Since you last saw him, Skjebne's handiwork has brought us many marvellous devices. That is his passion these days, Kell – to solve the puzzles of the many obscure artifacts that my traders bring to the town. But he will be happiest of all to know that you have come to his door!'

The guard stood aside and the two friends entered.

Kell stood at the threshold, dumbfounded. The room – one of the largest and best equipped in Edgetown, he would learn later – was packed floor to ceiling with stores and equipment of every kind. Here were instruments and mechanisms, weapons and tools of enormous variety: boxes were stacked high on shelves, and tables sagged under the weight of vats and bottles, jars and beakers containing mysterious liquids. A small firebox built into the far wall radiated a heat great enough to warm the entire room, and a network of pipes carried boiling water around to a number of outlets, creating a cacophany of rattles and hissings and clanks.

Skjebne had his back turned, leaning low over some intricate contrivance. There was a sudden crack and a spark and the object – an iron polyhedron built of many plates – trembled momentarily. Constellations of tiny lights flickered over its surface and then went out. The ball seemed to die back and become inanimate again.

'I fear that one day he will blow himself up through his meddlings, and my burg with it!' Alderamin said, loudly enough to distract Skjebne's attention.

Skjebne wiped his face with a cloth and turned, pushing the goggles from his eyes. He had an impertinent reply all ready to hand, though it went from his mind when he caught sight of the boy.

'Kell —' As though he didn't believe it — and then with certainty. 'Kell! Nobody told me — you're alive — you're here!'

'And hoping you won't blow me up too, *gaeleran*! I am so happy to see you.'

Skjebne came around his clutter of tables, and Kell was concerned to see him still limping from the time of his stabbing in Perth.

'It will never entirely mend.' He thumped his hip with his fist. 'Alderamin's physician tells me that the messages can't reach the muscles now, so they waste around the bone and don't know how to become strong again.'

'I am sorry to hear it, Skjebne —'

'So I have to while away my life in this dull prison, picking among these pieces of purposeless junk, growing more and more bored by the minute . . .'

Skjebne grinned and came and embraced Kell as a father might his son.

'I have thought about you every day since that terrible night in Thule when I feared the Demon had found you, or else you had burned in the fire . . . the circle was broken then and we were scattered. I believed that our brave journey had ended, and it was the greatest pain of all.'

'The journey has only just begun,' Kell said, pressed to his old mentor's thin shoulder. He felt Skjebne's brief nod.

'Now you're here I know that is true — and I have so much to show you! You have so much to learn!'

Kell smiled but could barely keep back a sigh. He was tired now, wearied by his journey and the emotions that had already washed through him like a storm tide.

'Starting tomorrow,' he promised. He looked hard at Skjebne and noticed new lines on his face and a slightly greater greying of his hair, and that brought home to him how much time had been lost. But the man's eyes still sparkled with energy, with the inquisitiveness that had brought him so far.

'And after tomorrow,' Alderamin broke in, 'we must begin final arrangements for the winter. The season is on the change now. Perhaps, Kell, you will help us prepare?'

'I will, and so will my friends – you will see,' he added, noticing the merchant's frown. 'If you come with me to the gates of the town, and have them drawn open . . .'

A short while later the three stood facing the darkness. Westward a waning yellow moon hung in a marbled sky. It was bitterly cold.

'These – friends,' Skjebne said tentatively. 'Did you meet them in Thule? Are they warriors? Artisans? Can you trust them?'

'Your questions will be answered, I promise. All I ask is your trust of me now. Hush . . . hush, Skjebne . . . I must concentrate.'

Kell was disturbed to find that even this short time among humankind had dulled his mind: the wulfen were like distant wraiths, like the memories of ghosts. He felt a brief though powerful fear that they had abandoned him and cut the silver synerthic cord that had joined them, and gone on their way.

But then the spirit of Fenrir appeared within him; thought–heard–felt–seen as a single impression of incredible clarity. And Kell understood that the pack had been hiding, even from the possible probing of men's minds. They had not understood that Alderamin's people lived isolated in their heads, unjoined and alone.

Come Fenrir, frio. Come Tir and Wyldewulf, Magula and all of my new-blood-kin. Be welcome among my olden friends . . .

For long moments there was nothing but the stillness of the night, and the faint broad track that led away from Edgetown following the turn of the river. Then, the faintest movement far away on the limit of what Kell could see.

Fenrir. Welcome. Join us!

'Stay here,' Kell told Alderamin and Skjebne. And the two men, nervous in the face of the unknown, dared not disobey him.

Kell walked out beyond the boundary walls; ten steps, twenty. Then he paused, and smiled; and the smile grew wider as Fenrir came loping towards him with all of a youngling's bright brashness. Kell knew that this was an important symbolic gesture on Magula's part, who was putting the pack's next generation into Kell's care.

The two friends made their greeting and waited together as Magula joined them, followed by the remainder of the pack down to the last *modor* bitchwulf, weary-eyed from a lifetime of whelpings.

All together they strode towards the gates of Edgetown while Skjebne and Alderamin, who had seen marvels in their time, were now struck breathless by what the boy Kell had achieved.

If Kell had learned one sure thing about the merchant, it was that he needed no excuse for revelry; though this home-coming was his reason to celebrate more! After a brief sleep, Alderamin roused his wives and the wives of his craftsmen and any of their children who were capable, and issued a cascade of instructions so that everything would be ready by the time that Kell was awake . . .

And it was the noise that woke him, a thunderous booming of belldrums close to his door; then the rattle of tambourettes; the cheerful reedy piping of truohorns and the steady chiming of the cluge, which somehow all came together to make a music that Kell found surprisingly uplifting despite the grogginess of sleep.

For a few strange moments he wondered where he was – in a warm dark room that smelt comfortingly of woodsmoke and spice: a glowing bed of ashes lay asmoulder in a central circular hearthplace; and the window was draped with a heavy red linen that hardly let in any fresh sunlight. Above him in the gloom, sturdy thatch whistled and hissed in the rising wind outside. This was no forest lair: he was inside – beneath roofbeams – in Edgetown, under Alderamin's care!

Excited and nervous, Kell scrambled out from under his sceatpelt blankets and refreshed himself quickly with the scented water and sweetsoap that he had been too tired to use the evening before. There was fruit in a nearby bowl and dried meats on a platter beside, but his appetite was for news and conversation and to see again the faces of those he had missed.

Kell pulled on the new leather breeches that Alderamin had supplied, then his thick, soft and very comfortable linen shirt and moxhide tunic: there were stout boots cross-laced to his knee, and a fine belt cleverly fashioned with secret slots and pockets containing jewels and coin – 'So you will never have need to beg again, as long as you wear it,' Alderamin had said almost crossly, as Kell told his story.

Lastly there was a stout leather sheath for his knife, while Hora's multiblade fitted into a scabbard strapped across Kell's back. And with his kit complete, Kell examined himself half critically and half in wry amusement in the polished steel speculum that hung on the wall by the bed. He had grown during his time as a prisoner in Thule: he was taller now, broader, and his face was losing the round innocence of childhood, so that his jawline seemed stronger and more angular. And his eyes too had changed; they had seen more of the world and knew its evil, and now possessed a darker cast. But today was a new day and the past did not need to weigh heavy on his shoulders!

Kell was thinking that his straggling hair was in serious need of cutting when someone hammered at his door, and there were scufflings at the threshold, and the sound of Alderamin's low laughter, unmistakably mischievous.

'Are you dressed, lad?'

'Alderamin, I – well, yes . . .'

The door swung open and Kell squinted into the sudden painful rectangle of daylight . . . the merchant didn't enter . . . but something did; an echo of the mischief, a glimmer, a rippling in the air that passed between Kell and the dying fire in the hearth. And even that subtlety, Kell felt, he had been deliberately allowed to see.

Just for an instant he was frightened and bemused, but then he understood as the emptiness beside him filled with form; colours, perfumes, prettiness, the spill of yellow hair that had grown greatly since Kell had last seen it, and the bright blue eyes he remembered even more clearly.

The girl chuckled and leant and kissed Kell's cheek before he had time to protest – that being the measure of how far she had grown in her confidence.

'Sebalrai,' Kell said, smiling himself to realise that his arrival at Edgetown was completed.

The festivities went on through the day. All of Alderamin's people were involved, and none felt guilty in the neglect of their tasks.

'This is an important time,' the merchant said, all swathed up in brockfur, his face flushed with wine and the heat of the bonfire that roared and crackled close by. He looked up at the heavens. 'This is the day on which the season pivots . . . can you feel the change in the wind, Kell? Not just its direction, but its smell and texture – its *gaest*. Now it carries the spirit of the winter and sings of the hard-long-dark.'

'I don't sense these things as clearly as you do, Alderamin,' Kell admitted, 'though the wulfen add weight to your truth. They too are aware of the changes.'

'The people need to be reminded that life is still a joy, even when the snows make us blind to the world.' Alderamin swigged another mouthful of wine. 'They must be reassured of our wealth of provisions, and that we are strong in the face of our enemies . . .'

'The enemies that caused you to build these boundary walls?'

The merchant nodded solemnly and shrugged, and his voice was thick with sorrow and disgust.

'The brigand bands have come this way several times now.

As the trade routes open up, so the roving thiefgangs prey on our rich caravans, like rooks flocking round a freshly ploughed furrow. It is an evil thing, this easy plundering of other men's hard labours. I despise it, and I will stamp it out when it comes to my door!'

'I don't blame you for that,' Kell said, 'but I think it is a pity that for safety's sake you have to wall yourselves in.'

'Aye, well, so it has to be . . . but there are threats that come more slyly and unseen – rumours and dark secrets, many of them from Thule; forebodings of the Tarazad's expansion through the land. That is one reason our friend Hora remained behind in the city, to ascertain the truth of it.'

Skjebne, who sat with them, spoke up.

'Whatever the truth, I think the Tarazad – or more precisely Helcyrian – use rumour and the fear it engenders as a weapon. Despite the military power the Shahini possess, she wields hearsay like a weapon, knowing that frightened people are weakened people. I also think that this is but one aspect of the deeper evil of weorthan, whose lies are so powerful that men sometimes never break free of its shackles . . .'

And so the conversation continued, ebbing and flowing like a tide; now taking a darker turn, now lifting towards lighter topics. As evening drew on and the last of the food and drink was consumed, the wulfen came tentatively into the courtyard which was the heart of the celebration, wisely judging the time of their appearance.

'Your friends are respectful as well as clever,' Skjebne told Kell with some admiration. 'The people are comfortably filled with meat and warmed by drink, and their hearts are light with the revelries. The mood is high – and look, they don't fear the beasts.'

Indeed that was so. Everyone in Edgetown had caught sight of the wulves, and had witnessed Kell and Skjebne and Alderamin approaching the animals to offer them morsels of food – and, apparently in Kell's case, actually to talk with them. They certainly did not seem to be the wild and savage creatures the merchantfolk were used to. Now, in a gesture of friendliness and peace, they had moved to the heart of the town . . . and it was Sebalrai through her trust in Kell who was the first to walk up close to the pack and make her greeting.

'She is a treasure more valuable to me than any jewel,' Alderamin said fondly, though only Skjebne noticed that Kell had failed completely to listen, since his gaze and his thoughts were fully fixed on the girl.

Some time in the night the snows of true winter began. The earlier cobwebs of cloud had thickened and massed; the wind had dropped; and a steady fall of flakes continued throughout the next day. But even before dawn mox-drawn ploughs were busy turning aside the drifts to keep the main streets of Edgetown clear. Similarly, the community's older children scrambled up on to the roofs with shovels and brooms to prevent the accumulation of snow that would otherwise collapse them under its weight.

Apart from these measures, the work of the people went on as usual. Firekeepers ensured that every house and workshop stayed warm: store minders apportioned provisions according to each family's need; *hyrdefolk* tended to the horses and the fowl, the sheep and moxen corralled within the compound — moxen that were simply beasts, with no mechanical elements like those Kell knew well from Perth. Edgetown became almost a tiny enclave in itself, walled by wood, roofed-in by grey overcast skies.

But while the humankin were content to outwait the winter, the pack could not remain so constrained.

We need to see the horizons, Magula told Kell just a few days after their arrival. *The world's wildness and ours is the same. We survive by it.*

But what of the Luparo? The land however wild will not hide you from the Slaughterer.

62

Even he cannot stop us from being wulfen. There was a great calmness in Magula's words, and a great wisdom that Kell fully appreciated.

Are you leaving us then? Kell could not keep the sadness out of his thoughts, yet even though he had been accepted into the pack he knew that the severity of the weather was likely to kill him. Besides (and he hid this from Magula as thoroughly as he could) there was another reason now why he felt the urge to stay.

We will go for a time. Your goodfolk have been kind to us and we would give something in return − our protection, should you need it, and fresh meat instead of the frozen kill you have stored in your earth-lockers.

So the arrangement was made. For days on end the pack would roam the hills: and especially when the Ice Moon was round and complete and so brilliant it outdazzled the stars, then Kell would hear the call of the wulfensong in his head, and sometimes in the air itself when he joined the sentinels on the walls of the town. And these were songs of freedom and hope, of the scalding violence of the hunt; of the past, impossibly far away; and of an equally distant future when (so the sagas prophesied) Man had vanished entirely from the world.

But these were only stories, and Kell wrestled inside himself to understand the nature of their truth, or whether in the end they were no different from weorthan dreams.

During these days he felt more comfortable in Skjebne's company, helping his friend to understand the array of strange devices he had been brought.

'Some of them are completely mysterious to me,' Skjebne admitted cheerfully, 'while others are used routinely but are still not fully understood − such as this.' He led Kell over to one of the worktables and showed him the metal polyhedron Kell had noticed earlier.

'I recognise it!'

'Good lad. It is like the orb we saw that accompanied

Zauraq of the wyrda, when we met him at the markstone outside Thule, with Verres the hog.'

'His orb floated in the air,' Kell teased. 'This one just lies about on your table.'

'Well, that is one of the problems I'm working on,' Skjebne explained slowly, with a towering patience. 'Hora has spoken with Zauraq, who had to confess that neither he nor any of his kinsmen knew the secret of the orb's motion. But when they learned of my interest in such matters –' and here Skjebne's eyes sparkled with anticipation – 'Zauraq has agreed to petition the *ealdormen* of the wyrda clan, for their greatest treasure is an object they call the Universal Wheel. It is uniquely wrought, about this size . . .' Skjebne made a round in the air with his hands. 'Skull size, and finely detailed with marks and sigils that may hold the key to the occult designs the wyrda warriors tattoo upon themselves.'

'But what has this got to do with –'

'Listen, listen!' Skjebne tutted. 'The Universal Wheel is more than a symbol. Hora has seen it once, when he travelled to the settlement of the wyrda for his initiation into the clan. And from his impression I believe that it is some kind of *controlling mechanism*, a contrivance, no less than the ice wain is a contrivance – something that can be dismantled and finally fathomed!'

Kell nodded and forced a thoughtful expression, but he needed to hold back his mirth at the thought of Skjebne taking apart the most sacred artifact of the Wyrda Craeftum.

'There is more to it,' Skjebne said, hurrying on. 'No living man knows how many of the iron orbs exist, or where they come from. But I have learned that when one of them ceases to function, or is destroyed, another appears as though from nowhere to take its place!'

'So there is a manufactory somewhere,' Kell said, 'and artisans who construct them.'

'Or a large but finite supply, so that as one orb becomes

inert, another is activated. And that will continue until they are all used up.'

'What has this to do with the mission of the wyrda – the – the –'

'The Sigel Rad,' Skjebne said. 'The Sun's Path.' He shrugged. 'The Wyrda Craeftum is a clan that has forgotten its own origins. Once long ago, perhaps even before the Ice itself, men understood the way. The orbs were created as useful tools, and the Universal Wheel acted as a governing force over them all, and perhaps over much more besides. But as the land froze and the enclave communities settled into themselves and became isolated, so the essential knowledge was lost and the wyrda fell back into pointless ritual. That is my belief.'

'I won't tell Hora you said that!'

'Hora would be the first to admit it. Ask him why he became wyrda. He has confessed to me that he suffered the initiation into the clan for the sake of adventure. "Skjebne", he said to me, "you're an intelligent and sensitive man. You understand that I was just a humble fisherman in Perth. Now I have the chance of travelling to far scapes, of seeing a little battle, of meeting exotic women . . ."' Skjebne shook his head sadly. 'I advised him to learn a safer and more honest trade, but he would have none of it.'

'If only he could be sensible like you,' Kell said, openly smiling now. And in this way through the months of the hard–long–dark Kell and Skjebne deepened their friendship and added to their knowledge. Some of their talk was frivolous and light-hearted, but at other times they fell into earnest discussions of all that was mysterious in the world, and how they would one day break open those secrets and lay them bare. Then in the heat of that excitement their work might be abandoned altogether as they sat and debated and laughed and argued deep into the night.

But despite dreaming large, they lived day by day. Kell spent many hours apprenticed to Skjebne, who made the boy work for his understanding. Kell's first big task was to tidy the workroom; to take every box and bottle from its place, and clean it, and put it back sparkling. And when Kell had grumbled, Skjebne asked him how *else* he was going to learn where essential items were kept.

Then there were the 'puzzle trays' that Skjebne set out for Kell, and which tested his patience to the limit. To begin with the trays held just a handful of items to be fixed into an otherwise almost intact device. But later Skjebne dismantled entire mechanisms, facing Kell with hundreds of components that had to be fitted together. And this work was long and frustrating, but it allowed him to understand the tiny crystal intelligences that lay at the core of many machines, and the jewelled threads that conveyed their dedicated thoughts, and the small packs of energy that allowed them to function. Moreover, Kell came to see that the memory crystals resembled weorthan glass, insofar as they spoke to his mind, just as his thoughts instructed the devices themselves.

'Skjebne . . . I think most of these instruments were designed to speak *directly* to the minds of men . . . but we lost the ability to listen!'

Kell's mentor was bent low over a workbench, using fine implements to ease apart two faces of argent metal. The hour was late and the day's work had been particularly long: Skjebne was barely listening.

'It's clear to me now.' Kell pushed aside his puzzle tray. 'As soon as we left Perth we encountered people who communicated freely with their thoughts – the Shore Folk, the wild wulfen in the forest. And that is the basic difference between their kind and ours. Skjebne, don't you see? In Perth our minds were controlled by weorthan, back and back through the ages. We saw what we were made to see, and our beliefs followed accordingly. But Outside, the races of the Ice developed their mental skills naturally – Magula once called it synerthy: thinking-together, all-minds-in-one. Why shouldn't machines and other artifacts share that ability?'

With delicate leverage Skjebne teased aside the argent planes to get to the delicate threadwork inside. He put down his instruments and rubbed his eyes tiredly.

'Well Kell, you may be right. It is an idea that is big and bold and you are a master of such notions.' He stood up stiffly and arched his back and yawned.

'And when you can use it to bring life to dead metals, I'll believe you.'

Kell lay curled in the little bubble of warmth that was his bed. He was going to dream – he knew that before it began. And he dreamed of a huge and complex building where there were many rooms – hundreds of rooms – linked by a labyrinth of passageways whose walls and ceilings twinkled with light.

At the beginning Kell drifted and felt utterly lost. But gradually, as his heart came to beat in rhythm with the pulsings of the lights, he allowed himself to see their complex patterns and be drawn by them more surely.

On and on Kell floated along a luminous pathway, noting as he went the unusual designs on the walls that remained tantalisingly just beyond his comprehension. Yet he knew that understanding was there, but for the audacity of his reach.

On and on – on and on to a place where the lights were converging, reddening with distance, surrounding a web of broken wires. Kell exerted his will towards them –

And was distracted by a voice calling from far off, urgently, insistently, so that his attention swung away from the glowing room –

Into the snow, into a soft relentless snowfall among pines . . . in the foothills not far from Edgetown . . . near a tradeway . . .

Kell! Kell!

. . . There was blood on the snow and a sharp and terrible sense of violence. Someone was there with him – Fenrir! Fenrir in such awful distress!

Kell felt his mind adjust to a new cadence. He saw his wulfen friend's face: Fenrir was showing his fighting teeth out of fear, not rage. Tir was bringing most of the rest of the pack to Edgetown; Magula and Wyldewulf were remaining behind.

Kell opened his eyes and acted instantly. He dragged on his clothes, slung on his weapons, wrapped himself round in a moxenhide cloak and ran out into the snowstorm, straight to Alderamin's home.

The door was answered by Alderamin's wife Jadhma, whose great gift was her calmness. She brought Kell inside and insisted he sat and drank some hot t'cha while she went to wake the master.

Presently the merchant appeared, half-befuddled by sleep but nonetheless concerned at Kell's state.

Quickly Kell told of the wulfencall from the depths of the forest, that awful song of death from the minds of every pack member, and how Fenrir and two others were staying behind because Kell had to go to them – he had to see for himself.

'I will help you all I can, of course,' Alderamin said; already he was calling for his clothes and horses and a posse of men. 'But the snowfall is heavy and the forest is huge.'

Kell offered his reassurance, and it was only through his gift of following Fenrir's grief-laden song that they arrived at the place of the butchery just as the first light was rising, grey and frigid, through dawn's iron fog.

There is only one left alive! Fenrir's thoughts were bright and splintered like glass shattered apart. Kell picked up a brief impression of another pack; male wulfen, bitches and younglings all dead.

They went through to the stand of trees where it had happened. Night lingered here, and Alderamin, following a few paces behind, lifted his firetar brand to cast light on the horror.

'By all that's good, how could this have happened?'

He counted fourteen carcasses, not one of which was complete. Limbs and heads lay scattered about and there was much blood sprayed over the snow and the brownblack trunks of the pines.

'Some animal, huge, powerful . . .' Alderamin's voice fell away and his eyes widened in shock, because his heart had been stirred by the memory of another night, years before, when his friend Lesath had been similarly slain, and the mind of his daughter Shaula locked into itself away from the monstrosity she'd glimpsed. 'But this can't be the same!'

'Be still,' Kell said with quiet authority, and the man did as he was told without argument.

The wulfen – Magula, Wyldewulf and Fenrir – had gathered around a she-wulf who was still, just barely, alive. Fenrir was making small whimperings as he suffered in sympathy with her pain. Magula leant and licked at the animal's wounds.

I wish Feoh were here! I wish she could make an ending of her torment!

She will die soon, Magula said, his thought shielded so that only the boy could hear. *But she does not wish to end until she has shown us what happened . . .*

And so it began, the brief dream vision that took Kell back to the bleak moortops in Magula's mind. For here, in the same way, the Slaughterer had come by with his face hidden in steel; and his retinue of serpents and dancing phantasms; and his spikes and blades that had chopped and lacerated and hacked off this branch of the great living tree of the wulfen breed.

And then, with a gentle dignity, the she-wulf's heart beat its last and she died, and in peace and perfection her soul joined with that of the Godwulf and she was gone.

Fenrir lifted his head and let out a mournful howl, not realising yet that no wulf is ever truly lost.

So. Magula's mind cut cleanly through. *We journeyed to*

Thule in search of the evil, but the evil has come abroad and found us out. It will not be long now until we must enter the field to face the Luparo, the slayer of wulves.

5

Luparo

'It is not your fight. Nor will Magula put you in danger by keeping his kin housed within your walls!'

Kell did his best to convey the pack leader's message, putting the same tone of determined finality into his voice as he'd picked up from Magula's thoughts.

It was late on the same day. For half of the forenoon Kell and Alderamin and the handful of men who'd accompanied them buried the remains of the slain wulfen pack in the forest where they had been found. But the she-wulf was brought back to Edgetown and her body placed in a quiet grave in the special place that Alderamin's folk had set aside for their own dead. It was a gesture of utmost respect and friendship, a great honour that Magula fully appreciated.

'And this is the stone on which I will carve her memorial, and you must guide me in its wording.' Alderamin held up the rounded rock that already had one face sawn and polished to receive the writing. His tone was equally adamant, and he grinned fiercely now through the bushy sable of his beard.

Magula tilted his fine proud head and tried to understand the strange expressions of this human *ealdor* who had shown them such kindness.

He does this for me, Kell explained, *as well as out of consideration for the wulfenkin. Alderamin realises what you have previously told me – that we didn't inherit the land from our fathers: we just borrow it from our children. He too despises the Tarazad who seek to destroy both the earth and our offspring . . .*

Kell went on to tell the story of Lesath and Shaula, and

71

how Feoh had brought the girl's mind from the place where the monster had chased it.

She dreamed of the demon, and the demon came to massacre her people.

But not the same demon, Magula replied. *And besides, the song of the Luparo is one of our most ancient. It is no recently conjured thing.*

I don't deny the truth of your sagas. I simply find it strange that now, at this special time as the world is opening, your nemesis should suddenly appear — as mine did, Kell thought to himself, remembering the night of the Ice Demon.

'I have a suggestion,' Alderamin interrupted loudly, quite rightly reading the silence of the wulf and the boy as messages passing between them. 'If the wulf Slaughterer is roaming the land for his prey, why not go out there to meet him, whatever he is? Why should he have the advantage of choosing the circumstances of the battle?'

Kell translated in his mind, even as Alderamin hurried on with his plan. 'The bulk of the pack can stay safe in Edgetown. I have enough capable people to defend our walls — and even more able she-wulfen will be here to help. A small swift hunting party can track down the Luparo, assess his weaknesses and strengths, and by that knowledge destroy him!'

Kell laughed at the audacity and Magula found himself confused by this show of mirth in the midst of such seriousness.

You must be tolerant. Humankin can laugh under all circumstances — it keeps us sane.

I will grant that the strategy is a good one. Out in the weald we are vulnerable. At least this way our younglings are better protected.

So it was assumed to be settled, even though Magula had not formally made any agreement — and he supposed this was another of the ways of the slow-eyed breed that he would never fully understand.

Since the hour was late, Alderamin suggested the wulfen

refresh themselves and rest well before they set out the next morning. Kell took the same advice and went to his quarters and slept.

And dreamed.

. . . The maze of glowing tunnels drew him on closer and closer to the room of broken threads. This time no deathcall disturbed him, and he saw clearly how the fibres had been damaged, and how not all of them now reached the chip of crystal at the centre of the conundrum.

With a swift assurance that was not entirely his own, Kell's hands mended the filaments and set the mind of the crystal free, so that he woke suddenly in a flash of light and understanding . . .

The fresh snow creaked under his boots as he hurried along the main street of Edgetown, across the open square through its windblown swirls of flakes, and into Skjebne's workrooms with their heat and oddly comforting chemical smells, and the man himself dozing at his bench.

'Skjebne! Skejebne, I know how to fix the iron orb!'

'Uh – wha?' Skjebne jerked awake and sat up surprised and dizzied. Kell had already set about his task, following the insight of his dream. If he had thought about it, the right way would have eluded him; but by letting some other, deeper understanding take him now, he could use Skjebne's tools adeptly. A few of the orb's metal plates came away quickly, and then he was inside the depths of the device. The passageways he had imagined were small jewelled conduits that slid out easily on their runners. Beyond was a latticework of threads leading to a core that contained the guiding intelligence of the orb.

And there, as he had seen them in slumber, the severed wires now lay before him.

'We must have heat, Skjebne, to melt them together . . .'

Skjebne needed no second telling. One of his most delicate implements was a fire-needle that Alderamin had procured for him on a trading mission. He fetched it over and handed it to Kell without a word, and marvelled at the boy's dexterity in touching one broken element to its partner to seal them and make them complete.

In a very short time the work was done. Kell reassembled the orb and carried it to a large empty table, and there set it down.

'I dreamed the answer,' he announced to his mentor proudly. 'And I have half a notion that the orb itself was guiding me – perhaps that is part of the orbs' cleverness, given to them when they were created.'

'Well . . .' Skjebne rubbed at his sleep-reddened eyes and yawned until his jaw cracked. 'It's certainly clever enough to lie there and do nothing. Perhaps it's just resting, as I should be doing . . .'

And he had neither time nor inclination to say any more; for there came a swift and sudden change of pressure in the room as the orb's field of influence grew. Kell felt his eardrums pop, and his skin was prickling as though in a dry summer heat with thunderclouds near. He laughed aloud to see the sparse strands of hair around Skjebne's shining pate standing up on their own, drawn out by the same energies.

'It's working,' the mentor said quietly, but with a note of caution as to what might happen next. 'Whatever engines drive the orb are connected to their source of power – and look, look!'

There was definite space between the polyhedron and the oak tabletop, and the charge in the air had intensified; the dust itself hummed and crackled, and both Kell and Skjebne wrinkled their noses at the smell of fire-scorched metals.

'Skjebne, do you think it's dangerous –'

But Skjebne was caught up in his fascination.

'Rise – rise!' he commanded, yet the orb remained obstinately still, resting lightly on its buffer of air. 'Go left! Go right! Bah, the machine is stubborn or stupid or both . . .'

'No no, like this –' Kell settled into a quiet state. The orb trembled, hesitated momentarily, then shot off sideways into a shelf of glassware that shattered in a cascade of fragments.

'Ah. I am not too familiar with it yet.' Kell projected stillness and the mechanism became calm. 'Remember how we learned to master the ice wain. You must ease into it; think your intention and be firm in that thinking.'

'Yes but I had control sticks then, something I could see and take hold of!'

'The wain was a simpler device. Look Skjebne, the soul of the orb wants to help us. It is like my multiblade weapon – its function is to carry out our instructions . . . and I suspect it too becomes attuned to the mind of its instructor as time passes.'

'Hora told me this orb had been inactive for a long time. But to the wyrda it is a holy relic, and through reverence they would not dispose of it.'

'Rightly so,' Kell said. 'For if one of these can be mended by simple means, then why not most of them – all of them even!'

Skjebne smiled at the boy's innocent optimism. Then his smile moderated, for that same strength had seen Kell succeed so far. In his beginner's mind, there were always many possibilities. And furthermore, he had not been afraid to join with the minds of other intelligences, whether they were constructed or natural. In doing so, he was prepared to learn from his dreams and theirs.

'Well, time will tell.' Skjebne came over and rested his hand on Kell's shoulder. 'But for now we have a wyrda orb ready to follow our bidding, if indeed there is anything in particular we would like it to do.'

'I have an idea about that,' Kell said, and explained what it was – so that shortly afterwards the two friends stood shivering at Skjebne's threshold while the orb rushed skywards through the driving snow and was instantly lost from their sight.

★

No one could know whether the device would carry out Kell's commands. At worst – and Kell felt a little hollow in his stomach to think about it – it would soar until its energies died, and then would be lost irretrievably. But if his plan worked he would have proved something to himself, and helped Skjebne and perhaps the whole clan of the Wyrda Craeftum in ways he had never imagined.

But that was for the future. Now the time had arrived when he must leave the warmth and safety of Edgetown to put Alderamin's scheme into action.

By earliest light he was dressed and armed and standing beside Magula not far from the gates of the town.

The snow has not eased, ealdor. Our going will be difficult.

It is a scouring wind, Kell. Its texture has changed – I can feel it. We will set out in a blizzard but make our way under blue skies. I have no doubts about that . . .

Moments later they were joined by Fenrir, Wyldewulf and Tir; and shortly after that by Hagen and Saeferth, two of Alderamin's most able and trusted kinsmen. Dressed in light leather armour and the white furs of the snowbeorn, they could move quickly and hide easily from sight when the enemy came into view.

'So, you are assembled,' Alderamin said as he approached them. He looked critically over his men, then with some concern at Kell. 'Remember that your first task is to assess the strength of the Luparo. There must be no conflict unless you are sure of his weaknesses, and only then when you have the advantage of surprise and the option of retreat . . .'

The wulfen listened patiently to this; but these were alien ways. In their own hearts they knew that the Slaughterer was a supernatural being that might never be overcome. And yet their own honour and the very life spark of their kind would not let them turn away from the contest.

'My feeling is that whatever the Luparo happens to be, he will have increased his strength through Tarazad forces. If such is the case, and if their power is too great, simply

76

return here and we will defend this ground as best we can . . .'

Even as Kell listened to the merchant's advice, he was aware of the impressions coming to him from the minds of the wulves: and he felt their pride and their fear and the fierce tenacity that had kept their breed alive since the arrival of the Ice.

'We thank you Alderamin,' Kell said when his friend's words were done and there was nothing left but farewells. 'I am here to give whatever assistance I can, and I know that Hagen and Saeferth will also be of help. But this matter is one that only the wulfen can resolve, so that at the end I have no choice but to follow their guidance.'

'Then they will do what they must, and you will aid them in your own way. Take every care,' Alderamin said. He stripped off his glove and he and Kell gripped hands in respect and in hope that this would not be their final parting. Then, as though to save himself from showing further emotion, he yelled loud orders to have the gates swung open, and would not watch as the travellers faded quickly into the drifting veils of snow.

For a short while their path took them along the bottom of the valley close to the river and they moved through a white blindness of freezing fog and steady snowfall. But soon Magula chose a little-used track that struck upwards into the forest gloom; up and up until they came to the edge of the trees. Beyond they could see that the cloud was thinning, rushing away on a westerly wind. The sky was blue and clean and a long way off, jagged and magnificent in their greys and golds and fanged peaks of ice, the Dawn Mountains followed the horizon in a huge curve of rock.

If the Luparo has come from Thule, he and his retinue must travel this way. There are not many passes that lead towards Edgetown.

I agree, Kell said, repeating the conversation in words for the sake of their human companions. *But if, as you say, the Slaughterer is a creature of myth, what has he to do with the Tarazad? And why does he need to use trade routes at all?*

These are human questions, framed by a human mind, Magula replied. *I am not sure they bear on our reality.*

Kell thought otherwise, though he kept his reflections to himself out of regard for the wulfen's beliefs.

Presently they rested in a small defile tucked away among the mountain's stony heights – as Magula had predicted, in brilliant sunshine. Alderamin had seen to it that chunks of raw moxen steak were included with the provisions, so that the four wulfen would not go wanting. Kell noticed that each animal took enough meat to satisfy politeness, but realised that they would be keener and faster with their stomachs virtually empty.

Then, a little past high-sun-time, the party pressed on along a ridge with the way back to Edgetown on their left, and a scape of ice-shattered rock and snowfields beyond and to their right.

We will go down to the canyons soon, Magula decided. *Already the air is colder and the night chill will be cruel . . .*

Kell nodded, taking the pack leader's word but detecting no change in the temperature yet. He noticed the puzzled glances that Hagen and Saeferth exchanged, and felt privileged to have learned, over these past moons, even this small amount from his wulfen companions and cousins.

Notice how it has happened, Fenrir said to Kell a little while later. They had paused on a broad sandstone shelf outlooking the vast spread of the land beneath. *The Ice came by and covered all but the topmost parts of this range. And then it withdrew, but left some of itself in the clefts and the hanging valleys and the higher canyons, where it remains to this day.*

Kell could clearly see the fragmented legacy of the Wintering.

Its presence affects the conditions here, chilling the wind as it sweeps across from where the sun rises, so that the snow lingers above the forest deeps further into the year . . . Sun and snow and wind mixed in this way make for a dangerous balance.

'Avalanche,' Hagen said, once Kell had passed on Fenrir's

thoughts. 'Winterscour. We hear its thunder sometimes even in Edgetown.'

'The whole snowfield becomes unstable around the time of the Reaping Moon,' added Saeferth. 'Alderamin will not send any caravans over the mountains then. There is still danger now, of course –' He gave a cheerful gap-toothed smile. 'But the hard–long–dark has locked the snow tight, by and large, so that we are only considerably at risk, rather than inevitably so . . .'

As Magula had advised, before very long they chose a route that took them down from the exposed spine of the mountain and away from the cutting wind whose blades had been sharpened by the waning afternoon. Kell had assumed that the wulfen were randomly searching for signs of the Luparo, but gradually he came to suspect that they were now following a definite trail: Fenrir particularly was becoming agitated, and Wyldewulf and Tir had fanned out, moving ahead and on a path parallel to the one the humankin chose.

Do you scent him? Kell asked at last, to test his impression. *Or are we jumping at nightmares?*

Fenrir swung his head to give Kell a bright goldeneyed look as he loped along beside. *We have always walked with great faith, great doubt, great endeavour. If the Slaughterer is near, he will not catch us by surprise.*

This was no clear answer, but obviously it was all that Kell was going to get. He put any scepticism to the back of his mind and, so that he could endure, set his thoughts as though this trek would be endless. His life narrowed down to this one step, then this one, then this –

And soon the sun touched the far peaks and its light splintered and went glittering across the whole sky. The track sloped down and the party descended into shadows – into a narrow gorge that channelled the smell of pine forest from the nearby valley below. The tension deepened steadily along with the gloom.

Then without warning Magula stood still. His eyes closed

and he lifted his face so that his muzzle pointed to the sky.

We have found him. His thought rang like a doombell in their heads. The men stopped. A moment later Wyldewulf came padding quickly towards them back down the trail.

Over the next rise. Snowfields, outcrop rock, some sparse tree cover. Forest far below – and there were other impressions, too swift and subtle and complex for Kell to understand.

Our fate is forked, Magula said. *We must on no account be caught in this canyon. But so far the Luparo seems not to have sensed us. We must move to more advantageous ground, and there decide whether to observe, or retreat, or attack . . .*

There was no argument to be made; no better sense to settle. Silently Saeferth and Hagen unslung their weapons and moved as quickly and quietly as they could, taking Wyldewulf's lead to the end of the gully and over a difficult lip of tumbled boulders. Briefly the low sun caught them in its full blaze before they gained new cover behind a rocky spur.

Below them was brief scree, then snow in broad blue-tinted swathes that swept down to the rounded base of the valley. Away to the left the pine forest was flung like a pelt across the slopes. More directly below, the distant forms of a terrible assembly were moving.

How do you know it is the Luparo? Kell queried, before Hagen pushed a metal shape into his hands; two tubes joined, which Kell could hang by a strap from his neck.

'Look into the glass. It brings the distance closer.'

Kell did so and was amazed and delighted to realise that here was an implement like a smaller version of Skjebne's beloved farscope; though with a lens for each eye the view was sharper and wider, so that the distant caravan became more clearly defined.

'Tarazad fighters,' Kell said. Now the link with Thule was confirmed. He could also make out pack moxen, and some warriors mounted on horseback; hounds and their human keepers . . . and an odd indistinctness that must have been the Slaughterer himself.

'He is veiled in mist,' Kell said; just a passing comment, but Fenrir snapped back angrily.

He is clearly visible! Awful – see the wulfenheads hung from his body. Their souls are trapped until the Slaughterer himself is slain. Awful, awful!

Without a word Kell passed the twinned farscopes back to Hagen, who checked Kell's perception and found it to be true.

'Saeferth?'

'There is only a blurring, a fogginess where anything might be so . . .'

So the humankin are as stupid and slow-eyed as we always knew them to be!

Tir's outburst drew a sharp growl of reprimand from Magula, who showed his fighting teeth in an open condemnation of his kinfellow's insult.

This dissent makes us weak like sun-rotted ice! Wyldewulf, give us the benefit of your assessment.

I think the Luparo is cunning, said the old wulf. *I think he is using our mythology against us.*

'But he doesn't know we are here!'

He knows well enough what always lies in the depths of wulfen minds. How the dread came to be there is a mystery for another time. But my feeling is that you see a fog because you are human, and we see our most profound fear because we are wulfen.

Your wisdom is forever valuable to us, Wyldewulf, Magula said. The pack leader gazed again at the caravan crawling along in the valley. His eyes, much sharper than Kell's ever could be even with the aid of the magnifying crystal, easily picked out the cruel wulfenhunter dogs chained to their masters' fists; and the Shahini men in their carapaces of leather armour hefting lance-like fire-hurling weapons; and, over-reaching all, the terrible ironclad form of the Luparo surrounded by his phantoms and serpentine tendrils of biting smoke. How could Kell fail to see it – or see it and not be cowed?

Tir stirred beside him and sniffed at the air.

It is too dangerous –

His comment had a beginning but no end. Out of nowhere came a fire that broke apart the rocks, and burned Hagen so that he died within a breath, and opened Tir like a flower. The others were hurled aside and sent sprawling.

Kell heard the whoosh of flame and then there was just a confusion of spinning rock fragments and a tingling blizzard of ice crystals. He heard Saeferth shouting close by, and Magula's howl of pure grief as he realised the death of his friend.

Move away! Move away!

His thought went out in alarm, because he knew that whatever had struck them would do so again in the same spot. He had not so much fear for the wulfen as for himself: they were fleet and powerful, while he was still dazed with the concussion of the attack, and shocked and blinded by ice spray and a hundred separate hurts that now seemed to grow in his flesh.

'This way, with me!'

Saeferth's strong arm and determined voice reached him at the same instant. Kell found himself swung clear and half-dragged at an upward angle across the snow.

From somewhere above came another crack like a fiercely snapping spark; and a whickering sound in the air; and then a dull boom and more cascades of snow; a waft of fiery air; a prolonged sizzling hiss of fading energies.

'Where are they! Where are they!' Kell cried in alarm. He was surrounded by a hurricane of spinning ice crystals, through which the afternoon sunshine blazed and made rainbows.

Saeferth pushed Kell down behind rocks and pointed upward through a cleft.

'There,' he said, with certainty and loathing mixed in equal measure.

Briefly Kell thought he was looking at more reflections made by the ice powder raised in the explosion . . . but the brilliant spot of light did not fade or fail; instead it drifted slowly across the deepening blue, and then swept down on a low swinging path once again.

'It's a sky gleam.' Kell felt dulled by despair, and his words sounded heavy, dispirited.

'Whatever you call it, the thing can spit.' Saeferth settled himself more solidly, hunkering down; propped his weapon in the V of the cleft and looked intently along the guidesights.

The sky gleam, accelerating rapidly, loosed a ball of fire at the low point of its parabola: a fizzing light that streaked off to the left and detonated with a loud bang. It blasted apart another knot of rock and sent loose scree rattling down.

Kell knew the gleam was firing at the wulfen. Their instinct would be to make for the trees, where they would be hidden somewhat from the senses of the machine. But to get there they needed to cross open ground, moving from one outcrop to the next with an ordeal between each. How Fenrir's heart must be racing with the terror of it!

'The gleams are not indestructible, Saeferth,' Kell said. He was hoping to give the man more confidence in his retaliation.

'This rifle your friend Skjebne supplied can penetrate steel armour. My greater concern is that there may be more than one of the "gleams". If so, our chances are drastically reduced.'

Then he put that possibility from his mind and made it as clear and empty as the sky; a great stillness and openness that held only his target and the inevitability of its destruction.

Kell heard a sharp clean crack and saw Saeferth jolt with the rifle's kickback. Simultaneously, it seemed, the sky gleam flew apart in a shower of flaming scraps that trailed twists of white smoke as they fell.

Saeferth gave a hiss of satisfaction and his eyes were bright with triumph.

'Can you reach the Luparo from here?' Kell dared to say.

'Probably − although the Tarazad will loose all their firepower on us now, and we should not be here to greet it. Also, from what I've learned of your wulfen friends, I think they would choose to defeat the Slaughterer more nobly.'

The words were well said, and Kell readily agreed. He scanned the heavens and no more gleams were visible. But in the valley, the tiny dark specks of the Tarazad men were mobilising quickly now, while the Luparo and the slower-moving moxen were making for cover.

'They'll be hidden soon. We will lose them . . .'

'Well . . .' Saeferth quickly assessed the situation, guessing the position of the wulfen as best he could. 'We need a stratagem that will rescue our companions, allow us to leave the valley safely, and perhaps deal a blow to the Luparo and his minions . . .'

And by the way he said it, Kell knew that Saeferth already had something in mind.

He watched fascinated as the old fighter unpacked a stocky metal tube and set it at an angle propped up by two struts. It was now pointing away from the enemy and towards the broad snowfields that were glowing silver-blue in the evening light.

'If you were wulfen I'd already know what you were planning,' Kell said with some irritation.

And Saeferth replied, 'If I were wulfen, I wouldn't have this equipment in the first place . . . it will feel unpleasant, Kell. Be ready.'

Kell nodded, but had no idea what was about to happen. Saeferth made a few swift adjustments to the mechanism's simple controls, then touched a red button.

'Cover your ears. Turn away −'

Kell obeyed automatically, but the *shunk* of the shell as it flew from the tube was still uncomfortably loud and close. He watched it sail in a high arc spiralling smoke, and drop and disappear into the slab-snow covering the slope some twenty furrowlengths below their position.

Then something happened – inside his chest, he thought, at the very centre of his heart. There was a tremor that seemed to make the whole world shiver very slightly, but very quickly. Kell instantly became nauseous; his stomach heaved and he stumbled like a drunken man. It reassured him mildly to note that Saeferth looked equally sickened.

By this time a clutch of Tarazad warriors was hurrying up the hillside: odd, gangly, insectile, they seemed to be strapped into jointed metal contrivances that amplified their bodies' movements and swept them along in great strides.

'*Hunta drengs*,' Saeferth said. 'I have seen them once before, in Thule. Usually they guard the core of the city and . . . def . . . rnn . . . ng . . .'

Saeferth's words crumbled and he pitched over as though in a faint. Kell too was helplessly felled as the ground moved underneath him. He scrambled clear of the overlooming rocks and saw the snowfield below him disintegrate. Great splits appeared, carving off immense blocks of packed snow, which under their own vast weight began to slide. Their momentum dredged away more snow from even lower down, so that within the space of just a few moments half the hillside was slipping, rolling, cascading in a colossal white wave towards the valley floor.

Kell experienced one wondrous moment of appreciation at the sheer scale of what was happening. A section of land bigger in area than the whole of Edgetown was shifting –

And then came the thunder, grinding upwards in an ever-growing roar that battered him physically: his head beat like a drum; knives pierced his ears; his teeth were attacked by tiny drills right at their roots. Kell screamed and screamed, giving up his pain to the heavens. Saeferth was screaming too and blood was trickling from his mouth.

Kell helped the man up and together they struggled in

agony through the unending fury of noise to the ridge, and over it into the haven of the little gulley they'd found out earlier.

Maybe Kell slept. His recollections were confused and fragmented. There was some vague memory of emptying his stomach privately behind some boulders. He thought that he had cried. He thought that Saeferth had laughed almost hysterically in his pain and at the fact that they'd survived. Then the man wept for a short time, and Kell too thought of brave Hagen and Tir and was similarly moved.

Night came on and the cold grew intense. Very sluggishly, Saeferth set up a makeshift camp. Skjebne had provided him with some flameless *ligetu* lamps that shone with a soft light; and with some heatstones that gave off warmth once you had struck them together. Then, sitting close because of the ordeal of the day, man and boy hunched down and cradled the heatstones and lost themselves in the peaceful glow of the lamps. They became part of the tiny bubble of light in the world's immense darkness.

A long time later, when moonlight washed the tops of the gully walls but the moon itself was not visible, Kell stirred. He heard a small crackling of stones; but immediately before that he had become aware of other presences nearby – the minds of his wulfen friends, Fenrir, Magula, Wyldewulf . . .

And now the animals came carefully closer, as though to reassure themselves that their companions, the warrior Saeferth and young Kell, were really alive and waiting. Magula was the first to show himself.

We thought the Luparo had brought doom on us all . . . The wulf blink-blinked in the light and looked from Kell to Saeferth, who was in the process of waking, and back to Kell again.

What terrible retribution you slow-eyes are capable of!

It was expressed with a passion that made Kell wince. He chose not to explain it to Saeferth, but the man frowned as though he understood something of the pack leader's feelings, despite his lack of syncrthic abilities.

Presently Fenrir and Wyldewulf joined them, and were glad to huddle round the heatstones as though to recover themselves from the shock of the day's events.

We buried Tir and Hagen under rocks, Magula commented at last. *Afterwards we searched through the valley, but found no trace of the Tarazad or their caravan . . . Nor did we detect any sign of the Luparo.*

There was no joy to these impressions, only a deep weariness that Kell had never encountered before. He passed on Magula's message to Saeferth.

'Even so, we will break camp early to return home, and there make ourselves ready.'

'For what?' Kell wanted to know.

'For the arrival of the Slaughterer. For it is a wise and very ancient wisdom that says — when you have seen the enemy defeated, be prepared against them.'

6

A Wild Hunt

The blood knows the truth.

Kell thought again of Magula's words as the weary and bedraggled party approached the gates of Edgetown. They had been met at the eastern markstone, and now runners going ahead of them ensured that the portals were opened promptly and Alderamin himself was there to greet them on their return.

In the warm and comfortable hearth hall they told their story. The merchant laughed hugely as Saeferth recounted the use of the sonic shell to bring on the winterscour.

'I have heard it told – from a trader who passes this way every few moons, and he heard it from an associate who once saw the very place – that there is an enclave to the north, empty of people, but filled with weapons of great power and variety. It was this trader who bartered me the weapon of sound. It can make whole armies sick to their stomachs! Alas –' Alderamin glanced at Saeferth and shrugged. 'I had but the one missile . . .'

The world is a more dangerous place than I ever thought! Kell passed this on to Magula and Fenrir and Wyldewulf, who were sitting nearby, but said nothing of it to any others.

'You have done a wonderful job, my friends!' Alderamin clapped his hands on Kell and Saeferth's shoulders. 'And we will eat and drink now and celebrate your victory, and mourn the loss of brave Hagen and Tir –'

And immediately Alderamin began issuing orders to that

effect. But the blood knows the truth, and Magula gave a sharp bark that stopped the merchant in his tracks.

Tell him, Kell. Saeferth knows the wise way. We did not find the body of the Luparo. And the Tarazad will soon learn of their hunting party's defeat – perhaps they know it already. Tell him to strengthen his defences, and to see that his women and children go to safety: not here, not in Edgetown, for wooden walls will mean nothing to the hunta drengs when they arrive. Tell him all of this and allow him to know that this era has ended, and the time has come to move on.

Kell did as he was bidden, and could hardly bear to look upon the change that came over the merchant. Alderamin's great boisterousness and energy faded; he seemed to sag and become a tired old man, beaten at last by life.

'But – but the Tarazad trade in our metals. Where else can they obtain the skills and the goods we supply?'

'They are a mindless swarm, driven by Helcyrian's outward urge,' Kell said, passing on the comments of the wulfen. 'Their industry takes a thousand forms, and the work of Edgetown affects only a few of them. The wulfen pack have lived in Thule among the Tarazad for a long time and realise the truth of this.'

And my feeling is that the Tarazad's main purpose is to uncover the secrets of weorthan, Magula added in Kell's mind. *That is why they tore the heart out of the hills. And that is why they will spread across the land, and very soon now. Helcyrian commands them, but Helcyrian is being guided from above, by a greater force . . .*

'I feel uneasy.' Alderamin looked about himself. 'I understand all you say, Kell, and I would argue against it. But something is warning me and I have no explanation for what I am feeling.'

'Is it enough to prompt you to action?' Kell asked, and under any other circumstances the boy's impertinence would not have gone unpunished. But now, after long thought, Alderamin simply nodded.

'It will break my heart – but yes, I will follow your advice.'

89

He looked into Magula's eyes and failed to see the sympathy there, or the hard bright glitter which told that endurance lay behind all feelings and all actions.

'The wulfen are creatures of the wilderness. Ask them for their guidance now. If the community is to leave, then it must be with the greatest possible chance of safety.'

Kell quickly passed on the request and was as swiftly answered.

'Our main advantage is that the hard–long–dark will soon be over: the next moon is the Budding Moon; longer light, warmer days. Magula also says that the people should split into small mobile groups, with the town's resources shared among them. Every group should be given weapons, and a mox, and a wain if enough are available. Every group should include at least one adult, man or woman, who can fight and whose orders will be obeyed without argument . . .'

'That allows us to separate,' Alderamin replied bitterly. 'Will we ever come together again? Will we ever know the peace that has existed in Edgetown?'

Does he have no deity to guide him? Where does his inspiration come from? Magula wanted to know.

Alderamin's god has betrayed him, as the All Mother betrayed us in Perth. I will not challenge him with that now . . . 'Magula also advises that the people of Edgetown should take as many routes as they can away from the valley: if you can avoid the main trade ways, so much the better.'

'If the Tarazad come this far for vengeance, what stops them from tracking us down wherever we go?'

Kell looked inwardly, and Alderamin soon noticed the change that came over his face. 'Magula says that the wulfen pack will remain behind to confuse the Tarazad hunters and inflict as much damage as possible. They don't do this out of simple generosity,' Kell added as Alderamin began to protest. 'Their own demon, the Luparo, is still alive in their hearts. Until they have overcome that, there will be no peaceful place for them in all the world.'

Alderamin ordered a huge bonfire to be lit in the centre of the town, and for a wooden platform to be erected before it. His wives and children went through the streets and called the whole community together; and, silhouetted by flames, he told his people what was going to happen. Kell watched their faces and was moved to tears by their expressions of horror and helplessness, and sometimes of overwhelming anger that they should be so ruined.

'Even before you argue, Kell, please realise that I will not be discouraged. I am going to stay here with you.'

Kell felt the gentle touch on his arm, and Sebalrai was with him, clearly afraid, but more powerfully determined.

'You belong to Alderamin's family –'

'They have looked after me. I am not a possession to be owned.'

'Sebalrai, the danger –'

'Chertan the brigand kept me in chains for years. He shackled me with punishments. Never again will I let anyone tell me what to do, or make me so fearful that I act against my heart's wish.'

Standing nearby, Skjebne shook his head sadly. 'Alas Kell, you might as well argue with the breeze. Sebalrai will go wherever she wants, and there is nothing that you or I can do about it.'

'Besides which,' said the girl, 'I have a most useful skill, which I may be able to teach you –'

So saying, she vanished from his sight. And although Kell could still feel the gentle pressure of her fingers, he could not convince his eyes that she was there. Then she was gone entirely, making Kell panic briefly as he swept his hands around in search of her.

'See how you need to know where she is.' Skjebne gave a wicked grin. 'See how you want her back so much.'

Sebalrai reappeared laughing, but then became serious

because this was a troubled night, and because Kell was angry with her decision.

They listened to the rest of Alderamin's instructions, and when he had finished they returned to Skjebne's rooms together with Magula and Fenrir who sniffed distastefully at the miasma of chemical stinks.

'I will need to leave most of this behind,' Skjebne said with a sigh. 'But the fruits of my work are in my head, and noted down for the future.'

He went to a cupboard and pulled out a leather haversack, and tipped its contents out on the table.

'It's weorthan!' Kell was horrified. 'You have been putting your thoughts into the weorthan crystal –'

'Listen before you judge,' Skjebne said sternly. 'When we showed you the underground caverns in Perth, we came to a room. You called it a place of stories. In there were thousands of crystal coins containing a huge quantity of knowledge from past times. Do you remember that – yes of course you do, clearly. I said then and I say now that there was no trace of the All Mother in the glass, and yet it was weorthan glass all the same. And I say more. The mind of the ice wains we used to escape were minds embedded in weorthan. Can you not understand, Kell, that weorthan itself is not evil. What is evil or good is the way in which it is used!'

'I am deeply suspicious of it.'

'Of course you are, because of your own experience of it. And I am suspicious of the uses to which it is put, because of my experience. I also make the point, Kell, that the best way to learn to plough is to spend time with a ploughman. If I am to understand weorthan, then I must keep it by me . . . and so instead of trying me, help me to pack up what I need!'

They worked through till morning, and then slept briefly. By the time a hazy, brassy sun had lifted above the ramparts of Edgetown the first groups of people were ready to leave.

Kell shared their sadness as he stood in the still frosty air and watched the gates open and the mox-drawn waggons begin to pull away. Wulfen escorts from Magula's pack ran and scampered ahead: they had agreed to accompany the travellers for a while, guiding them away from any Tarazad patrols that may have been combing the area. Then they would return to the abandoned town, and wait for their own wierd to unfold.

Alderamin stayed at the threshold and made his farewell to every soul that left his protection. But Skjebne rather tetchily said there was no point in him doing the same.

'I will stay here with you, Kell, because I know your way is bound to the wulfen, at least for now. But it would be prudent to make ready for a swift departure if circumstances bring us to that. Aside from which –' and here Skjebne's smile darkened – 'I have a few arrangements to make for our Tarazad friends should they choose to knock on our door.'

For the rest of the morning Kell and Skjebne laboured together, loading what they needed into two backpacks, carriable with some effort.

'If Sebalrai does indeed stay with us, then she can carry some provisions. And if we travel with the wulfen, then using a mox will not be appropriate. We can take only what is essential.'

By mid-afternoon the last of the Edgetown families had gone and Alderamin retreated to his hearth hall for a final time – not to bemoan his circumstances, but to reflect the fortunate tumbling of fate that allowed his people another chance of life. He had his family close about him, and for some while Sebalrai sat with them to explain her decision.

'I still can't understand you,' Kell said afterwards. Night had come and Sebalrai had joined him on the ramparts where he was helping to keep watch. The day's fair weather had held: a worn moon seemed to be dissolving its light across a lace-covered sky, entangling a few bright stars. Apart from the sputter of the firetar brands below in the streets, and the woosh and hollow calling of nightravens out on the hunt, the land was quiet.

93

The girl sat, a faint ghost, beside him. Her hair glowed softly and her pale face was looking up at his, but Kell could not make out her expression, much less her thoughts.

'I mean, Alderamin's is a *proper* family. Besides, he has reputation and influence in this region. Once he has moved beyond the immediate danger of the Tarazad, the likelihood is he'll establish another town which will flourish in time like the next season's growth . . .'

'Nevertheless, I have made up my mind –'

'I mean, I don't even know where I'm going! I have a journey but no destination, and I travel with a wulfpack and a half-crippled *gaeleran* so possessed by his bag of weorthan that he cannot bear to leave it behind!' Kell sighed with exasperation. 'It just doesn't seem sensible that you should come with us.'

Sebalrai slid her hand on his arm. 'Everything you have said is about yourself and how *you* feel. It lets me see what your world looks like. But not once have you realised how *I* feel and what life looks like to me. I understand everything you say: there will be only Skjebne, the wulfen, the wilderness and doubt.'

'Yes – yes!'

'And still I choose it, and you will not dissuade me, Kell. And some day you may come to realise my feelings.'

She might have said more – Kell had the impression she wanted to – but something made her move away. She turned side on, then seemed to turn again and become a thin line like the edge of a shadow, and then she had vanished entirely and Kell did not see her again that night.

Later he roused from the oddest sleep. He had not been awake, and yet his eyes had kept watch over the eastern approach to the town. Someone had been using them on his behalf – Fenrir, he knew a second later; whose physical self was curled in a corner of the caravanserai close to where Alderamin's mox-wain was waiting to depart. He felt the wulf's presence withdraw, and a moment later heard the creaking of the ladder below as Saeferth came up to join him.

'It will be light soon,' the soldier said. He was armoured and cloaked in furs and his breath smoked in the leaden air. 'I am going with Alderamin's wain. Despite your wulfen-friends' offer to act as a rearguard here, we think you should be on your way too. The longer you leave it, the more time the Tarazad have to assemble a greater force to attack. Will you ask your friend Magula what he thinks of this?'

Kell nodded and the movement dizzied him. He stumbled and then jolted upright as a spark seemed to leap in his brain.

'What's the matter boy?'

The woods were rushing by him and he burned with the fire of too much running. But his blood was strong and his heart, like a fist, was clenched and angry and sure in its power.

'Wulfen –' was all he managed to say: the vision consumed him briefly. The trees loomed over and the hard ground drummed with the rhythm of his running, and the predawn mist flew aside and then swirled back to conceal him. He was linked, suddenly and completely, with one of the wulfen pack; an outprowler sweep-searching the woods.

'The Tarazad are coming,' he told Saeferth without seeing him properly. Through the mist loomed a wall of shadow – the eastern ramparts of the town.

Kell tore himself free with an effort. He looked over the parapet into the distance, and a few moments later caught sight of a young silver wulf – Eodor was his name – pounding along the track with his red tongue lolling.

'Open the gates! Warn the people –'

Kell scrambled for his multiblade, nearly tripping over its strap as he reached for it beside him. Saeferth made a calming gesture.

'Hasten slowly. Live longer.' He smiled and unslung his own weapon, a device like the fire-rod that Hora used to favour. Saeferth settled himself with the weapon aimed ready, and waited.

Below in the town the few remaining warriors were gathering. Alderamin came bustling out of the hearth hall with weaponry of his own, while Jadhma and Shaula and the rest of his family hurried towards the protection of the wain. Of the wulfen there was no sign, and Kell guessed they were busy with their own defensive preparations. Skjebne appeared, clattering with wargear, and hurried as best he could towards the ladders.

'Wait, I'll help you!'

Kell clambered down and took hold of some of the kit.

'At least if I am to die,' Skjebne said grinning like a horse, 'I will try out some of these untested armaments!'

A little way off two men hauled open the gates and Eodor streaked through at full speed. Kell caught sight of tall spindly things moving rapidly along the track behind him; the hunta drengs.

'Hold the gates!' Skjebne yelled. He hefted a tube on to his shoulder and warned Kell to stand well clear. Immediately afterwards a projectile *whooshed* away at a tremendous velocity through the mist.

The guards, startled and unsure, pushed the gates closed again, so that Skjebne failed to see the accuracy of his shot. But they all heard the enormous *boom* that resounded through the valley and sent the roosting corvus flocks lifting like a cloud out of the elms.

But just a few seconds later Saeferth and the other few men with him on the ramparts began firing rapidly. And a moment after that something thudded with a huge impact into the oaken walls of the town. Saeferth changed the angle of the weapon and began shooting directly downward at whatever was climbing up from below.

Leaving Skjebne (who seemed amply equipped to defend himself), Kell climbed the ladder and joined the front fighters. He looked over the edge and saw the hunta drengs closely for the first time . . . and they were just men, armoured and anonymous and clad in their skeletons of metal which extended their limbs and their power. Frightening and without thought of their own, relentless and deadly, ferocious and tragic. But just men.

The leading dreng fell away as Saeferth's onslaught penetrated its armour. It smashed to the ground and lay twitching. The one coming up just behind it looked like a giant beetle, its back and head shielded over. Saeferth waited until it reached the top of the wooden wall, its silhouette standing proud, then he fired the rod and kept firing in a cacophony of sizzling light until the dreng dropped back out of sight.

'There are not very many of them,' he shouted so all could hear. 'This is what's left of the Luparo's hunting party. Fight on!'

'Why do they attack when they are so few?' Kell wanted to know.

'They have little mind of their own,' Saeferth hazarded. 'A dreng dies and its neighbour fails to learn. These are not warriors, but ants.'

'Why would men choose this life?'

Saeferth smiled at the way Kell could question in the midst of conflict. 'They don't choose it, any more than your mox once chose the soil you commanded it to plough.'

'At least my mox thought to wander off sometimes,' Kell said with feeling.

'Three more!' yelled one of the soldiers a short way along the wall. Saeferth broke off what he was going to say and ran to his neighbour's assistance. Kell heard the heavy wooden *chunk-chunk* as the dreng's clawed skeleton hooked into the wood, then the rapid thudding as it ran up the vertical face. He leaned over the better to see –

And another dreng, just below, swiped at him and caught him a glancing blow with the edge of its metal hand.

Kell spun away, stunned; landed heavily on the walkway

97

and rolled to its very edge. Below him the ground tilted; packed earth and piled snow streaked with dirt, ice-crust, a running man . . .

Blood trickled rapidly across one eye and over the bridge of Kell's nose. A dull pain in his temple grew as the first bright agony faded. He lay dizzily, loose-limbed, and watched in total helplessness as the dreng climbed over the rampart and stepped lightly down to the platform. It drew a long plain sword from a sheath of concentric iron rings, the metal lifting free with a musical note.

Kell waved his hand about ludicrously searching for his multiblade, for his knife . . .

Another head loomed behind the helmeted head of the dreng; huge and dark and round. Kell thought that perhaps the commander of the Tarazad force had come to watch the pathetic easy finish of one stupid hopeless ineffectual boy.

The dreng raised its blade for the deathblow.

And the object behind it swept forward and hit the armoured soldier with a clang and sent him tumbling over the edge, where he landed with a crash and lay still. Immediately three wulfen buck were upon the dreng to make sure of its death.

And above Kell in the mist a dark orb hung, sparkling with a dust of jewelled lights.

'Pretending you have lost a fight does not deceive the Tarazad,' Hora's voice said with a wonderful clarity. 'Next time just remember to strike first!'

'Hora – where are you?' Kell was light-headed with pain and joy and relief at being alive. He made no effort to stand until Hora snapped a brief order for him to do so.

'The skirmish isn't over yet – though there are but three or four of the dreng warriors left.'

'You can see that? You can see me?'

'You worked a fine magic on the orb – with its help it has to be said. I can see many things through it now . . . as for where I am; upon a fell, around six days' travel from

98

Edgetown. I'm sorry I am not there to fight with you in the flesh, but the orb makes a reasonable mace as you've seen! Circumstances have changed and we must meet, Kell, and the sphere will guide you. Have done with the Tarazad there and come with Skjebne north-eastwards through the forest and over the pass that Alderamin calls *Feallanstan*, the Tumblestones . . . are you still with your wulfen friends?'

'Yes!'

'Then they will protect you on the way –'

'But what about Thule? What about Helcyrian and the Tarazad over-running the land?'

'All strands of a spider's web lead to the centre. Have some patience Kell and be content to know that our work will take us towards that end. Be quick now, for every day is precious.'

With that, the orb made a half-spin and then lifted silently into the opalescent fog, presumably to search out any further hunta drengs sneaking towards the town. At last, feeling foolish in the extreme, Kell dragged himself up and walked the battlement to where Saeferth was attending to a wounded friend.

'You have the most remarkable guardians,' the soldier said, having witnessed the encounter. 'The last time I saw that sphere it was a useless metal ball lying on Skjebne's work-bench.'

'He did his best,' Kell said with no hint of arrogance. 'But I think we must all learn that the world works by the deft use of the mind and not just through capable hands.'

Kell helped Saeferth to carry their injured companion to the ground. The fighting seemed to be over now: in the distance came the howl and snarling of wulfen as the last of the drengs was dispatched. Shortly afterwards Alderamin appeared, puffing with the efforts of the combat.

'We lost two men, Aethgar and Wayd. And there are a few injured, who we can accommodate in one of our wains.'

He looked around himself and Kell saw his eyes moisten, and he glanced away.

'I think you were right, Saeferth,' Alderamin said. 'These drengs were just what remained of the Luparo's escort. Others will follow them, many more than we can withstand. And though it hurts me to say it, I think the time has come for me to leave my beloved burg.'

'I will see to it the wains are ready.' Saeferth smiled at Kell fondly. 'And you will go on with the wulfen?'

'To meet with Hora and, I suppose, his wyrda fellows.' He briefly recounted what Hora had said.

'Then travel well,' Alderamin told him, 'and make your own path. Let us be quick now, for time is short.'

And so it was that soon afterwards Kell and Skjebne and Sebalrai watched Alderamin's caravan of two wains and four riders on horseback lumber away into the mist. They became shadows, then vanished entirely and were lost to Kell's sight. Sebalrai wept openly and would not be consoled, but Kell pushed the hot tears back, realising he would be weeping selfishly out of loss while denying what had to be done.

Fenrir ran swiftly up to them to report that the way was clear and Magula and the pack now waited in the shelter of the trees and were ready to leave the valley.

Minutes later Kell stopped to heft his backpack more comfortably on his shoulders. He gazed through the thickening trees and looked his last upon Edgetown, and decided in that moment it would forever be known as Alderamin's Land.

The soulless drengs and the wulfen were as far apart in their natures as Kell could imagine. If what Hora said was true then the hordes of Helcyrian obeyed without thought or reflection, whereas the wulfen were highly independent within the compass of their lives.

It surprised him, therefore, when Magula readily agreed to accompany Kell and his friends to the place that Hora had described.

As I explained to you earlier, Kell, the world is a web in which we all live.

With Helcyrian at the centre —

Oh no . . . The wulf seemed to smile in his thoughts. *The anwealda of Thule is but a place where a few threads cross. We have not seen the centre yet, neither you nor I in the flesh or in our dreams. But the point I make is that paths cross with a purpose. That is the essence of Wierd. I remind you that it was no accident you spared Fenrir's life and that we accepted you as brooor into the pack. For now, your way is our way also. And your friend Hora undoubtedly has powerful knowledge, which may be of use to us all.*

So Magula felt the matter was settled, though Kell was intrigued and a little unnerved by his image of the web and the recollections it brought of his earlier days in the gardens of Perth: playing in the leafy tunnels the bushes made, happening upon such a web woven across, and then the startlement, always, as a fat spider ran from some unexpected angle to defend its centre. Perhaps it was there in green innocence where Kell learned his first fear, where the demons first came to his mind . . .

He let the thoughts go because they were a distraction to him, and the world outside was not without dangers of its own.

They were a good half-day's travel from Edgetown now, moving through the high forests in the direction that Hora had advised. Magula found a promontory and mapped the wind, and warned that snow was sweeping westward — short flurries rather than the steady fall of the past few days.

It will not trouble us too much among the trees, but when we come to more open ground the going will be harder —

For us. Kell added. *Not for you.*

Friend Skjebne is in pain from his old injury, but he hides the suffering well. Young Sebalrai is simply happy to be in your company, while you are fit and strong from your time with us in the wilderness . . .

And Magula went on to outline his plan — and although

Skjebne protested and became as cantankerous as Kell had ever seen him, in the end he recognised the honour and respect that was being shown by the wulfen in allowing themselves to be yoked. Besides which, the stretcher was deliciously comfortable, and Wyldewulf seemed able to pull it without effort for hours at a time. In the forest, especially along the *heorot* tracks, the travelling was easy and smooth: across rougher ground Kell took up the rear struts and helped manoeuvre the litter over obstacles.

They journeyed in this fashion throughout the next day. Beyond the trees the snowsqualls howled and whistled, and only a gentle powdering of crystals flickered down to the level of the ground. Wyldewulf with his burden, Sebalrai, Kell and the bitchwulfen and their younglings stayed together while the rest of the pack scouted near and far for any signs of danger.

After many hours of such travel, and as the forest started to darken, Fenrir appeared and was soon joined by Wulfmaer, Hyld and the other buck wulves who drifted from the trees like ghosts, with the silence and subtlety of the mist.

Finally Magula himself arrived and matched Kell's pace with an easy loping stride.

Do you suppose Hora's orb is still somewhere near, and watching over us? he wanted to know.

I saw it vanish into the fog. I thought Hora had called it back to him . . . Why?

It could help us now, Magula said. *Because we are being hunted.*

The Luparo. Fenrir was near, moving up close beside Kell and the pack leader. *The utewulfen, the outrunners, have detected him. He smells our blood!*

Fenrir! Magula's strident thought was accompanied by a flashing glare and a show of teeth. *Now is the time to be strong.*

What can we do?

Most of the pack are not aware of his presence yet. Hyld who first detected the Slaughterer's stink held his thoughts fast, in secret, and has told only a few of us.

Skjebne still has weapons –

It is not just that. There is the playing-out of the prophecies, the Wierd, Fenrir's ordeal . . .

Then that is a limitation you have placed upon yourselves, Kell said with all the daring he could muster. *Does Wierd speak of Fenrir battling with the Luparo alone? Or could it be that reference is only made of him overcoming the Slaughterer, without mention of the means?*

Kell detected the wulf's hesitation in the afterglow of his anger that a mere slow-eyes should question the character of Wierd . . . but then, wasn't that part of the nature of the Way – that its endless interpretation led men and wulfen alike to their own destinations?

We are made by what we choose, Kell said more gently, without the passion of his earlier feeling. *What use will Fenrir's corpse be to us, and the Luparo left alive to terrorise your pack? You know yourself – for I have felt these thoughts – that the survival of the wulfen informs your every decision and action –*

There is the question of honour, Magula replied. Kell felt it like a flinching limb, like a reflex that existed now because it had existed for so long, whether its purpose was valid or not. Magula said it because he had always said it, without thinking any further.

You hide from the storm to survive the storm! You hunt the wild boar as a pack to eat boar meat and live! What's the difference now? Where is your action all-one-together when you need it!

Never in his life had Magula been spoken to like this. In the past he had inflicted a swift and severe punishment on arrogant whelps who spoke out of turn in questioning his authority . . . and yet now he sat and his eyes reflected the stillness of his mind as he settled this matter inside. For Kell had not challenged his leadership. He had questioned more profoundly than that, endeavouring to give power rather than take it away. And it was true enough that every pack strove to be independent, for reliance on others had meant reliance on their weaknesses. But already, within the single cycle of a moon, the wulfen had changed their ways remarkably: they had taken the shelter and food and friendship of Alderamin's humankin, and fought with them against the Tarazad . . . and had Magula and others not worked with Hagen and Saeferth already to try to prevent the Slaughterer's advance? Where was pride and honour when you lay on the ground with your lifeblood spilling out over the snow, in the name of tradition?

Magula sniffed the air and knew the world around him. He touched his muzzle to the ground, hunkered down and put an ear to the earth. Then he stood and regarded his pack steadfastly.

There are men moving in the forests – hunta drengs probably. And the Luparo will not be far from them. Listen carefully to us now, for we do not have much time . . .

The endless trees made striding difficult. Though there were faint tracks through the winter-rotted undergrowth, these had been caused by smaller creatures moving across their feeding grounds; and they were animals that ran to survive, so the paths often led through the most inconvenient territory as far as a pursuer was concerned.

Even so, the warrior's armour driven by its magic fire made him strong. If branches hung in his way, he tore them aside. If a boulder – one of the wandering stones brought by the Ice – ever blocked his progress, he leaped over it or shattered it with a bolt of force. And if the cowardly *feond* fled for his life, then it was a simple matter to urge the machinery on faster and faster until the struggling prey squirmed and shrieked its last in the trap-hooks of his immense iron gauntlet.

Such was the unstoppable might of the Shahini Tarazad when it was unleashed upon the world.

Now the dreng pushed through the pines with a new determination, for there were wulfenprints peppering the snow – many of them, the entire pack perhaps running quickly towards the Blackfall Cliffs, where the mountain sheared off and there was only the awful drop to the unvisited valley below. Soon they would realise their error and have to turn back upon themselves, or else follow the path of their weakness over the edge.

Inside his all-enclosing helmet, the dreng warrior laughed at the inevitability of the result; and the voice of Helcyrian urged him on to his greatness, and the fire of the Sustren surged through his blood. The weorthan put pictures in his head, and now he followed its vision and let out a deafening ululating cry through the darkness, to terrify his prey even more.

The trail split, and the wulfen spoor broke both ways. No matter, his *gefera* were moving up behind to take the other track. And behind them all strode the Luparo, whose blades would slice the last wulfen belly before the darkness was done.

The dreng took the left hand path, hurrying, hurrying now with the imagined smell of blood and the promise of another victory . . . but he slowed when the number of pawprints dwindled; six wulf, four, one . . .

And there ahead in the snow lay a man's head looking at him. What killing had already occurred?

The head laughed and the man rose up and pointed a stubby-looking weapon.

The dawn lifted through the earth and the faint veils of mist became ever brighter until the dreng's eyes were seared and he knew only blindness.

He shrieked, lashing out.

A weight crashed down on his shoulders. Another hurled itself at his chest and clung to the framework of steel ribs of his outer skeleton. The wulfen were attacking him! He roared. He clawed at the beast on the front of him and ripped it free. But another took its place, and another. More wulfen dropped from the trees – where wulfen had never climbed before! – and the dreng began to buckle under the animals' collective weight.

He knew that if he went down he would never rise. This

was the way of Wierd. Desperately the soldier prayed to the Sustren and sought strength and advice from his weorthan. But the terrible light had damaged the glass and he saw only stars drifting across – drifting forever across –

He felt fierce jaws wrenching at his armour, twisting the steel itself. The noise of the animals' snarling went on and on. Something pulled at his faceplate with enormous force. He cried out. The faceplate tore away –

There was but a second of intensely hot pain and an overwhelming fear. And then the soldier was truly among the beautiful stars, his soul floating free.

Kell heard the dreadful cry of the dreng as it died, and steeled himself. At the same time a rush of energy and excitement swept through him. For rituals bound the Tarazad, as they did the wulfen.

Deeper in the forest, another of the hunta warriors met his end. Magula had scented six of them, and if the plan ran its course they would all be slain within minutes. For many seasons the Tarazad had learned the wulfen ways; protected themselves against the songs that lured men to their doom; devised weapons to snare and destroy fleeing animals – not creatures that thought in advance, and schemed, and were co-ordinated in their defences. No wulf had ever climbed a tree to ambush a hunter. No wulf had ever before worked with humankin. No wulf had ever dared to turn and face the myth of the Luparo. It ran in the blood. And the blood knew the truth.

Well, the heart made the blood move, but the mind made the blood change. Now Kell and Fenrir and loyal Wyldewulf clung to the high branches of a stout pine and listened to the soft crepitation of the snow crystals as they filtered down through the tree canopy.

And presently out of that sound came another; the steady thud-thud-thud of the Luparo stalking along the path.

The dreng may have alerted him to this ploy, Kell warned. *Be ready on the ground, Fenrir.*

And the young wulf complied, slithering down a short way and then leaping six or so spans to the earth.

As it came on, the Luparo bellowed. But it was no more fearsome than the challenge of the aurok that Magula had bested. And as it came on dazzling lights blazed out from its armoured body. But they were nowhere near as bright as the sunburst weapon Skjebne had used.

And there in the centre of the light as it spread through the forest mists stood the Luparo's vast form. Smoke wreathed around it, and in the smoke were serpents and demons and the trapped souls of the wulfenslain!

No Fenrir, no! The Slaughterer is trying to mislead your mind –
He has come from the start of time to destroy me!

Kell felt his friend's terror, because he had himself run blindly from the Ice Demon in Thule. But that had been before he'd understood the deceptiveness of weorthan and the way its lies could be spoken directly into the brain.

Remember when we fought the hunta at Edgetown! Kell kept his thoughts firm and keen as a blade. *These were creatures who ran up the sheer walls of the compound, and spat fire, and whose pace could outdistance a horse. But we looked into their eyes and saw only men –*

And the demons driving the men!

We don't know what Helcyrian is. But the drengs are just men. And the Luparo is just another dreng.

The Slaughterer let out a saw-toothed shriek as it spotted the young wulf cowering back in the shadows. It made a spitting sound like fat dropped on a hot skillet. It held its vast hands out and repeatedly clenched the fingers with a cold hard rattling of metal. Then, with great deliberation, it swept aside its cloak and drew out the great double-headed axe with which to split the *huntung* in two.

Spiritedly the wulfling jumped into the middle of the path, its hackles raised. It showed its fighting teeth with a low drawn-out snarl. Its eyes gleamed with sheer ferocity – which was nothing in itself – but behind the bright rage was a dwindling fear, and behind that fear a sharp intelligence was working.

Through the power of the weorthan the Luparo spoke to the other drengs in the forest and called their names, and gave them their orders . . .

But in answer there was only the faint hissing of the voiceless dark and, from close by, the lifting howl of a wulf.

Inside the armour the Slaughterer tensed and swung the axe as it lumbered forward. The wulfling danced and skipped clear like a flick of silvery light. The Luparo swung again and clove the mist, the outer blade thudding into a tree. Ice crystals showered down – and something else – another attacker that landed on the Slaughterer's back.

Instinctively the Luparo reached round to rip its opponent free. But the little wulf leaped up and snapped at its face. In that moment's pause Kell stood astride the Luparo's shoulders and drove Hora's multiblade down through the steel plates – just a knucklespan wide, into the narrow space between the Slaughterer's body and the inner face of the armour.

The Luparo bent forward suddenly and Kell was thrown clear and went flying through the air. Luckily he'd kept the presence of mind to hold on to the multiblade's handle, and the weapon slipped free with a *zing* of sliding steel. He landed roughly and had the breath knocked from him for a while.

Fenrir leaped a second time, not to inflict damage but to taunt. The Slaughterer was fighting in the confined space where the heorot ran. Trees restricted his span and sweep. Every axe stroke seemed to end with the blade embedded in a soft trunk, and then the bothersome fatherless wulfwhelp would spin at him again, all slashing claws and snapping fangs. Once Luparo clipped him with a spiked glove and the animal went sprawling with a yelp of sudden pain –

That's when things changed, and he lost sight of the human boy who had stupidly come up against him. He was an unexpected enemy, to be sure, but he knew the road to agony and had run away from it now.

Littlewulf regained its legs and barked and snarled — feinted forward and leaped aside.

Another wulf, much bigger, came streaking along the track behind it and launched itself into the air. It struck the Luparo full force, square on, and sent the Slaughterer stumbling backwards. His heels kicked against something behind him in the way, that wriggled clear as he fell —

The scruffy *beom*! But how was he there? He had been nowhere in sight!

And then a girl seemed to swirl out of the mist beside him. So fragile. Those sad and pretty eyes —

The Luparo fell back against the multiblade that Kell had driven at an angle into the earth; the Slaughterer's sheer weight sending the spearpoint clean through. Such an ancient simple childish trick!

Luparo laughed and blood sprayed on the inside of his helmet.

Almost reverently the two human youths came forward. The Slaughterer's arms lay beside him like two useless logs, for the spear had damaged his spine and there was no feeling in his limbs, as there had been none in his heart. He prayed to the Sustren for solace and help, and his calls went unanswered.

Kell snicked his knife from its sheath and worked on the fiercely contoured faceplate until it came loose. Underneath lay the face of a bearded man, glassy eyed, strong featured. His lips were smeared with blood.

Silently Magula and the rest of the pack emerged from the trees. Their killing fury was over now and they walked quietly up to the fallen idol and looked upon him with a gaze that meant nothing to the Luparo. Wulfen eyes had always been beyond his understanding.

But now his own sight was failing, yet his attention was drawn to the boy and the girl who swam in the fluttering illumination cast by his armour. All around him his machinery was dying, as he must die now, as belief in him died now.

He opened his bloodied mouth and spoke in a tongue that Sebalrai could understand –

'*Nemnao hy sylfe . . .*' They name themselves. It was his mark of honour to the creatures who had defeated him.

And he tried to say more but his time was spent.

Kell and all the others stood aside as Fenrir leaped lightly on to the Slaughterer's chest, waiting just a moment beyond what tradition demanded before lunging forward to tear out his throat.

7

The Universal Wheel

Snowtops plumed in the endless wind that blew over the huddled backs of the mountains. Kell allowed himself a brief moment to marvel at the great banners of ice dust curling like smoke across the blue sky – a perfect sky, empty of gleams . . .

For the past three days he, Skjebne, Sebalrai and the wulfen pack had kept to the trees and narrow gullies. After the death of the Luparo, sky gleams had all but swarmed through the rest of that night and for most of the following day. Gradually they had thinned out, but that in itself might be a ploy to lull the travellers into a false sense of security. A single gleam, high up almost beyond vision, might still spot movement on the ground.

'Though their eyes don't seem able to penetrate tree cover,' Skjebne speculated. 'Which I find odd. Perhaps they are ancient machines, constructed before or during the onset of the Ice.'

He stood beside Kell now and swept the small twinned farscopes across the horizons. The instrument was a parting gift from Alderamin, who knew it would delight Skjebne's technical mind.

'Do you suppose they have a rudimentary intelligence like Hora's iron orb?'

Skjebne shrugged, and Kell could see the frustration in the gesture.

'I don't know. But one day I shall have one lying on a workbench, and by my own hand I will find out its best-kept secrets!'

And they both laughed at the note of mischief in the older man's voice. It was a comment typical of Skjebne; his curiosity knew no bounds. But it spoke of a time perhaps far in the future, when the Tarazad — and what lay behind the Tarazad — had been understood and overcome.

For now, the strange little group of wulfen and humankin struggled on, following Hora's only-just-adequate directions. The Tumblestones lay almost two days behind them, and they had yet to catch sight of the orb that was to lead them the rest of the way.

But more than these things added to their disquiet: the wulves had moved further beyond their territory than ever before, and although they were not apprehensive of any others they might meet (in fact there had been no sign of other wulfen), the land was new and unfamiliar to them, and some of the ealdorwulves seemed hesitant about going on.

At least we are moving away from the Tarazad, who are highly dangerous to us now!

Magula's argument carried little force.

Thule was a place we understood, a devil we knew, replied Hrothwulf, a big buck animal, the oldest in the pack. *There were endless places to hide and find food . . .*

So, it was easy. Magula's disdain was carefully calculated: he knew that too much of it would cause conflict. *You know the wulfen way, Hrothwulf. We do what we have to, not what feels comfortable.* He lifted his paw and stretched out his spread of black claws. *It is what has kept the edge of survival sharp in our souls.*

Hrothwulf and the few other dissenters followed him of course, but even without Magula saying so Kell knew that he would not be able to rely upon the company of the pack indefinitely.

As for Fenrir he still walked as though stunned, reliving the glorious triumph over the Slaughterer's blades. No matter that the wulfen prophecies made no mention of human help, he was the one chosen by Wierd to put a final end to the shadow that had been cast over his kind. His had been the last blood, if not the first. And upon the completion of the act, he had put his muzzle to Kell's face and smeared it with the blood of the kill, thereby perfecting their friendship.

Now the group moved on, turning away from the breath-taking prospect of the windscoured peaks. The sun was sweeping low to the west and the shadows of the mountains behind them already cast a wing of twilight into the sky. With no cloud, and with such a cutting wind, tonight's cold would be cruel and the need for shelter was great.

They found it in a little corrie, part of which contained a small deep lake of the purest water. It was crusted over with ice, but Skjebne's fire-rod burned a hole through that very quickly. Sebalrai and Kell slung hides across two uprights of rock to give some protection from the wind and any scouting sky gleams: ligetu lamps were lit beneath, placed in a half-circle about a pile of heatstones. Further rocks were shifted to help break the wind's sharpness, and the wulfen nestled among these on the fringes of the lamps' yellow glow.

'What if Hora has met with some mishap?' Skjebne wondered, once Sebalrai had fallen asleep. He could scarcely imagine the big old mox coming to any harm; but the possibility of continuing without him needed to be mentioned.

'We'll give him another day to make contact with us. If by then we have heard nothing, we'll speak with Magula to decide what to do . . .'

Skjebne nodded at this wisdom, without realising that Kell's comments came through sheer weariness and not from any philosophical consideration.

So presently they all slept, and the eyes of the two guard-wulfen looking out from rocks nearby protected them all.

Kell was woken early, well before the sun cleared the peaks. The air was needle sharp and the world was filled with a brittle and delicate light. It was the most exquisite shade of indigo; and in the east, just above the summits, a waning crescent moon was slowly being washed away by the dawn. Wulfen called it the She-Wulf-Claw-Moon on account of the sweep and sharpness of its curve.

Heoden, one of the lookouts, touched Kell's face with her ice-cold nose once again and backed away a few steps – out of nervousness or respect Kell thought at first, until he saw the black disc of Hora's iron orb hovering in the air a furrowlength away. At least, he hoped it was Hora's machine . . .

Kell scrambled for his weapon and the orb swung closer in a shallow arc.

'You're jumpier than a reed-hare in heat!' Hora's voice declared boomingly. Skjebne roused with a groan: Sebalrai jolted and flickered from sight. All of the wulfen were hidden, alerted when Heoden's keen eyes had first caught sight of the orb dropping fast from the heavens.

'We expected you two days ago,' Kell grumbled, feeling annoyed at his sudden awakening. 'We were concerned –'

'Don't be concerned for yourselves or for me.' The timbre of Hora's words had changed now, and Kell knew then that things were not right.

'Alderamin . . . ?'

'I have no news of Alderamin. This sphere and others have been searching for him with no success. But some of the other caravans have been savagely attacked, and as for Edgetown itself . . .'

The orb moved closer, and Kell was intrigued to see that sunken into one of the facets was a shining screen, such as he'd seen in the ice wain they had ridden in from Perth.

'Another of the orb's powers; to soak up images and give them back later, like the weorthan discs we found . . .'

Kell recognised the valley in the scene, though he was

looking upon it from a great height, and the trees and where Edgetown had been were wreathed in great drifts of smoke.

Where Edgetown had been! Now there was not a building left standing, and earth had been dredged by some huge force and flung about in all directions.

'This is not Tarazad damage, but damage *to* the Tarazad.' Skjebne was grinning as he said it. 'There were many explosive substances stored in my workrooms. It was a simple matter to connect them to a crystal that counted out time like coins in the hand. Once the hours were spent, the explosives gave up their fire and light in a heartbeat. There is nothing so mean, but so glorious, as revenge . . .'

'Well, events have tears,' Hora warned, sounding like one of Kell's old tutors. 'Now that the Tarazad have been hurt in this way, their resurgence has been widespread. There was fighting in Thule. Some people have been killed, including Elhaz, who was wyrda. Others have left –'

'There are no wyrda in Thule now?'

'None, Skjebne. We left because of the trouble – and because your work on the orb was even more successful than you could have known.'

Hora went on to explain that for the first time in living memory – indeed, for the first time in the written history of the wyrda – the central symbol of the Craeftum, the Universal Wheel, had spoken to them and answered their prayers.

'It was not in a language that we understood, if in fact it was any language at all! But the complex rings that compose the Wheel have moved, and there were patterns of lights such as you may have noticed on this orb. And – and other things have happened . . .'

'Other things, Hora?' Skjebne felt a mischievous sense of amusement at Hora's awe and discomfort. Back in Perth he had been a fisherman, and anything beyond his understanding he had attributed to the All Mother's work. Now out here in the wider world there were other gods, another level of the unknown to puzzle over and pray to and fear.

'More orbs have been appearing. Others, dormant for ages, have come to life. And we are being given directions . . .'

'That's interesting.'

'Some of the wyrda eolder have been dreaming of a high place, a plateau, which I will take you to when we meet. Vague stories have long circulated through the Craeftum that such a hidden plain existed, but no one knew for sure and no wyrda ever sought to find it.'

'It sounds as though now it is finding you,' Skjebne said. 'Perhaps because human minds have joined with the Wheel, it is responding to human intelligence.'

'Whatever your explanations, Skjebne,' Hora said, 'you have made the Sigel Rad clearer for us, and because of that the wyrda will always be in your debt.'

'Thank you Hora.' He glanced wryly at Kell. 'I think we may yet need to avail ourselves of your help. So, we will travel to the plateau you spoke of?'

'Yes. Fwthark and I will rendezvous with you soon – the orb will stay with you now as a guide. At the meeting place we are to be joined by Zauraq, who you remember. He will bring the Wheel there to us. This is a unique and sacred honour, Skjebne. Special dispensation was given by Thorbyorg, First Eolder of the Craeftum, to release the Wheel from its keeping-place at Uthgaroar. It is being entrusted to us in the hope, in the anticipation, that by taking it to the hidden plain we can further understand its purpose and power.'

'That honour is fully appreciated,' Skjebne said. 'And be reassured that we will do our best to live up to it, and with pleasure. How far are we from you now?'

'The orb can span the distance in the time it takes me to drain a juggon of beer –'

'Oh, we are very close then!'

'A day's hike for you if the weather stays fair.'

'As it will, my wulfen friends tell me. Then we will see you soon, Hora, to embark on the next step of the journey that Wierd has planned for us.'

When the wind keened round the contours of the rocks and caught the travellers unawares, it made them shiver with the cold. But the sun was pleasantly warm, and for much of the day Kell and his friends could dispense with their moxenfur overcloaks and stay comfortable in tunics and shirts. At times their progress was slowed by the cumbersome arrangement of Skjebne's stretcher: because of the rocky ground Kell, with Sebalrai often assisting, needed to bear the load at the back. But Wyldewulf supported the bulk of the weight effortlessly and without complaint.

By the evening of that day, with the sun still shining brilliantly between the mountain peaks, the iron orb led the party over a final rise. There below, flecks of spectacular colour in a rocky grey canyon, the wyrda men waited.

'A dozen of them,' Skjebne said smiling; 'and Hora too.' He scanned the gorge with his farscopes and easily picked out his friend. 'We must let them know we've arrived . . .'

Kell conveyed Skjebne's intention to Magula, who let out a wonderful wailing call of greeting which was answered by a flurry of waves and a few gruff and suspicious growls from the clutch of armoured boars the wyrda group had brought with them.

Hora and Fwthark, according to clan etiquette, clambered up the wall of the defile to meet the newcomers and offer the salute of welcome. Then Hora embraced Kell and Skjebne, lifting him off the stretcher to carry him down to the floor of the gorge.

Soon after, with a robust fire burning and pots of the strong spiced drink called *wyrtgemang* bubbling on the stones, the company gathered to hear more of Hora's news. The wulfen, who could not be persuaded otherwise, stayed away from the light and settled invisibly among the rocks – though the humankin knew that the pack was closely attuned to Kell's mind and so understood all that was said. Nearby around a nucleus of heatstones, the boars and their wyrda keepers and the company's horses formed a separate group.

'The *hyrdemen* are a sullen lot,' Hora confessed quietly. 'In the end there is little to distinguish between a boar-keeper and his animal.'

'Or a fisherman and his fish,' Skjebne teased, out of sheer pleasure at meeting his good friend again.

And so the sun dropped below the peaks and the cold, like a mailed fist, gripped the land. Early stars appeared, and Kell cast amongst them apprehensively.

'Forget your worries, *brooor*. Drink some spice and they'll vanish anyway . . .'

'I am concerned about the Tarazad and the sky gleams they control.'

Hora nodded and leaned away, his leathern chest-armour creaking. 'Hwaet!' He alerted the iron orb hovering nearby and beckoned it closer.

'What you and Skjebne have done has opened a marvellous doorway for the wyrda. See how the orbs look out for one another.'

At some invisible signal, or perhaps simply guessing its master's intention, the orb transformed into a glittering sphere of light. At least, that was Kell's first, brief, startled impression. Then he saw that a number of the outer facets had folded inwards to reveal a panoply of screens whose viewpoints formed a dizzying panorama.

'It's still full daytime there!' he said, pointing at one of the windows.

'That orb is the most distant from us, beyond the mountain rim. The sun is still above the horizon there. But elsewhere the other orbs circle this canyon. Their eyes are higher and see more clearly than ours. These two are sweeping the heavens above for signs of Tarazad presence. And so the enemy will not approach us undetected.'

Kell smiled as though reassured. But he had not yet come to share Hora's deep reliance upon unknown devices, and so asked Magula and the other guardwulfen to stay well alert . . .

'And now, Hora,' said Skjebne, whose interest was getting the better of him. 'You made mention of a certain Wheel that has been brought . . .'

Hora stirred uneasily. Since Skjebne and Kell had known him in Perth, Hora's initiation into the Wyrda Craeftum had given him blood-red hair and a landscape of unusual tattoos – but his discomfort in confronting the mysterious was very familiar to them both.

'We are afraid,' he admitted in a low voice. 'Even the eoldermen are fearful of what might occur if we tamper with the Wheel.'

Skjebne protested. 'You said we made the Sigel Rad clearer for you!'

'Aye, but now the road is real, it is here: it is not just a matter of celebrating the legends.'

Skjebne reached out and gripped Hora's hand tightly and found it to be shaking. He knew that the man had spoken of the deepest fears in his heart.

'If you believe Wierd, then you have been on that road all of your life, without knowing it. Now, all that has changed is that you *do* know.'

'But where will it lead?' Hora wondered with a little child's timidity. And none of the other wyrda made comment, because they felt exactly the same.

'It leads to where you have always wanted to be . . .'

'As a small boy, I was always happiest out on the lake, sometimes just drifting over the waters, other times casting my net wide.' He smiled as yesterday shone in his mind.

'Then perhaps that is both your journey and your arrival.'

'You confuse me with puzzles, Skjebne!'

'Then I apologise, because life should more often be a reality to be enjoyed rather than a puzzle to be solved. So forget your worries. Drink some spice and they'll vanish anyway.'

They supped companionably and talked of other things. Later in the night, with sleep still a distant prospect, Skjebne's patience was rewarded. Hora seemed to settle something inside himself. He turned aside to speak briefly with Fwthark, who then stood and entered one of the *feldhus* shelters erected nearby; structures of canvas and sticks that glowed warmly with yellow ligetu light. A minute later he reappeared, and beside him was Zauraq carrying the Universal Wheel.

An unexpected silence fell upon the gathering, for by the flickering flames all could see that the Wheel was a very beautiful thing.

Skjebne reached out to accept it, but Zauraq kept back.

'It is a hallowed object,' he said.

'To understand it is not to disrespect it.' Skjebne replied. His hands held steady, and after another moment's hesitation the warrior passed the Wheel over to his care.

'Wonderful, amazing . . .' Skjebne turned it this way and that, allowing Kell and Sebalrai to gather close and see its intricate construction.

From what Kell could make out, the Universal Wheel was a series of nested globes; not solid spheres, but woven rings made of age-dulled steel, jewelled and etched and intricately inlaid with gold and speculum wires: wheel within wheel within wheel spun together with astonishing complexity. The innermost rings were tiny and almost hidden from sight.

'The wielders and wrights of this work were masters of their craft,' Skjebne said with admiration clear in his voice.

'Tonight it is quiescent,' Hora said. 'But recently some of the inner circles have moved of their own accord, and tiny lights have glittered – yet no consequences seem to have followed.'

'Maybe the Wheel's activity is itself a consequence of the events in which we are involved. Think of that –' Skjebne's face lit at the idea. 'What if we did not so much react to the Wheel, *as it responds directly to our actions!*'

'Why should the gods dance like puppets to the tunes of men?' Zauraq wanted to know. Skjebne smiled at him cheerfully.

'Puppets? Dance? Your language is your limitation, friend. Might it not be that the wyrda and the gods of the wyrda are engaged in a creative evolution, both endeavouring to know the other more truly? If that is so, then the Wheel, where so many circles conjoin, is an apt meeting place of understandings.'

'You remind me of the eolder with your high-sounding words,' Zauraq said grumpily.

'Then I take that as the greatest compliment . . .'

Your companion Skjebne is clever. He wins battles without fighting.

Magula, intrigued by the talk of the Wheel and what it represented, had moved closer to the circle of light. Now he came up beside Kell, looking cautiously but never fearfully at the gang of boars not far away. Though he had bested the aurok, which was much larger, the savage *eofor* had the greater anger. Besides this, they were too stupid to die quickly. Magula had once seen two of them fighting for reasons he never discovered: and with lumps bitten out of them and standing in their own pools of blood, the machinery of their tusked jaws had kept working, even reflexively after death, when all shreds of meaning and purpose had left them. To all wulfen the boars of the wyrda – surely not a natural product of the land – were dreadful dangerous monstrosities never to be trusted.

Even so, Magula pitched just a little disdain into his gaze and forced his muscles to relax, so that he gave the impression of sitting casually with the humankin and equal among them.

Skjebne is as elegant in his way with the wyrda as you are with the eofor, Kell said as he traced the path of thought in the wulf's mind.

I did not think he believed in the gods.

But the wyrda do, and he would never insult that belief.

Now Zauraq had settled himself down by the fire and sipped at a goblet of wyrtgemang; just enough to satisfy ceremony but not enough to tempt intoxication. Having been entrusted with the Wheel, he would keep it in his sight until the day that sight, and his life, were taken from him.

'What do you make of it, Skjebne?' asked Hora, who was determined to see this meeting of talents bear fruit.

'It is a mechanism – crafted by men –' And here Zauraq snorted with disapproval and seemed on the point of storming away. 'Crafted by men with god-given intelligence, I have no doubt. There are makers' marks; at least that is what I take them to be . . . and yes, many other etchings of a mysterious nature but surely with logic behind them . . . and there . . . the eye at the centre . . .'

The I at the centre, Kell thought, and smiled at his momentary misunderstanding.

'I think it is weorthan glass –' There was a murmur of unease among the company. Skjebne looked up and faced them determinedly. 'You may disagree, but I am simply telling you my opinion . . . I think it is weorthan, for our experience has been that when crystal has been worked by men or by the gods, they have infused it with meanings. None of you can deny that a crystal lies at the heart of the Wheel. Why would it be put there if it were simply an inert substance? And you say that the Wheel has spoken to you – it has attempted to offer up some of its secrets. What part of it reacted to your wish for understanding? And look at these wires. Not just decoration, I'm convinced. I have seen filaments like these before, in other devices, and I know that information flows along them.'

'When you put it like that,' Hora said, easing things over, 'it seems very clear and obvious.'

'I may be entirely wrong, of course. But we must go armed with some kind of supposition.'

'And if we do suppose the weorthan eye can respond to us, what then?' Kell said, wanting to draw Skjebne further into speaking his ideas.

'I would like to understand how it does so. I would like to learn the language of the Wheel.'

'All of which will take time.' Hora drained the last of his spice and glanced at the sky. 'Is there any more you would tell us now, Skjebne?'

'I could talk for hours, though it would be based on what I guess rather than what I know and have seen. I think I should examine the Wheel more carefully by daylight. Besides, we have all travelled hard and we are tired, and good judgement wanes as weariness grows.'

So saying, he handed the Wheel back to Zauraq and gave a small bow.

'We sleep then,' Hora declared. 'And at first light tomorrow continue on our journey.'

Quietly, quickly, speaking among themselves, the wyrda men moved away from the fire to their tents.

'I have spoken optimistically.' Skjebne shook his head and leaned over to Kell. 'But without a codex, translating the sigils on the Wheel could take a lifetime!'

'For all that Zauraq grumbles and disputes, I think he knows you are the wyrda's best chance of understanding.'

'Well, maybe so.' Skjebne stirred himself and stood up stiffly, wincing at the pain in his leg. 'Goodnight to you Kell, and to you Sebalrai . . .' He paused and smiled gently at the girl. 'I hope you don't mind travelling with a muddled old fool like me, whose ideas are like the clouds, impressively large but of little substance! I should really be like you; listen more, talk less. I could learn a lot that way . . . yes indeed . . . talk less, much less . . .'

Sebalrai grinned at Skjebne's antics as he made his way to

his bed, but her smile faded when she saw the seriousness in Kell's face.

'Too much spice wine. But underneath he is burdened. Skjebne knows that through Hora the wyrda have come to have faith in his abilities; more faith perhaps than he has in himself.'

'Faith and doubt are two sides of the same coin. I know that from my own life,' Sebalrai said.

'And I should know it from mine.' Kell watched the play of firelight in Sebalrai's eyes and was beguiled. 'I'm glad you chose to travel with us,' he said after a pause. 'And I hope we all find what we're looking for.'

Briefly he touched her hand and then, realising that Magula was still close by and watching them impassively, he stumbled out some confused words about being very sleepy now and needing to rest, and hurried away to his tent.

Deep in the night. The eye. The I at the centre.

Mysteriously he stood on a beach and felt sad with the knowledge that Faras and his people had at long last followed their Wierd and entered the ocean for good. It was the way they had been changing when he met them; soon they would alter beyond recognition and be free in the world . . .

Way out in the green swell of the sea the Seetus bulged from the deeps. No, it *was* the sea, or at least an inseparable part of it. For without life to swim in it, what use would the water be?

Don't taste the salt, came the huge, benign and thunderously silent voice.

Be the salt.

Since the beginning nothing has been kept from you.

It is only you that has closed your eye to the fact.

The I at the centre . . .

Kell turned away and the shore was whipped from him like swiftly lifting mist.

Now he recognised the dream, for it was the one he had

dreamed in order to understand the orb in Skjebne's work-shop. But now there was more, an immense amount more.

He flew along passages at incredible speed. He noticed pulses of light gleaming within the speculum threads that Skjebne had spoken of. He *became* the light and was aware of a universe of movement and complexity around him; wheels within wheels within wheels. And as he flew he knew that the rings which made up the Wheel were eternally spinning into new configurations, even as they remembered their ancient patterns.

Like a spark, like a particle of fire from the sun, Kell's presence surged through endless tunnels and passages, turning corners without slowing, plunging into swarms of similar particles and sweeping through them like a cloud without touching any and without being damaged himself. And all the while he felt that understanding was rising through him as a bubble of air lifts from the bed of a pond. But the bubble never reached the surface and burst; it just came closer and closer, filling Kell with tension. He clenched his jaws with the frustration of it and moaned low in his chest with an anguish –

The moan turned into a deep rumble of the ground and into the wailing howl of a wulf simultaneously.

Kell's eyes flared open. The air prickled and danced with blue sparks; it itched on every part of his skin. The sides of the tent flapped slowly, as though under water.

Outside the guardwulfen were baying in alarm, and now came the shouts of men and a terrible sepulchral sound that Kell had never heard before. It was the noise of an eofor in fear.

Almost instinctively Kell grabbed the multiblade that lay beside him – but it cracked and sparked and little lightnings ran along its length, its very touch stinging him repeatedly.

He left it and ran outside and was aware of a general confusion; men shouting, wulves leaping about in the dark; horses stamping and the awful loud grunting of the boars . . .

In the centre of it all stood Sebalrai, quite still, with her head tilted upwards and her arms raised to the heavens.

Kell followed the path of her gaze and was numbed by the sight of an immense black hole in the sky –

Then his mind readjusted and his breath stopped. For it was not a hole. It was a huge iron globe, bigger than Alderamin's hearth-hall; vast and silent and hanging there above them, blocking out the stars.

8

Adventures With
Impossible Figures

In that moment when almost the whole assembly stood paralysed believing they would die, Zauraq was the only one to show some presence of mind. Daring as he had never done before, he took his eyes from the monstrous globe, reached into the leather pouch at his belt and lifted out the Universal Wheel.

'By the Rad, it is alive . . .'

Then they all saw that was true. Tiny lights twinkled over its surface in mimicry of the sky; slowing, halting for a moment, then speeding up in scintillant waves that swept around the circumference of the Wheel again and again –

And as if in final confirmation of the reality of the gods, the patterns were repeated on a colossal scale across the sky globe itself, and the encampment was washed with rainbows.

Zauraq, Hora and the other wyrda gasped in their astonishment. Sebalrai began laughing, laughing until she cried with it. She kept her face upturned and let the light pour in. Skjebne came over to Kell and put a hand on his shoulder and gripped it hard.

'Young friend, I think that if you had any part in this spectacle, you should decide what you want to do next . . .'

'That's easier said than done,' Kell gabbled out. He told Skjebne of his dream. 'But that was only in my head – an idea.'

'All things are ideas before they are expressed in the world. Let your idea run free and have the sky globe do what you will.'

'But the orb is huge!'

'Only small minds are impressed by size alone. Go on. Deep down you know what to do.'

Kell forced himself to relax – then abandoned trying, as though he was the water in the stream that already knew its way.

With the gentlest of sighs the orb settled down through the air. Its brilliancy faded until only a few silver pinpoints of twinkling light marked out its dimensions, making it look to Kell like a scattered swarm of ligetu moths wheeling around a sphere of blackness.

'It's coming to us!' Zauraq announced. Hora had automatically reached for his sword, then laughed as he realised how ridiculous that was. Instead, he propped his hands on his hips and let his heart swell with the sense of momentous occasion the night had brought.

The orb descended as naturally and as quietly as a leaf from a tree until it was less than one span above the ground. Then it stopped instantly with no sign of its mechanism of support, save for a slight agitation in the stones beneath.

Kell walked towards it and held out his hand – which Zauraq snatched away with a stern and angry look.

'This is a divine vessel. You will not profane it with your touch.'

Kell felt a huge anger rising, the outcome of all the angers he had ever known against the small-mindedness of people in blocking his way.

'The boy is just curious,' Hora said, trying to mend the rift. 'We are all curious.'

'Even so, curiosity is nothing. This vessel is holy.'

Unnoticed, Fenrir crept up to stand close behind Kell, for just on the other side of the smouldering fire Zauraq's boar Verres was tensing against his chain.

'Leave him Zauraq,' Skjebne said warningly. 'If it wasn't for Kell your sacred ship would not have berthed in this harbour at all!'

Kell could see that the situation was becoming serious, and Zauraq's face was dark with outrage.

'Wait. What good does it do any of us to be mood-proud here at the feet of the gods? Will we stand at this crossroads arguing while the Sun's Way is yet to be travelled?'

'You are still not permitted to desecrate the orb!' Zauraq's voice towered and Fenrir let out a soft, low, menacing snarl.

'Then we are all voyagers without a ship.'

Kell waved his hand, and quite unexpectedly, and terrifyingly as far as the wyrda were concerned, the great sphere shuddered and rose, and kept on rising until it became a suddenly blazing star, caught in the sun's invisible light cast up from beyond the horizon.

'I am only a boy, Zauraq, green in my seasons – but I understand the symbolism of the Wheel. It is the coincidence of us all being here now that has brought the globe to our camp. Not one of us by ourselves could have achieved this. All the people in my life, and all the things they have said, have given me insight. I was reminded of that in my dreaming tonight. I learned again that the orb is receptive to our minds. But you are Keeper of the Wheel, the highest honour of the wyrda. Yet, if you are so care-laden that you prevent the instrument from doing its work, then you have disrespected that honour – and you know that the eolder would agree with me!'

Zauraq had never been spoken to like this, and certainly not by a youth. He had lopped heads for less. But there was sound sense in the whelp's words and he would only diminish himself by denying them angrily now.

And so, without arguing his stand – and without openly embracing Kell's view – he placed the Wheel gently in the boy's hands and watched the magic work again: lights speckled the Wheel's ancient metals, and deep inside a few smaller rings turned minutely. There was a breath of icy cold air, and Zauraq looked up to see that the globe had returned.

No one could find sleep again that night, and through the remaining hours towards dawn the whole assembly came together to discuss the implications of what had occurred.

Zauraq and a few other wyrda men favoured returning to Uthgaroar to tell the eolder of this wonderful event . . . and perhaps it would even be possible to entice the globe itself to make the journey . . .

Skjebne smiled inwardly at the tentative way Zauraq made this suggestion, and how he cast a sidelong look in Kell's direction as he spoke.

Magula said that now the wyrda had a most wonderful weapon to use against the Tarazad – though being wulfen his opinion was not considered openly by the wyrda warriors, oaklike in their traditions and pride.

'Well we can't just sit here sipping spice and mouthing like a bunch of toothless *ealdmodor*!' Skjebne's patience was at an end, and he laughed almost bitterly at this ridiculous situation of men bickering in the shadow of the sky globe.

'Look – it waits for us! It is a ship. It was built to journey! And don't we have a port of call in mind, a certain precious valley that the wyrda speak about in their sagas?'

'Yes, but . . .' Hora looked up at the mighty orb, seemingly even larger and more solid now in the morning's first faint fiery light. 'It means going inside.'

'I don't intend to cling on to the *outside*, Hora!'

'I have a suggestion,' Kell said, and in light of earlier events, all listened. 'I propose that Zauraq enters the globe – the honour of being first should be his. I secondly propose that Zauraq nominates those others he would like to accompany him, choosing them for the particular abilities and practical skills they can bring to this situation. Finally, I think we should delay any decision about what to do next until we have learned more of what the globe has to teach us. That is my suggestion.'

'Exactly what I was about to say,' Skjebne chirped up. 'I agree completely!' And again he found himself admiring

Kell's cleverness in manoevering Zauraq into an illusion of choice.

The matter was settled in the next minute. Zauraq asked Hora to go with him into the sphere, since it was Hora's intervention that had brought Kell to this place. Kell himself was invited, and Skjebne because of his knowledge of machines. Magula was asked to represent the wulfen, but named Fenrir in his place; for Fenrir's heart was more open to wonder, and his future was more closely bound to the orb.

'And when we have entered,' Hora said, 'what then?'

'We become as nosy as fisherman gossiping in a tavern,' Skjebne told him. Hora laughed, satisfied with the answer.

As the day brightened Hora and Zauraq, following the wyrda way, put on their wargear and looked splendid and fearsome and proud. Kell saw no need for weapons, but carried his knife anyway as a symbol of good luck and the multiblade in case his impression of safety was wrong. Skjebne took his farscopes and a little pouch of tools. He looked like a child set free in a toyroom.

'You won't be able to dismantle the sphere with those,' Kell quipped, showing only how nervous he was.

Together they approached the vessel and none could fail to be moved by the vast silent structure with the uppermost hemisphere illuminated by bright morning sunshine and the other still sunken in shadow.

'How do we –' Hora started to say. But in the same way that the globe, somehow, had known they were coming to the canyon, so it understood their intentions now. A doorway appeared as elegantly and quietly as a flower unfolding; a ramp swung down like a gesturing hand, and the interior of the orb lay before them.

'Zauraq, please. The honour is yours,' Skjebne said, noting the man's apprehension.

'What should I do with the Wheel?'

'The Wheel will tell you,' Kell answered, easy in his assurance. 'For now, let us go and meet your gods.'

He failed to appreciate his own sarcasm or see the cautionary glance Skjebne gave him, but it was in any case forgotten moments later. A broad passageway led through the craft, and Zauraq and Hora were almost overwhelmed to see its walls decorated with the patterns and symbols they had carried on their bodies since joining the Wyrda Craeftum. The moment was full and tense with significance and mystery.

Within a dozen paces the vessel responded to their presence. Where the walls had been motionless, now they pulsed with rhythms of light indicating the path that the pilgrims should follow. Beside Kell, Fenrir's nose was reading the air and his eyes were darting everywhere, but his thought-voice was calm as he reported there was no discernible danger.

'It is clear to me,' Skjebne said, partly to conquer the silence, 'that both the wyrda gods and the men who lived before the Ice were very advanced in their foreseeing. They must have realised that the peoples would be scattered across the land as the cold intensified its grip. Knowledge would be misunderstood, fragmented or lost. And so they made their devices sensitive to the mind, so that even now, all this time later, the orb's intelligence recognises our thoughts and guides us.'

'I still don't know how that's done.' Hora looked at Kell frankly. 'Here is this youngling able to summon the orb out of the night – while all the wisdom of the wyrda have not been able to achieve it throughout our history. In fact, we did not even know of its existence!'

'Neither did I,' Kell said with equal honesty. 'But I knew that greatness lay within the Wheel, as you and your wyrda kin must have done, eh Hora?'

'Sensitively said, boy.' For the first time Zauraq's face showed the trace of a smile.

'By the same token,' Hora added, brightening, 'the orb's defences have not killed us yet. It leads me to think we may survive this day!'

Their journey to the heart of the craft did not take them long. On the way they saw a number of sealed portals which, just for now, they passed by. The time for coming to know this domain in all its fantastic detail lay in the future. Soon the pulsations of light ebbed away and the path opened ahead and they came to a roughly spherical room just big enough to accommodate them all. The jewellery of the walls and their arrays of shining eyes struck Zauraq speechless, but Skjebne exclaimed aloud at the sense of familiarity with the place.

'It's like the ice-wain! Bigger, more complicated – but not essentially different.'

'Surely the wyrda gods didn't inhabit Perth in the past?'

Skjebne smiled at Hora's naivety. 'Maybe they left their mark everywhere. Who is to say? But clearly they understood our ways – look, these controls are built for human hands.'

Skjebne moved eagerly towards one of the two seats facing the forward wall; then remembered the occasion and stood aside for Zauraq and Hora.

'I suspect you can follow the Rad in some comfort, *brooor*. Sit, and give your commands.'

They did so and the huge ship seemed to settle around them expectantly.

'But we have not prepared,' Hora declared. It was almost a wail of desperation. 'We have not consulted the eolder-men!'

'They would likely tell you to take hold of your courage in one hand, your wits in the other, and let Wierd show you the way!' Skjebne leaned close. 'This orb *came from somewhere*. Let us find out where . . .'

Perhaps the thought flickered through Hora's mind, or in any event the intention of it. However it was, there was a distant sigh and the vessel seemed to shift fractionally and its fabric hummed with power. Some of the eye-screens whirled in a sudden change of perspective . . .

And outside the remaining wulfen and the other wyrda watched in wonder as the craft rose smoothly upward and swooped away into the distance, leaving a slipstream of thunder across the sky.

'We're moving,' Skjebne announced with as much calm as he could gather in himself. 'Look at that . . .'

They gazed at the screens more closely and made out the panorama of the mountains slowly drifting past. The orb was moving at an immense height, way above the tallest peaks; yet there had been no impression of ascent, nor was there any of speed at that moment.

'Some of the other eyes are dimmed,' Hora noticed. 'Others are illuminated but blank —'

'And some show scenes I don't recognise.' Kell indicated several viewpoints; one of rocks, another of a place of trees, a third that appeared to be the inside of a cluttered room.

'Remember the orb you sent to Edgetown, Hora? Remember how it too showed you the world in the glass . . .'

'The pictures are reflected here! You think so?'

Skjebne nodded definitely. 'Aye. You said yourself the orbs seem to appear when they're needed. Others are lost or presumed inactive. I think we're looking out through some of their eyes now . . . these must be subsidiary orbs that belong to this great sphere.'

'There are many of the small orbs in Uthgaroar,' Zauraq said. 'But I don't recognise any landmarks there . . .'

'Well, I have some thoughts about that – but one small step at a time.' And Skjebne smiled and winked at Kell and would say no more on the matter.

As the minutes passed and the landscape below sailed slowly by, and nothing seemed to change within the vessel itself, the travellers turned their attention away and talked of other things.

Zauraq told them more of the wyrda sagas, and particularly of the valley they would presumably be visiting.

'It is central to the understanding of the Sigel Rad, for the stories say that the gods came and went from the land at this point.'

'In orbs like these I wonder?' Skjebne said. Zauraq let that go, involved as he was in his story.

'The Ice was already encroaching on the world, and to follow the Sun's Way was to escape its terrible grip. Some sagas reveal that the first wyrda initiates used their skills to prepare for the earliest journeys away from the reach of the cold – though the same legends speak of other ordeals whose origins and meanings are obscure.'

It occurred to Kell to ask why the Sigel Rad held any importance for the wyrda if the Ice was indeed now receding from the land . . . but then he checked himself, remembering the powerful forces that had drawn him to find an escape from Perth, even with its promise of pain and torment and death. He had gone anyway, partly because the All Mother said he should not!

'And what lies at the end of the Sigel Rad?' he wondered instead. And it was Hora who chose to reply.

'I have come to see that the Rad is not just a way, Kell. It is a way of life. Do you understand that? If you had not yet escaped from the enclave, you would still be seeking an escape. Even as an old man stumbling towards his death, *you would still be seeking a way out!*'

Hora said this with some passion and Kell nodded in firm agreement. Each of them who had left with Kano – indeed all of the dispossessed of Perth – must have let that same energy run in their blood.

Perhaps that is the way of all thinking life. Fenrir's thought came quietly and secretly into Kell's mind. *Because being alive is itself a moving thing, like the air and the water and the swing of the sun, we are all, always, restless.*

It may be so, little brave brooor. But, you know, even though I dreamed with such anger to be free of Perth, some small part of me would go back there – at least for a time . . .

To see how much it has changed?

Kell turned and looked into the wulf's startling amber eyes.

No. To see how much I have changed.

135

They sailed like wisp, weightlessly and, so it might have been to any onlooker, without purpose across the sky. Below them the land in all its varied scapes drifted slowly by. It was like the light–patterns forming in the eye of the ice–wain, a casual accumulation of detail. Sometimes the orb – for obscure reasons of its own – swung close to the ground and flashed among the crags and valleys of the wilderness. At other times it moved at an immense height, so that the mountains looked like crinkled paper and glaciers no more than a frozen spill of milk. And Kell smiled to himself to recall what Skjebne had earlier said; that only small minds are impressed by the size of things. For he wondered now if they ceased to be impressed only because they grew bored.

For the best part of a day the journey continued. Skjebne noticed that sometimes the sun shone from one screen, and soon thereafter from another.

'I think the orb is searching,' he said at last, voicing his observation aloud.

'You mean you think the vessel does not know which way to go!' Again the note of outrage in Zauraq's voice at this supposed sacrilege made Kell tense with irritation. But Skjebne had grown used to the man's sensitivity and had an answer ready, and was able to keep the right balance of deference in his reply.

'Oh, it knows where to go – it is simply returning home. But it made the outward journey very quickly. My guess is that the orb is taking this opportunity to explore. It may have been dormant for ages; the land is likely to have changed. It is finding its way about. It is doing the intelligent thing, Zauraq, and without reference to our unworthy selves.'

'So it doesn't obey our commands exactly, and without question?' This seemed a far more serious point to Kell.

'Well, not on this occasion I think,' Skjebne said. 'But consider. If the mind of the vessel obeyed blindly, then it would be only as effective as our common sense allowed . . .'

'I see what you mean.'

'By bringing its own understandings to bear on our, ah, *requests*, it keeps us safer.'

'I like to think so too,' Zauraq chipped in, with an affirmatory nod from Hora. 'The gods were never at our beck and call.'

And Skjebne smiled and did not rise to the bait – if Zauraq even realised it was bait.

Towards the end of the day the orb brought the travellers to a huge range of mountains that seemed to have been formed – or constructed – as a series of nested circles. The outermost ramparts, whether by the design of nature or man, protected the inner valleys from the worst ravages of the Ice. Now, at the start of the brief softer season, they were dark and green with woodland, and streaked with the silver of a thousand cascading streams.

The orb flew above them, soaring down from time to time like a hawk seeking out its familiar territories. Then it slowed until it hung silently above the steep drop of some forested cliffs that became vague and vanished in the distance into white veils of wet mist.

'Is this it!' Zauraq stirred himself and scrambled to stare at the screens –

And at that moment the visions in the eyes of the orb faded; a door opened and a pathway of light drew the voyagers to another part of the craft . . .

To a room that was made entirely of glass, above, below and to the sides. Now how this wonder was accomplished was a mystery to Skjebne and the others, and would always remain so. But so powerful was the illusion that they might have been standing in mid-air, several hundred spans above the invisible ground. Speckling rain lashed at the glass, and gangs of black corvus birds circled warily, one attempting to peck at this vast curiosity that had descended into its world.

'I would like to hear their cries,' Skjebne said in passing –

and then the group suddenly started as the harsh cawings echoed loudly around them.

Kell glanced nervously back at the doorway they had just passed through. It was still there, with the lighted corridor beyond, and the only thing that spoilt the perfection of this marvellous chamber.

'I am reminded of weorthan glass,' Kell said, moving close to Skjebne so that Zauraq could not hear.' Standing here as though in the air itself, in this globe of crystal, does not fit with the natural laws . . .'

'With the natural laws that we know about,' Skjebne corrected him. 'We have lived our whole lives out of ignorance, Kell; moving forward from a state of little knowing into a state of knowing a little more. Who can say what the creators of the orbs achieved before they disappeared from the world? *If* they disappeared from the world,' he added wryly. 'You see, more ignorance.'

'But how –'

'Something's happening!' Hora cried out. And it was no sooner said than the misty gorge and the corvus birds and the shadows of the tall cliffs dropped away as the orb soared high into the clean upslanting sunlight of the late afternoon. It did this without any sound or, as far as its occupants were concerned, without any sense of motion or acceleration. With perfect ease the land changed its configuration, so that the circling mountains became symmetrical; ringed rock separated by valley deeps and, at the centre, a high plateau almost on a level with the highest peaks. This patch of ground, raised halfway to the sky, was marked with several large constructions and the ruined or half-ruined outlines of other buildings; collapsed pyramids, delicately balanced towers, and many edifices of more conventional design, made mainly of the hard grey granite from which the mountains themselves were composed.

The entire settlement was exciting and intriguing to the eye. But it was the largest of the structures that caused Kell and his friends to gasp in amazement. For they were domes of even greater size than the orb in which they stood. There were three of them – one destroyed by fire, one intact, and one unfolded like the bracts of a seed; the very shell, perhaps, from which this vessel had hatched.

'This is truly the work of giants!' Zauraq was breathing quickly. Kell held back his impulse to argue. Over the past dozen moons or so he had lost his faith in 'the gods'. And indeed, if they were 'giants' who had built these marvels, stone upon stone, why did they let them tumble to ruin? Why did they leave the minds of the orbs to function alone? Why did they abandon mortal people to come out into the world with only the strengths that human minds and flesh possessed?

Fenrir had followed Kell's drift of ideas, and now interrupted.

The Godwulf is never seen, but he is always with us –

Then why did Magula risk his life against the aurok to speak with one who never leaves you anyway!

The wulf recoiled from Kell's sudden sharp anger, then apologised for having intruded. Kell sighed. Perhaps he was more scared than he cared to admit.

And I'm sorry too, Fenrir. I know pitifully little about your kin. Who am I to criticise?

You are one who was betrayed by your god. Ours has never done that, because the Godwulf is made of all our souls.

Then the Godwulf amounts to an accumulation of what you are. Which is the way any human god should be. If there were giants in this land, then they were men whose dreams gave them stature.

That may well be so . . . I know pitifully little about your kin. Who am I to criticise?

Kell smiled and gently nodded his thanks to the young wulf for this wisdom.

'So what do we do now?' Hora asked without much hope of an answer; and neither he nor the others knew of the meanings that had passed between Kell and his wulfen friend.

'We have come here to learn,' Skjebne said. 'It seems clear to me that we have arrived at the orb's place of origin. When our will in combination with the Universal Wheel stirred the mind of the orb, then it came from here directly to the valley where we were camped.'

'And those other two?'

'One burned, Zauraq, the Rad knows how long ago,' Hora said. 'But the third . . .'

'Still complete.' Skejbne grinned. 'Perhaps with another orb inside.'

'Then these are riches beyond our dreams.'

'If you mean that here lies a wealth of possibilities, I agree.' Skjebne squinted into the sun which was now caught in the cleft between two peaks. 'We have some little time left. Enough, perhaps, for a brief trip outside?'

This was a temptation that none of them could resist. And it was easily accomplished, since no sooner had their resolution to explore passed through their minds than the orb drifted downwards and came to rest at a man's height above the grassy ground.

Quickly now for time was short, and with the impulsiveness of excited children, the group hurried back to the room of controls, and from there along the lighted passage to the outermost doorway. They found the ramp already laid down before them, and a cool clean breeze blowing steadily up into their faces.

'Perhaps Zauraq would care to go first?' Skjebne indicated the short step down to the ground.

'Before you do . . .' Kell looked distracted and was concentrating intently. 'Fenrir is telling me . . . he is reading the breeze . . . he says there are things here which are unfamiliar to him . . .'

'This is to be expected.' Skjebne breathed on the lenses of his farscopes and wiped them gently with a soft cloth.

'People?' Hora wondered.

'People – no, not people – he doesn't know.'

'We are armed, and we will not wander far from the vessel. And we will keep the hatchway open,' Skjebne added as an afterthought. 'What is the point in being here if we do not see with our own eyes?'

So the balance of decision tipped and Zauraq, with Verres leashed close beside him, went forward and stepped down to the ground, assisted to the last by the strange forces of the orb which delivered them to the earth without weight or impact.

Hora followed, then Skjebne and Fenrir and Kell. Skjebne immediately gazed through his farscopes and brought the distances closer.

'It is a beautiful place,' he whispered; though Kell, to himself, was touched by a sense of tragedy and loneliness. This had little connection with the fire-gutted dome, which spoke of some single violent event in the past: it was more to do with the almost soundless wind that blew endlessly over the abandoned stones, and the short grasses that grew between them with their tiny yellow flowers trembling; and the clouds that curled meaninglessly around the pinnacles that had cast their shadows over this ground for uncountable ages. There was an emptiness here. An aura of defeat.

I am proud of you. Fenrir stepped softly into Kell's mind, remembering his earlier trespass. *Magula often reminds us that nothing is too insignificant to observe.*

But these are just my daydreams . . .

You know enough now, Kell, to realise that these thoughts which seem to rise idly into our awareness come as much from outside as from within. The world teaches us without saying anything. We simply have to notice what is there.

Now you sound just like Skjebne! Kell laughed at his own comparison and Skjebne, standing nearby, turned and looked at him in puzzlement.

They walked a short way from the orb, Zauraq in the lead with Verres snuffling the ground ahead of him. Hora took up his usual position as rear guard, while Fenrir scouted this way and that among the ruins to explore the wider area.

'This place has been left to itself for a long time,' Skjebne said, reaching out to touch the lichen-tainted stones. 'Perhaps since before the Ice itself advanced.'

'If so,' Hora said, 'the glaciers did not reach this far. The settlement is out in the open, not buried under the ground like Perth.'

'Then where did the people go? And why?'

An idea occurred to Kell. 'If the orb has been here as long as the buildings, then maybe it knows. Perhaps the answers lie in its memory.'

'More explorations,' Skjebne said brightly. 'In good time.'

By now the sun had passed behind the bulk of the mountains and cast glorious fans of gold and pinkish light towards the zenith. Behind the group, the orb loomed huge in the gathering darkness; and even as they turned to reassure themselves it was still there, they saw the outer hull sparkle into life with moving patterns of tiny lights. It was a wonderful, mystical sight that made their hearts swell with wonderment in realising their own insignificance.

'Hwaet!' Zauraq called to them from a little distance away. 'Verres has found something here. Bring light – bring light!'

'I have a ligetu lamp,' Skjebne replied, and while he fiddled with the mechanism there came the musical *clink-clink* of sparkstones being struck, and then a crackling whoosh as Hora's firetar torch ignited.

They hurried over to where Zauraq was struggling to restrain the boar. Verres was dragging on his leash, grunting at the lip of a tunnel or shaft that was sunk at a steep angle into the ground. The boar was speaking rapidly in a language that meant nothing to Skjebne or Kell.

'Why is he agitated?' Skjebne wanted to know.

'I tumbled some stones into it. They went on and on – hold, Battlebright, hold! – Verres says he smells the stink of life down there . . .'

Hora's firebrand was making the shadows jump. Skjebne leaned over the brink of the shaft and thrust the ligetu lamp as

142

far down as he dared. Its white glow illuminated the smooth stone walls of the tunnel for a little way before it was engulfed by the darkness.

'Move your torch away, Hora,' Skjebne said tetchily. 'I think I can see . . . something . . .'

And indeed, when Hora withdrew, Skjebne and then all of them could make out that the darkness in the depths of the shaft was glittering with stars.

Beware! It was a warning from Fenrir. *They mass in their thousands!*

And now, accompanying that strange sight, came the first sound they had heard apart from the voiceless wind's whispering across the tops: a cacophony of chittering squeaks that grew louder and more clamorous as the stars far below moved and swirled and then rushed forward.

A storm of noise and shadows erupted from the tunnel a moment later. Skjebne cried out in horror and surprise, and even Verres squealed in dismay at the sight of this new enemy –

Bats, clouds of them – the Hreaomus horde –

But not *bats*, Kell realised in absolute horror. For each small winged being had a human face. Some were tortured by terror and pain, others fierce and sharp with rage.

Blindingly, making a terrible din, they swarmed about. Hora waved his firebrand feebly. Verres snapped and growled. Fenrir leaped and caught one of the struggling creatures in his jaws.

And another swept swiftly down and before Kell could act latched itself upon his chest.

9

The Skymaster

The *hreaomus*, the bat-that-was-not, seemed fully grown, though it was as slight as a doll and weighed no more than a lightly packed food pouch. Beneath its black silky fur it was pale skinned and felt like a fragile construction of sticks as Kell swatted and tugged to remove it. But the animal was tenacious, while the shock of feeling its sharp needle-like claws in his flesh filled Kell with a paralysis of loathing.

All around its kin swirled like dark smoke and the noise of their pandemonium was unbearable. Through a haze Kell watched his friends fighting for their lives – poor Verres had vanished beneath a crawling mass of the things: Skjebne swung the ligetu lamp in a spectacular circle over his head; Hora and Zauraq wielded firebrands and swords with a deadly aim; while Fenrir battled with such elegance and ferocity that he had actually created a space about himself, for not one of the horde dared to risk his flashing fangs and crushing jaws.

Kell's attacker alternated between fluttering its membranous wings and lashing out with thin cruel claws at his face. It spat at him, and its mouth writhed and it let out a gabble of squeals which Kell somehow knew was a language.

That realisation stunned him even more, but he had no time to react to it, for a second animal hooked into his hair and without preamble swung round to the side of Kell's face and bit into him in the fleshy part of his cheek –

There was a sharp and momentary pain. Then came a numbing cold that spread through Kell's face and neck with the speed of his circulating blood. Following this was a langour of profound uncaring about what might happen to him next; for the night was unseasonably warm and the sky was exquisitely blue, and everything that happened had a rightness about it . . . for this was his Wierd and the centre of the cosmos smiled with a human face . . .

The ground vanished strangely and reappeared flat against Kell's back. He understood vaguely that he had fallen down. One of the bat-things still hung in his hair; the other scurried in a spiderlike way and crouched over him. And he bore them no hatred for they, like he, had only been trying to live . . .

There was a snarl, brief and low and savage, and a silver-grey blur flashed across and the bat was gone. The other managed a thin piping shriek before it too was broken between Fenrir's jaws.

Stir yourself slow-eyes! They will smother us else.

Slow eyes that at least take time to see. Kell thought that sounded very wise, like something old Gifu might have said to him once as they gazed across the sunny plains and terraces of Perth . . .

Fenrir barked – he actually barked – and with a desperate urgency took hold of Kell's sleeve in his teeth and began dragging him towards the orb – which, a second later, turned into a new sun and flooded the plateau with light.

This was something the Hreaomus could not stand, for they were children of the night. Like dust in a sudden whirl-wind they broke apart. Many hundreds of them swept back down into the shaft, while the rest sprayed outwards into the greater darkness among the mountains in search of the cliff-gnats and miscellany of insects which more usually provided their food. Before Kell realised where the new brilliance had come from, the horde had dispersed and the sky was once again clean.

'Their saliva must have this effect.' That was Skjebne's voice, typically sounding more fascinated than concerned.

'Or perhaps it is a venom. Some folks must be more susceptible than others . . . Can you speak, Kell?'

Kell spoke, or thought he did. But Skjebne just shook his head and shrugged and looked somewhere beyond, at Hora or Zauraq perhaps.

'Let's get him back aboard the vessel.'

I am still here with you, Fenrir reassured. *Your thoughts are peculiar and come in fragments . . . but that is a completely normal state of affairs.*

Then Kell wanted to laugh though his mouth was too numb to move. He felt himself lifted and had a brief glimpse of Zauraq tending to a battle-bitten Verres: luckily the boar's armour had protected him effectively and had probably saved his life. Even so, he was looking mightily sorry for himself and made the most of his master's concerns.

He is not a brainless stone, that one. Fenrir again. *The old eofor will take advantage of this situation for the next half moon!*

The quality of the light now changed. The day switched off and the air ceased to smell of the grass and the stones. Kell was inside the orb, carried easily by Hora to one of the sleeping areas they had discovered during their journey. He felt himself laid down, but not the weight of the blanket that was pulled up over his body. Hora vanished. Skjebne was there – and gone again. Time was dancing and he was aware of little except the intense and desolate face of the small winged man, and the skittering sound of his voice, and what he had been trying to say.

Kell woke next morning having fully returned to his senses, with a fierce thirst and a drumming headache that lasted all through the forenoon. Hora had been keeping watch from dawn, and now the big man smiled like a father and placed his heavy warrior's hand down on Kell's forehead.

'Your fevers have broken. You sweated and babbled all night, I'm told – it was like listening to Skjebne prattling on!'

'Well Kell is back now and you'll get more sense from him ... what of the Hreaomus?'

'They came back just before dawn – warily, for the orb's beams had frightened them thoroughly. It was our ill luck that we were caught out after sunset, since it seems that as the darkness falls the swarms rise.'

'Maybe that's why there are no people here.'

'Perhaps.' Hora smiled tiredly, as though he had not slept well. 'Skjebne is full of theories, each new one trying to outdo all the others.'

'Well, you can only have good ideas by having lots of ideas.' Kell tested his muscles and they followed his will. He sat up stiffly in bed and his head boomed. 'What is Skjebne doing now?'

'Playing with some new-found toys. Come along, I will take you to where he is.'

Hora assisted Kell along the passageway to the room of screens. Fenrir was there also, watching with his head cocked in curiosity as Skjebne worked the controls.

All of the screens were moving, or rather their visions were; though the orb was presumably motionless, still hanging a man-height above the ground. So Kell too was gripped by fascination – and then the solution came to him as he saw one of the small, head-sized orbs floating across one of the viewpoints.

'There are many of them, Kell! Maybe hundreds of the little orbs stored around the vessel. And see, they can all be guided. Yet they also have their own intelligence, which is a fragment of the mother-orb's mind. It would be impossible for a man to keep track of all of the little ones: you could not make decisions quickly enough. And so you define your intention broadly and the orbs carry out your wishes through using their own initiative. It is a marvellous and most sensible arrangement.'

'I can see how it would –'

'And there is a greater magic!' Skjebne swept on, caught up

in his excitement. He reached towards the console and a part of it came away. 'Oh, it isn't broken. I found this out by accident while you rested . . . though the orb slept not, and I suspect it was guiding my searches. Now, come with me, quickly now – oh, Hora, maybe you'd better carry him again or he'll take all the day to get there . . .'

Skjebne bustled out and Kell held up his hand as the warrior came over.

'No Hora, enough is enough. The feeling is back in my limbs and I have a mind to make my own way.'

'I would not dream of arguing,' Hora said, and watched with patience while Kell limped and hobbled and dragged himself out of the chamber.

They followed Skjebne to the crystal room which they had discovered the day before. Stepping through the doorway it seemed to Kell then that he was walking in the air ten spans above the ground, with the ruins of the settlement spread out before him. In the distance, the huge domed structures glowed a butter-gold in the early sunshine. Nearer by, the shaft from which the Hreaomus had risen seemed an innocent portal cloaked in black.

'Now –' Skjebne wielded his instrument of control. 'Behold!'

Instantly, completely and perfectly, the entire panorama had changed. Now they all drifted closer to the earth, among the very ruins they had just been observing from afar. Kell looked down and the grass floated by itself beneath his feet.

'The entire room has become the eye of one of the orbs.' Skjebne chuckled like some old wizard at the successful casting of a spell. 'And with no effort I can select the view from any orb. Perhaps when my knowledge is greater we can see the world through many eyes at once!'

'This is making my head spin,' Hora groaned.

'It means we can learn of places where it would be too dangerous for us to go in the flesh . . .'

'Like the shaft of the Hreaomus . . .' Kell matched Skjebne glance for glance. And both were mischievous.

The rest of the group was gathered (Zauraq arriving last, since he had just been coddling poor Verres by feeding him his breakfast of shredded mutton and milk). Skjebne had demonstrated the marvellous powers of the crystal room to all of them earlier, as Kell had slept. Now he simply used his control device –

And they stood at ground level looking into the gloom of the shaft.

'It is so real, it frightens me,' Kell admitted with no disgrace.

Not real to me, Fenrir responded. *I cannot read the wind. I cannot smell the stone and the shadow. I am not connected to this place!*

It is enough for our purposes now. Fret not brooor. Let Skjebne work his tricks.

The little orb moved. The world shifted, and Hora staggered on his feet and chuckled sheepishly. The shaft's portal passed around them, and then they were inside. Lights came on – ligetu beams from the orb – and by that glow the group of friends watched the smooth grey stones of the tunnel walls drift by. This monotonous passage went on for many minutes, until the shaft split and Skjebne chose the right-hand path.

Soon after the tunnel opened out and the stone gave way to some other substance: greyish white and smooth and remarkably free of the grime of the ages. It looked like a kind of ceramic. And whereas previously there had been no clue to the settlement's builders, now the orbs' creators began to reveal their presence.

Designs of great complexity and beauty inlaid with metals of various lustres were cut into the walls. It was Zauraq, within seconds, who noticed that the patterns matched the tattoos that he and Hora and all of the Wyrda Craeftum wore.

'This is where the knowledge started,' suggested Skjebne.

149

'And you and the wyrda before you have been preserving that wisdom in your own flesh down through the generations.'

'It is still no clearer to us,' Hora said a shade wearily. And his friend nodded and smiled and held up the hand of patience.

'Not yet, *beorn*, not yet . . .'

But Hora grew even more dismayed as the orb moved further along the tunnels. The unusual designs did not come to an end or even repeat themselves as some decorative motif; instead, they simply continued unfolding far beyond the simple sketches the wyrda bore on their bodies. And it seemed clear to him – as it did to Zauraq who fell into the same gloomy silence – that for all this time the bond-brothers of the Craeftum had been carrying the imprint of only a partial knowledge, a tiny fraction of what the dome builders had known and tried to communicate. And in the privacy of his own mind, just briefly before the good fortune of this discovery came home to him, Hora was overwhelmed with a sense of the smallness of the wyrda's endeavour, and how pitiable it had been until now.

'Of course,' Skjebne said, sensing something of his friend's despondency, 'now that we have the orb we can return here many times to explore and to decipher these glyphs completely.'

'Aye, and as an old man I can watch my sons start out on the Sun's Road, and wave them a feeble goodbye . . .'

Kell at that moment was tempted to grow very annoyed with Hora, who was wallowing in self-pity as Verres might flounder in mud. They had escaped from Perth only a handful of seasons ago, and yet all of this had happened. So much, so quickly. How could Hora inside himself turn what had been a series of marvellous revelations and adventures into bitter disappointments?

But pointing this out to his friend could wait, and Kell's irritation became meaningless, since without any warning the tunnel ended and the little orb floated into a vast cathedral space, so huge that its lights were instantly lost in the darkness and picked out just occasional glints and reflections – though for minutes at a time the device sailed through a blackness empty of any detail, except when a flash of white lightning broke with a flicker that was almost too quick for the eye.

'Have I been too clever or not clever enough in allowing our small adventurer to go this far on its own?' Skjebne reviewed the control device helplessly as he looked for a solution to this predicament. 'I fear we have lost the orb. It will drift in this void forever.'

'Not if . . .' The idea struck Kell as so absurd he hardly dared speak it. And yet the orbs, the small scouts and the mother machine had all been sensitive to human minds so far. So why should it not be the same in their place of origin?

Kell said nothing further to the others, but concentrated his vision and then let it go. Fenrir caught something of his intention and was amused by its audacity: this youngling would truly make his mark upon the world . . .

Then the room in which they stood filled with brilliance as the whole vast arena bloomed with light.

The little orb's visual mechanisms took a moment to adjust. All of the watchers cried out in pain at the brilliance, and it took some time for them to realise what had happened. But when they did, their astonishment was complete.

All around the incredible cavern thousands of lamps were shining; ligetu lamps Skjebne considered, or perhaps some other more esoteric illumination. It was like looking at a city that spread entirely around the inner surface of a sphere – as though Odal had been built all across the skies of Perth.

But the comparison was only a superficial one, since it was clear from the outset that this was not a place of habitation. The entire chamber had been constructed to house machinery of enormous proportions; principally a cluster of huge reflective globes connected by filigrees of crackling fire. Mostly these lightnings leaped between the globes themselves, but occasionally thin blue streamers would streak jaggedly and apparently at random to strike the inner surface of the cavern with a spray of sparks and further runnels and zigzaggings of flame.

'How long has this continued?' Skjebne wondered half to himself. 'Surely not from the time the place was created?'

'Maybe the city is waking.' Kell said. 'Maybe it has been waiting for lifetimes for the wyrda to return.'

'And the wyrda would be overjoyed by it – if we knew what to do!'

'My feeling, Hora, is that the dome builders made things to be easily fathomed and worked.' Kell felt that perhaps he was speaking out of his depth, but with the experience behind him of knowing that the mother orb and this colossal chamber were responsive to human thoughts.

'The span of time and our long isolation have made this place and its knowledge appear mysterious. But look, we are learning moment by moment. One day all this will seem as familiar and commonplace as the wharves and taverns at Odal!'

'I would be there now, to down a juggon of ale or two,' Hora said. But his mood had lightened and he made no further disagreement.

The scale and power and beauty of the chamber filled with its lightnings caused them to linger there for a long time. But presently Skjebne's curiosity was aroused by what else lay beneath the plateau's windblown ruins. He used the control device and sent the little orb swirling back along its way through the tunnels to the point where they had first divided. And to satisfy a suspicion, he directed the orb along the left-hand fork until he found what he had been looking for. The place where the Hreaomus horde lived by day.

Fortunately the orb's means of propulsion was silent, and the creatures remained undisturbed. The orb came upon them clinging to the walls and ceiling of a rough-hewn cave in their thousands, like large black bunches of some grotesque fruit. They were very like bats, save for their startlingly human faces which were exquisitely formed right down to little pointed teeth and clear, piercing, intelligent eyes which opened as the lights of the orb drifted by them.

'They know what they are,' Kell said. 'These are not mindless simulacra of men. These are people in their own right, heirs to the earth as much as the wulfen or ourselves.'

'Why are they like this?' Hora held up his big capable fisherman's hands. 'Why aren't they like us? Why aren't all peoples the same?'

Skjebne shrugged the comment away. 'Might as well ask why all flowers and fruits and animals differ. Lucky for us there are many forms of things – would you want to live in a cave, hanging by your toenails?'

Hora shut up at this no-answer and felt that his question had been disdained.

'I think the idea will come back to haunt us,' Kell told him, as Skjebne directed the orb in a cursory way around the rest of the cave and then brought it back to the surface.

They had spent the best part of half a day wandering the subterranean passages and caverns. While there was still light, and before hunger got the better of them, they decided the orb should now visit the domes, for these were the central point of the complex.

Firstly, Skjebne directed the little orb high above the plateau, where it hung in the blue sky like a brilliant miniscule star. In the quiet of the crystal room, the company hovered there with it, gazing down upon the uncanny symmetry of the ringed mountains and the immense misty scapes that surrounded them and dwindled away to the distance.

Then the orb dropped in a controlled and breathtaking fall, making Kell gasp with the thrill of it and Skjebne stagger with dizziness.

'Carry on,' Hora grumbled, 'if you want to see my breakfast on the floor!'

But Skjebne was hardly listening. With his confidence growing, he sent the orb swooping around the opened flower of the first dome, and in among the mighty steel petals from which – he supposed – the mother orb had come.

There was enough evidence to suggest that it had. Foremostly the proportions of the shell matched the size of the mother orb: it could have nestled within the protective bracts for ages shielded against the worst weathers. Secondly, inside the shell and at its base was a cradle suitable for supporting the orb – or at least for delivering power, since gleaming metal contacts protruded through the floor, and there were suggestions of mighty cables leading away from the central point; cordage as thick as a man's torso. Finally, though circumstantially, the mother orb had delivered them here to this lonely plateau. Why else, unless as they suspected it was coming home?

To test their deductions, Skjebne took the wandering eye of the orb to the place of devastation close by. It was hardly more than a charred crater in the earth, empty even of fragments. Perhaps the sphere that had been housed here had successfully sailed skywards before disaster overtook the site. However it had been, no clues were left to decipher.

And so finally Skjebne directed their viewpoint to the third and final dome. By this time the afternoon was well advanced and the structure glowed with glorious red–gold low–slanting sunlight. It looked to Kell's eye like a colossal ball of chalk, perfectly carved, but left out for so long that its surface was blotched now by lichenous growths of many shades of green and brown and russet.

'How do we get in?'

'We'll give you a hatchet and you can hack out a doorway for us,' Skjebne said. He was still caught in the mood of his earlier thoughts, which were that the supposedly wise and dedicated Wyrda Craeftum should count among their number mox-brained oafs like Hora and Zauraq. How could they follow the Sigel Rad, when they couldn't even grasp the simple elegance of their transport?

'The dome is seamless,' Kell spoke up in Hora's defence. 'But I think it knows what to do . . .'

Fenrir could already feel the focused intention of Kell's mind, supported by Skjebne's more knowledge-laden but not necessarily wiser intellect. He could sense too the *onweardnes* of this place, the presence of the conscious but unliving forces that had maintained it since the earliest times, and which was now fulfilling its purpose at the feeble promptings of these newcomers.

Still, Fenrir could not help but admire his friends' human endeavour, however slow-eyed it may be. They were a stubbornly determined breed, misguided in many ways, with the erratic curiosity of wulfen-whelps, thoroughly infuriating! But they had qualities of nobility and honour and a selflessness like a wulf's backbone, flexible and strong. Quite likely they would prevail. And if so, then by the Godwulf Fenrir hoped the world was wide enough to accommodate both Kell's kin and his own.

These were deep and intimate thoughts. Fenrir found himself drawn back to the outside world by a low rumbling that his ribs sensed first. Skjebne made a little sound of surprise, but tentatively, as if he had been startled by something inside his own head.

'Look at that.'

Kell pointed and they all saw that the smooth chalky surface of the dome was now flawed by a million hairline fractures. Simultaneously the material itself was disintegrating, powdering into clouds even as curved chunks of it dropped away, most of them evaporating in the fall.

The little eye withdrew so the process could be seen in its entirety. Sure enough, an outer shell was sloughing off, creating great billows of dust that glowed and flamed in the evening sunshine. A light steady breeze blew the dust eastwards, so that within a very short time the façade was gone to nothing and the huge metallic inner bracts were revealed; beautifully polished, reflecting back the world; the mountains, the sky, the mother orb that hovered there to witness this marvel.

And presently, according to a plan that had been laid down hundreds of generations before when the Earth was very different, those bracts began to open.

Gauda, the guardwulf that night, had seen nothing to report or to alarm him. Once, in the hours of deepest darkness before the Silver Blade Moon had risen, he'd glimpsed a bright star sailing serenely and on a steady path far beyond the mountains. He had heard tell from the humankin that they feared such sky gleams. But this one was so far away and so briefly noticed before it vanished again that he gave it no credence, and went back to his pastime of imagining the Godwulf in various configurations made up of the stars in the sky.

At last the thin morning moon came up like a shave of ice from the mountain, and the dawn's first painfully beautiful blue touched the heavens. Pale frost dusted the rocks and the sleeping shelters of the slow-eye and even Gauda's shaggy silver-grey pelt, so still and silently had he kept watch.

Now he roused and shook himself and stretched and let out a deep cleansing breath that steamed about his head. The day was brightening, his duty was over and he looked forward to a morning's light sleep before, perhaps, a little hunting that afternoon.

On the rock where he perched the frost-glitter changed in its brilliancy. Sunrise was approaching. Gauda looked eastwards and gave a yelp of surprise and confusion. The great orb in which Fenrir had travelled was returning, coming in fast underlit by the still-invisible sun. But beside it and a little behind there was *another* sphere, equally impressive; from this angle looking like a big black hole cut into the sky.

Gauda's alert swept through the sleeping wulfen and

within a few moments Magula and Wyldewulf and the rest of them had gathered, a few howling loudly to rouse the rest of the camp.

So it was that the whole company gathered as the nearer orb swung in to the narrow valley and grew huge and settled on a cushion of shimmering air, while its twin hung higher, just within the shadow of the mountains.

The ramp opened down like a gesturing hand and the first face to appear was Fenrir's, grinning like a buck at the beginning of spring. Then followed Kell and Skjebne, helped a little by Hora; then Zauraq and the lumbering Verres tugging at his chains. It was a triumphant company, safely returned.

Within a short while of the first greetings – gentle and shy and tentative between Sebalrai and Kell – the night's fast was broken and *wyrtegemang* and wayberry wine were brought out in high celebration: for this was an occasion of the most profound importance for the Wyrda Craeftum, and with implications for all the kin of the earth.

With great solemnity (though Kell felt light-hearted and crackling with excitement) Zauraq lifted the Universal Wheel and noted how its arrangement had changed in the last few days.

'I have produced a thought,' Skjebne said, leaning over towards Kell. The man stank of spice and, being unaccustomed to drinking wine this early on, found his words running together like water.

Sebalrai chuckled as Skjebne draped a brotherly arm around Kell, and at Kell's disapproving expression.

'So, this thought of yours . . .'

Skjebne lifted a swaying finger. 'The Wheel mirrors the changes we have caused. In that case we acted with our minds directly on the mind of the orb. But it is also true – and I feel this most strongly – that we can exert control by manipulating the Wheel itself . . . it is a bit like the control mechanism I used earlier . . . if only we knew how to do it.'

'Like a puzzle ring!' Sebalrai said brightly. 'Like this.'

She slipped a ring from her finger. Plain and simple silver twisted a few times about, but with a complexity concealed. The linked circles seemed to come apart beneath Sebalrai's dexterous touch, and then were reassembled into a delightful sphere of speculum wire with a tiny red stone at its centre.

'The ruby is invisible when the rings are put back as they were. Alderamin gave me this soon after he welcomed me into his family.' She blushed slightly. 'All of his daughters possess one.'

'Intriguing.' Skjebne forced himself to focus. 'So what looks like a ring is really a sphere of interlaced circles. And the Wheel, a sphere of interlaced circles . . .'

'Is a puzzle unsolved – something much more, on another level of being.'

'Yes, yes Kell. All down the years the wyrda *eolder* have assumed that the Wheel is as it is, and no more . . . but it is implicate; folded into a simple shape –'

'But why?'

'For ease of carrying, to preserve its secrets, who knows? Ha! Who knows! Certainly not the wyrda. So, I think our next step must be to journey to Uthgaroar and seek permission from the First Eolder to pick and poke and pry a little more, eh? Using the orb it will take us less than a day to get there.'

'At this rate we'll be travelling the Sun's Way for them!' Kell said. And suddenly Skjebne's eyes were clear and his mind was utterly concentrated.

'I think someone has to,' he said with a great intensity. 'For their sake, I think someone has to.'

10

Uthgaroar

The miraculous is often concealed in quietness. Gifu had told that to Kell once, as they'd sat on the terraces high above Perth and watched the tall wheat waving in the wind. So the wisdom was reaffirmed as the great orb – 'Skymaster' Skjebne had named it – lifted out of the valley in utter silence; turned slowly once, and then shot away at enormous velocity to the west and the north . . .

The marvel of it was that although the wyrda men had visited Uthgaroar for their ritual of initiation, they only knew where it was relative to the valley where they'd assembled, and only then from the viewpoint of a man on the ground. But somehow the mind of the orb had studied their knowledge, as Alderamin might read one of his story-stones, and by that means understood the way to the home of the clan.

It had been no easy matter to persuade Magula and the other wulfen to come aboard, for to do this detached them from the land in which they were rooted. But Fenrir set the example by his confidence and courage; and besides, the elderwulfen like Wyldewulf were not going to be bested by some strutting pup! And so they came carefully into the sphere – Magula sniffing the atmosphere at great length before he allowed his pack to enter. And once, as they were taken to the crystal room to reap the best of the journey, he stopped and cocked his head and listened, but said nothing: for sometimes Wierd does not like her secrets to be revealed at an inappropriate time.

Not all of them stayed in the room of crystal, however.

Fwthark discovered a terror of heights — at least, of heights from which he could not descend by himself. And Sebalrai, whose imagination had never prepared her for this, chose to go to the sleeping quarters until she had steeled herself to the view of the world far below. Several wulves likewise sought out quiet corners in other rooms, tolerating this ordeal for love of their leader and his wishes.

Kell and Skjebne, Hora and Zauraq, however, delighted again at the wonderful panoramas that drifted into their sight: great mountain ridges and the deep folds of valleys; forest pelts flung across curvaceous hills; lakes and rivers; flood plains and lofty plateaux. Sometimes they spotted features that were clearly artificial. On the distant horizon, Kell noticed the ramparts of some vast fortification. It looked to be carved from the hills, though on reflection might have been formed by glacial erosion over great spans of time. Shortly afterwards, Skjebne noticed a cluster of remarkably symmetrical hemispheres, and close by them, foreshortened by distance, a pit or hole that could easily have swallowed the whole of Edgetown. At first Skjebne tried to see these more sharply using his farscopes. But the orb cast its magics again with elegance, and a portion of the crystal wall rippled briefly and magnified the view for the travellers' convenience. Even so, it was still not possible to discern what the landmarks might mean.

'Well,' Kell said airily, 'let's just take a brief diversion . . .' He exercised his will — but the orb would not be distracted. Kell's expression of haughty frustration caused Skjebne to break into laughter.

'I think it's pointless railing against the Skymaster's determination. Obviously on this occasion reaching Uthgaroar takes priority over satisfying our casual nosiness!'

Kell was not pleased but Skjebne let the issue be: the boy would learn that his judgement was not always the soundest.

So they settled themselves to enjoy what their route showed them of the world. 'But one day,' Kell said with a quiet resolve, 'I will rein in this orb as I did with my mox, for it can journey in the twinkling of an eye to far-off lands. And I will see those lands, Skjebne, and I will come to learn their names.'

Before long the Skymaster, and its companion orb following the same path a minute behind, encountered storm clouds gathering over a range of hills that bordered a lake whose bright silver waters resembled scored steel. It would have been no hardship for the vessel to sail right through the heart of the lightning, but it chose instead to rise over it into the dazzling sunshine, up and up to such an altitude that the horizon bent like a lightly drawn bow and the blue of the sky above deepened.

'How high can it go?' murmured Skjebne, and felt his heart thrill and clutch, for this was no idle thought.

'Look there!' Kell pointed upwards and his friends followed his gaze. They saw, at an even greater height, a drifting star, so far away that no details were visible.

I witnessed something like it in the before-dawn-time of my watch, said Gauda, whose comment went to Fenrir and Magula and Kell simultaneously. There was no more that the wulf could add, and the orb gave no indication of wanting to pursue the mystery; and so a mystery it remained. And soon afterwards Skymaster swooped down through the sky on a long arc towards a range of sandy-coloured mountains which Zauraq recognised as the region around Uthgaroar.

The company busied themselves for journey's end. Skjebne wished to send a little orb ahead of them to alert the people of their arrival. On this occasion Skymaster was compliant and a moment later the tiny speck flashed away towards the ground like a stone from a catapult.

'Will you bring the rest of your kin to the outer hatchway, please?' Skjebne addressed Magula directly, though the idea was conveyed through Kell. Kell then hurried to find Sebalrai, and cajoled her to return with him to the crystal room to observe their approach to the village.

It was built on a series of broad terraces cut into the sandstone rock: the lowermost terrace was still many hundreds of spans above the narrow rubble-filled valley it overlooked, through which a rapid river ran. Many of the dwellings were small; family houses perhaps, though larger structures could be seen — hearth-halls most likely, Kell thought, or workshops or store chambers. These climbed the slopes like stone steps towards a complex of much-weathered and probably ancient carvings of complex yet archaic design. Above these stood a desolate place, shaped by the hand of man and fallen now to ruin. Kell could make out more tumbled buildings and rain-melted statuary, and massive blocks of masonry that had no obvious purpose. And there seemed to be caves and clefts in the uppermost levels of the rock face, although Kell was equally persuaded these were shadows cast by the trickster light.

All through the journey the great orb had made no sound. But now there came a deep sigh through the whole fabric of the ship, which swung about in a broad half-circle so that the buildings of Uthgaroar moved out of sight.

'Come on,' said Kell, 'let's join the wulfen. We're almost there.'

He walked quickly towards the outer hatch, to Sebalrai's embarrassment. She stayed back to assist Skjebne whose hip was stiff and painful from his journey out of Edgetown.

'I am sorry. Sometimes he doesn't think of others.'

Skjebne patted the girl's shoulder and accepted her offer of support. 'He is excited and young and eager for more of life. I understand that. There is nothing to forgive.'

Courtesy as much as common sense dictated that Zauraq should stand at the head of the party and be the first man visible when the hatchway swung down. He held the Universal Wheel cupped in both hands. Hora tended to Verres, flanked by Fwthark and his own boar, the powerful Heorrenda. And although Verres tugged and grunted most bad-temperedly at being leashed by someone other than his master, Hora knew that he was handling the animal well. He looked forward to the time when Uthgaroar's eoldermen granted him an eofor of his own.

Clustered behind them were Kell and Skjebne and Sebalrai, with the wulfen back in the shadows. That was the right order of things, the order in which the travellers would be introduced to the wyrda people.

Not one of them aboard sensed the moment when the orb came to rest. Indeed, they were all startled when the hatch began to descend with a hiss of equalising pressures, admitting the lemony light of the desolate tops. Cold mountain air blew in, tainted by the woodsmoke of Uthgaroar's many hearth-fires. There was movement outside; soldiers bristling, some exclamations of surprise and gasps of astonishment. Kell strained to see past Hora and the others, and looked upon the fierce tattooed faces and red hair of the wyrda that had come up to meet them.

Zauraq said a few sentences in an obscure tongue, then explained briefly in clearer language what had happened since the eoldermen had put the Wheel into his care. Now he handed it back to a retainer, and Skjebne's heart sank a little to wonder if he would ever be allowed to examine it again, let alone take it apart.

'What we have learned, and where we have been, would not have been possible without the help of these friends,' Zauraq said to the head of the wyrda delegation, who was obviously Thorbyorg, the First Eolder. Zauraq stood aside and indicated the others should climb down from the orb.

Thorbyorg of Uthgaroar was aged, yet still imposing and powerful, with a shaggy fleece of hair and beard dyed red in the traditional way of the wyrda and strung here and there with small brass beads which, Kell supposed, were a mark of authority. He was a big, broad-shouldered man, rough edged and twisted a little with a wastage in the bones; but still he stood solid with the high pride of his warrior clan and their dreams of the Sun's Way. His eyes were as blue as lapis and flecked with gold, and mixed both hardness and kindness in a way that Kell found quite remarkable. Beside him stood a lean youth, an assistant perhaps, who carried a tall spear with an ash-leaf head topped with an iron orb. The assistant remained attentive to his master's merest movement or word.

'All the kin of Uthgaroar welcome you. By this act of bringing two of the Great Orbs to our hearth you have taken us into childhood again, where all dreams are possible.'

'We are delighted to meet with the child-again people of the wyrda,' Skjebne said with a diplomat's artistry. 'We too feel elated by the way Wierd has carried us along. Our streams meet here, and now we flow together with a sense of honour.'

'There is much to discuss,' Thorbyorg said – and here Skjebne noticed an ominous clouding of the First Eolder's eyes – 'and not all of it bodes well for our futures. You will know that there is a darkness creeping over the land. But even so the elements of light have assembled here, and we must respect them and celebrate them now.'

So saying, Thorbyorg, accompanied by his *gefera*, whose name was Garulf, led the new arrivals along the stony path towards the longhouse where the hearth of the community was always kept stoked up and warm. The whole population of Uthgaroar lined the way, and some of them gasped aloud, though not in horror, at the strange appearance of the visitors – for here was a thin man of little hair whose face was lean and drawn, perhaps through the pain of his injured leg, yet whose eyes sparked and flittered with an endless curiosity. And here, incredibly, walked a pretty girl of such shyness that she seemed actually to fade from the sight of the onlookers, so completely for some of them that they carried no memory of ever having seen her. And by her side was a tall beaming boy, scruffy haired, dressed like a peasant but with something much more in his demeanour. This lad, on the brink of his manhood now, was armed with a multiblade and a valuable jewelled knife – but the look in his eyes was sharper than its cutting edge, and brighter than the sea-washed garnets on its hilt.

Most amazingly of all, however, striding behind this impressive human company, came the wulves – not the thin, grey, desperate scavengers that scoured the tops and were a constant nuisance to the wyrda peoples: these were prime beasts, well fed and immaculately self-groomed, whose pelts shone with the varied lustres of the most precious metals. At their head strode a massive creature whose fur was the colour of flame-brushed silver and whose eyes and bearing spoke of a towering pride in his nature. Here was a being that marked the essence of life: his existence was in itself a triumph over the cruel ravages of the Ice. He was closely flanked by a younger, slightly smaller and leaner animal; but this wulfling drew a hush around him as he passed, for his spirit equalled that of Thorbyorg himself, and swept by the mind as softly and profoundly as a whispered prophecy.

So the assembly moved on and left the villagers stunned, not least so because behind them, beyond the flattened summit of the mountain, hung two of the orbs of the Sigel Rad, spoken of in the sagas but never seen until this day by any wyrda eye save the handful of men who had found them. The first orb, in which the visitors had arrived, sat cushioned on a rippling of air just a span above the ground. Its companion, seemingly identical in every way, held steady further off like an ornamental rivet hammered into the blue shield of the sky.

Many of the wyrda community chose to stay outside the longhouse and marvel at this spectacle of the orbs. But an equal number followed the procession into the sturdy hall built of mountain stone, and there gathered as best they could given their numbers around the glorious fire, as men had done since the time when they first had mind to call themselves men.

Thorbyorg eased himself into a sturdy *setl* built of age-darkened oak: no trees grew this high among the tops, and generations ago many wyrda had laboured for many days to carry the heartwood up to this place. How effortless it would have been with the aid of the orbs! Thorbyorg sighed and shook his head a little tiredly, and then put the past from his thoughts. He gave some instructions to Garulf, and the young lad sent others bustling to bring food and *wyrtegemang* and a delicious honeyed drink of impressive richness and flavour, which Garulf told the guests was called *meodu*. Then, having attended to these formalities, Thorbyorg began to speak about what troubled him.

'You must know that the wyrda's Wierd has been hard,' the First Eolder said. 'How long could anyone continue following a dream with little hope of ever waking to its reality?'

'Are you saying that the notion of the orbs and the Sigel Rad has been nothing more than a small hope?' Skjebne said brazenly. But this seemed a time for forthrightness and honesty. Skjebne and the others all felt that never before had Thorbyorg voiced his feelings in this manner.

The man's expression was ambiguous, but his eyes remained fixed on Skjebne, for he was sharp-minded, very astute, and would not be deceived by an old warrior whose most cruel battles had been with his faith.

'We have been sustained by the inspiration of the Universal Wheel, of course. And the smaller orbs, the gadfly spheres with their mysterious ways, have always been in our company. All of these things have suggested something beyond themselves. But our existence has been shaped largely by the sagas . . . but stories are not stones that shelter you, or weapons that can protect you, or vessels to carry you on to your destiny –'

'They are all of these things!' Skjebne declared, too outraged momentarily to notice Thorbyorg's smile of amusement and tolerance. 'We ourselves are stories, little motifs and chapters in the great book of Wierd, the Tale-Of-All-There-

Is. And what fills me with wonder again and again is that while we make our mark on the world day by day, in one sense we are already written and complete. And our telling never ends in the mind of creation.'

'Can you hold the proof of that in your hand?' came Thorbyorg's challenge.

'Do you love and honour your ancestors?' Skjebne replied.

'Of course I do!'

'Can you hold the proof of that in your hand?'

The First Eolder laughed, not scathingly or with any sham of politness for Skjebne's clever wit: Thorbyorg had been well answered, and his respect for the man grew by the moment.

'So you are saying that faith is proof in itself. Well, I have been tested over the long years and found wanting – though there is one thing which has kept my heart stout in this matter, and we will speak of it later. But today we have the orbs and witnessed their connection with the Universal Wheel, whose powers and meanings have always tantalised us. Our business here must be to discuss what steps we take now, and how far you are prepared to battle beside us . . .'

There was a note of query in his voice that Skjebne warmly appreciated: the First Eolder was not presuming that he would now take charge of the orbs, leaving the visitors with no influence in the matter. Clearly Thorbyorg realised that they were all equally woven into the world's way, and that their coming together was no accidental or superficial thing.

'I presume you refer to the Shahini Tarazad?'

Thorbyorg nodded. 'We too have experienced the voracity and ruthlessness of the Tarazad – the plundering falcon, and Hora has conveyed something of your incursions into Thule.'

'Our purpose was – uh . . .' Kell paused, not quite knowing if this was allowed according to the protocol of wyrda conversations. 'A companion of ours, a young girl named Shamra –'

'I have been told of her. And have no fear, Kell. If it were not for your search you would not have met Zauraq; Hora would not have chosen the wyrda way; you would not have journeyed to the plateau of the orbs . . .' The eolder smiled and shrugged lightly as though casting off Kell's doubts for him.

'I think it is important for you to continue seeking Shamra, and since you discovered the spheres, it is only right that you use them as you think fit in finding her.'

This was more than Kell and Skjebne could have hoped for.

'That is very gracious of you, Thorbyorg,' Skjebne said.

'It is the way things must be. I also feel that you should continue on your path with some urgency –'

'All we know is that Shamra was taken in a sky-borne vessel eastwards.' Skjebne briefly told of the incident during the time they spent with Faras and the Shore People. 'We thought she was bound for Thule, but we now realise she has travelled much further. One of our friends, Feoh, set out ahead of us to find her. During this time Kell was missing and we believed him dead; and I was recovering from my wounds in Edgetown . . .'

'All of these things are like little tiles in the grand mosaic.' Thorbyorg chuckled deep in his throat. 'Hora has told me of Feoh; that she has the gifts of mind-sight and healing. I believe she has deep intuition, so that to locate Shamra you must find Feoh first.'

'Easier said than done –'

'You have the great orbs and their many eyes which can wander the land at your will. Also,' Thorbyorg said, 'I think it is no coincidence that Feoh was drawn to Thule. For as you may know, the city is ruled by a seeress called Helcyrian. She belongs to a sisterhood of women with similar gifts. They call themselves the Sustren and their influence spans this entire continent. They wear the mantle of secrecy and superstition about them, and the fear that engenders is enhanced by the

Tarazad drengs, whose minds are washed by weorthan light and are not their own.'

'Are you saying we should return to Thule and speak with Helcyrian?' Kell wondered.

Thorbyorg gave a smile that was as hard and vicious as a blade. 'I doubt she will grant you an audience. My suggestion actually is that you go to Thule to find out what you can about Feoh's connection with the Sustren. And whether you learn nothing or much, together we will take the first opportunity to wipe Thule from the land.'

None of these plans or any others that were discussed during the rest of the day reached any final agreement. Thorbyorg recommended that all parties should sleep on the matter and make decisions by the clear light of a new day.

'Look there. Kell and Sebalrai are already doing so!' Skjebne and Thorbyorg laughed quietly at the sight of the two younglings leaning against one another, breathing softly in slumber. Others too had dozed, torn between the need for rest and the wish to attend the discussions of the eolder and his guests.

'Well, let's make an end to talking for tonight,' Thorbyorg suggested. He sipped the last of the meodu from his stone goblet and set the vessel down gently. 'But before you go to your bed, Skjebne – I said earlier that there was one thing more than any other that had kept my belief alive in the wisdom of the sagas.'

'You did . . . is it a book? Is it an instrument you wish me to look at?' Despite his own weariness, Skjebne's curiosity danced within him at the prospect.

'Ah, patience, patience my friend.' The eolder pushed himself heavily up from the settle and beckoned Skjebne to follow. Those among the Uthgaroar people who remained awake also rose and bowed towards the two men as Thorbyorg led his new friend to the doorway that opened out into the night.

'Put on these furs. It's cold.'

Skjebne grunted under the weight of the pelts that Thorbyorg handed him at the threshold. He struggled into them and was instantly warmed as though he had surrounded himself with heatstones.

They stepped out and the freezing pure crystal air bit at their lips and their eyes. A thin wind streamed up over the raw stones of the lower reaches. It whistled past the men and went on its way, moaning like someone lost in despair over the heights.

'Just stand. Just wait.' Thorbyorg's breath made brief smokes. 'The night will come to you.'

And that is how it was. For as Skjebne's eyes adjusted to the dark, so the stars appeared in their thousands.

'I see –' Skjebne checked himself because he could barely believe what he was seeing. 'They have colours!'

'Every one different, if you look with sufficient care.' Thorbyorg nodded and let his gaze drift across the heaven. 'Wyrda legend has it that each star is the soul of a slain warrior. I think that is just a little fanciful myself.'

Skjebne smiled to himself. 'I am most impressed, *gaeleran*. Thank you for showing me the stars as I have never seen them before.'

'Oh, this is nothing.' Thorbyorg nudged Skjebne and handed him a small flask of meodu that had been hidden in the fur of his gauntlet.

'Fortify yourself with a little more liquor, for we have a short climb yet before I can show you the Eye of the Rad.'

So saying, the eolder trudged his way along the stony path with Skjebne just a pace behind though labouring rather more since, unlike Thorbyorg, he had not made this journey many thousands of times before. But after only ten steps Skjebne stopped dead, dumbfounded by the spectacle of a star streaking across the sky and leaving behind it a fading feathery light.

'Did you see that! Thorbyorg, I would swear by –'

'No need to swear by anything, friend Skjebne. You have seen an arrow star. They are very common. In fact, at certain times of the cycle they come in swarms. Sometimes you hear them fluttering and swishing through the air at a great height. Twice in the recorded history of Uthgaroar an arrow star has come to earth and proved to be nothing more than fragments of cindered rock. These, however, are much prized since some people believe the sky-stones bring down the knowledge of heaven with them.'

I would rather go and find out for myself, Skjebne thought, though he said nothing to Thorbyorg whose apparent touch of cynicism might have run deep.

They went on their way and at last, after long minutes of hard walking up the increasingly difficult slope, Thorbyorg rounded a crooked shoulder of gritstone and stepped with Skjebne out of the perpetual wind.

They had come to a quiet sheltered place away from the faint light generated by the home fires of the settlement. Lower down to the left Skjebne could see the Skymaster; a dark ball of shadow defined by tiny sparkling gleams, just as if it were mimicking the sky. The other orb, which had not yet been named, was out of sight.

Briefly Skjebne thought that Skymaster's roundedness had influenced his eye, for just a few steps ahead another curved shape presented itself, seemingly crafted from rock. It looked like a skullcap nestled into the ground, but impressive in size and twice the height of a man. Then he was reminded of the domed housing of the great orbs, and wondered if the same people had constructed this building.

'It was here when the first wyrda came to these tops and decided to settle,' Thorbyorg explained. 'Those early dwellers – perhaps wiser than us and perhaps more innocent – believed it was a shrine. Well, that might be correct. Judge for yourself. Come along!'

His manner became brisk and almost impatient. Skjebne did as he was told. Thorbyorg's pace did not lessen: he continued walking right up to the curved surface of the structure, put out his hand as though to test its solidity – and apparently walked right through. Skjebne imitated the action (yet without the same certainty of outcome) and found that a curving doorway had silently swung aside. He found himself inside a faintly lit empty chamber whose flat floor and smoothly fashioned walls and ceiling formed a perfect hemisphere.

'Where is the light coming from?'

Thorbyorg slipped off his fur mantle and let it fall. 'From the fabric of the building itself.'

'Is it ligetu light?'

'No one knows. Nor have even the most determined and inquisitive eolder discovered any rooms connected to this one, nor any means by which it can function. But its purpose is clear . . .'

Thorbyorg's words were only just spoken, when the nature of the interior was transformed. What little Skjebne could see by the pale ambient glow showed that the surfaces were featureless and grey. Now the greyness faded and the room grew dark, and the stars came out all around them and far beneath their feet.

But what stars! Not the dim glimmers Skjebne had glimpsed outside. These were so numerous that they swept like smoke in every direction in veils and clusters, whirls and sigils of pure flame. Nearby, just as silently open-mouthed as his companion, Thorbyorg was silhouetted by stars; and now their colours were obvious, a part of the infinite variety of the jewelled heavens.

'This is where the Sigel Rad leads, or so my heart tells me when my mind begins again to doubt. This is where the wyrda long to go, to the place where all the gods become as small and unknowing as a newborn child.'

'I would make no argument against that,' Skjebne replied in the same hushed way. And then his attention was drawn back to the breathtaking brilliancy of the night – but like no night that had ever shone down upon this or any other scape trodden by men. Nothing he had ever seen or imagined could have prepared him for this vision, let alone have explained it. He felt tears of humility and awe spring to his eyes, and realised that all men and all things were like dust blown by time along the infinite shoreline of space.

He had no idea how long he stood there, or where his thoughts had come from nor where they might lead. But at some point Skjebne considered that this situation was not entirely unfamiliar to him. Briefly he fought to deny it and then let acceptance wash over him to realise that this place was essentially the same as the crystal room aboard the Skymaster.

Kell knew that his mentor had changed. For a little while it disturbed him, but then it elated him although he was not able to say why.

He thinks of things I do not understand, Fenrir said when Kell had passed on this impression. *I sense that he and Thorbyorg have talked for most of the night . . . I do not have the forms in my head to shape the concepts they discussed.*

No doubt Skjebne will explain it all to me in his own good time, Kell replied. He felt mildly irritated not to know what ideas had passed between the two men.

Moreover, as the break-fast ended and most of the wulfen left the longhouse to see to their grooming and toilet, Kell grew even more upset to realise that agreements had been made between Skjebne and Thorbyorg in which he had played no part.

'The First Eolder has agreed to allow a *gedryht* of wyrda men to come with us to Thule, and there aid us as we need,' Skjebne said crisply.

'But we have the orbs. We have the wulfen –'

'The wulfen have the right to follow their own path if they choose. We can use the orbs to take them wherever they wish to go, and that is some repayment for the help they have given to us. The point is that while Thorbyorg will let us make use of the machines, one day we must return them to complete their original purpose.'

'And what might that purpose be?' Kell said acidly.

'You will find out one day . . . but now our way lies east through Thule, and on in search of Feoh and Shamra. That is a dangerous road. Wyrda companions can protect us. In return we can help them to understand the orbs: these will take them to their destiny, but not us to ours. If we were to perish in Thule, what would become of the orbs then? It is necessary we decide on these things together.'

'As you are seeking my opinion now?' Kell replied harshly.

'I don't believe I am seeking it at all. The matter is settled,' Skjebne said more quietly, in a reasonable tone; a subtler weapon entirely.

He is baiting you, brooor. It's part of his teaching –

But Kell would have none of Fenrir's explanations. In an outrage he stood and turned his back on Skjebne and Thorbyorg, brushing by Sebalrai and storming his way through the busy hall and outside, where the air was less stifling.

Kell's temper told him that he had been snubbed and that Skjebne was stupid for doing so. It was also irrational that he should have listened to Kell so carefully and followed his advice with such trust suddenly to ignore it now . . .

And in the that fury a little serpent writhed. It was the jealousy Kell felt of Skjebne for being taken into Thorbyorg's confidence and shown the secrets of the wyrda, for that was surely what had occurred. The two men had talked as men and chewed over the possible future and settled the steps they would take. How could they dare to do such a thing by themselves!

But this was one voice in Kell's head, and all people are made of many parts. He knew too that he was only a boy who had started humbly and might end in just the same way. If in the years to come his life contributed to the greater pattern and was recognised, then that should be enough to satisfy his soul . . .

Kell found himself smiling at the contradictions that sped through his mind and the feelings that followed these conflicts. The day had already taught a good lesson. Let the old head-nodders do whatever they wanted; it was bound to suit Kell's purposes in the end!

He had been walking upward along the winding path to the place where the Skymaster rested. Now Kell could see the hull of the machine looming impressively through the cloud-mist that hung and stirred about the rocks. The wind direction had changed in the night, bringing warm moist air up from the valleys. Kell could smell the stones and damp dust and even the odour that came off the sphere; it was beyond comparison but very distinctive, something he would remember for as long as he lived.

Briefly he looked for the companion sphere, but that was entirely cloaked by cloud somewhere above. Kell set his stride and entered the Skymaster with a sense of coming home. The portal was already open and had been since the arrival. It was a symbol to the people of Uthgaroar that they were always welcome here.

He wondered how many had gathered up the courage to board the vessel. There seemed to be nobody present just now . . . except there were tiny noises coming from the room of controls . . . maybe the machine's secret workings. Kell stepped cautiously and drew out his knife and held it before him.

But the chamber was empty. Quite a number of the crystal screens were aglow, but most showed only fog. One revealed the viewpoint of a little orb that drifted about the settlement – the smiling face of a small boy appeared, and then his hand as he reached out to touch this miracle passing him by. He spoke and the orb drew back and showed a girl of similar features; his sister, unmarked by wyrda tattoos and the garish dye the warriors wore.

Kell wondered if he might startle the children, for he was in a prankster mood. If he could project his voice from the machine . . .

He cast about and saw jewelled studs and bosses arranged below the screen. One of those. He went to press it and froze as a shadow passed across his hand –

– turned and was struck hard in the face by something dark with wings . . . with wings and a human face.

Kell had no time to defend himself or run before the creature fastened on him and sank its teeth into his neck.

11

The Dreamhoard

In return for blood came understanding and a cool numbness in Kell's throat that was like the touch of the Ice itself. Immediately he knew that one — and maybe more — of the Hreaomus horde had stowed aboard the ship; but it was only a solitary creature that chose to attack him now.

Its name was Tsep.

Kell fell backwards and barely felt his body hit the floor. The langour was upon him; an acceptance, almost a bliss of allowance.

You are too small to bleed me dry, hunta! Kell said in the easy way his thoughts were flowing. And not without humour, for the notion of this homunculus daring to challenge something so much larger than itself was perversely amusing . . .

But then came a darker reply — of thousands of these almost-men bringing down an aurok-like beast of the high plateaux. Their sheer weight made its legs collapse. Their venom chilled its blood and closed its body down and then its mind. And then it was nothing, only a feeding-trough.

Kell's scream lived and died in silence. He was incapable of sound. Tsep's thoughts murmured to him softly, and without any basis of fact Kell knew that this little predator could kill him with ease . . . and that it was the only hreaomus to have entered the orb, locked by sunlight inside.

Then my companions will discover my body — and hunt you down — and break you under their heel!

Tsep lifted its head and grimaced at Kell with a bloody

mouth. It liked the way the boy spun fear into anger: he was well on the road towards courage.

I take what I need and spare you the rest. Tsep licked its lips with a long red tongue and sat on Kell's chest with its head cocked. *It makes no sense to kill the tree just to eat an apple.*

You are still dead –

Only if silverfur snares me!

Tsep lifted lightly with a flutter of membranous wings and gave a chittering laugh as Fenrir leaped by snarling and missed with a snap of jaws on the empty air.

Skjebne has poisons. He can suffocate this tick and have done!

Fenrir stood over Kell, whose flesh was now filled with a tingling fire. The wulf touched his tongue-tip to his friend's wound and read the message of Tsep's venom.

It subdues the body's whisperings to itself. The brain stops. The victim becomes a dead burg . . .

These were Fenrir's understandings, translated in the only way he knew.

You will live, added the wulf. He swung his head up to look at the parasite and glared his hatred of its entire kind.

Especially since I never take selfishly.

With a huge audacity Tsep glided down from the high shelf where it had perched. It moved out of Kell's sight and landed close in front of Fenrir, folded its thin and delicate arms and challenged the wulf to attack. But along with the insult came the clear impression of many chambers within the orb that Tsep had explored, and which were yet unknown to all others.

The place of the eyes! Kell said with a shock. His limbs were recovering, but his head thumped horribly. Clearly Tsep had shown him the treasure room where scores of small orbs were in storage. Silent, patient, waiting to awake. He sat up and gazed groggily at the creature that had bested him but drew no triumph from the encounter.

You are frightened little cousin . . . you are cut off from your kin.

It's true. Tsep's eyes never wavered. *Nor will they take me into the swarm again now that I have been tainted by the smell of others, and by strange far places.*

Then you are lost, Fenrir said with a hard edge. Tsep showed its needle teeth.

Like both of you, I seek to find my way. I have given you sight of valuable things. I have no comprehension of them, but I know where they are. I can take you there in return for the shelter of this cavern, and for living blood to sustain me.

He can be useful to us, Kell said. Besides, the advantage of revealing new chambers in the orb to Skjebne and Thorbyorg would help Kell to restore some pride in himself!

Now the effects of the bane were rapidly fading and Kell was able to haul himself to his knees. He wiped a smear of blood and water from the sore spot on his neck and rubbed his soiled hand on his tunic. He saw the provocation go from Tsep's face and realised that in the manikin's drinking something had passed between them.

An affinity.

The decision took time, for significance has no relationship to size. Tsep could sit comfortably in Thorbyorg's hand, and yet the introduction of this small animal that first shared its roots with humankind might prove to be momentous.

With thoughts as clear as a mountain stream, and rather liking all the attention, Tsep explained that the existence of the Hreaomus at the High Place of the orbs was a coincidence. As the explorers had discovered, the plateau was a hive of caverns and tunnels and fantastical chambers. Nothing moved there usually save the Hreaomus themselves; except that occasionally the immense machinery sustaining the orbs would wake and adjust itself and then fall quiet again. This might happen once in a generation, or perhaps not at all within the lifespan of one of the swarm.

As for the Hreaomus and their place in the world . . . all that Tsep could say concerned the Origin Dreams. Alas, his kind did not own anything as impressive as the wyrda sagas or the elegant dance of the wulfensong. Wierd was a concept they had heard of, but did not believe in.

An intelligent hand created the orbs, Tsep told them. *As it created us. Huddled in the darkness of deep caverns, the Origin Dreams occasionally sweep through our minds. We dream that all things come from the same soil. But we were taken and changed, very long ago when the Ice was still tightening its grip on the world. We dream that there was desperation in our making, for the cold was the great enemy and no one alive knew quite how to battle with it. We dream that our creators turned to minds that were already dead, since it was believed that the primary questions of life might once have been answered long before, but those answers were forgotten or hidden away . . .*

However it was, we were born out of darkness into darkness. And like the orbs, and like the humble sword, we were wrought to a purpose that cannot be changed.

And what is the purpose you obey with such blindness? Skjebne wanted to know.

Tsep answered simply. *To outlive the Ice.*

'Well Tsep of the Hreaomus, your story is both tragic and noble,' Thorbyorg said, 'And since I trust and admire Kell, with whom you have struck a useful bargain, I add my weight to his decision. Let the pact be made.'

The winged man would be offered protection and what nourishment it needed. In return, Tsep would reveal the concealed ways of the orb and be of whatever use he could. The pledge was not universal. Fenrir still regarded the man-bat with loathing; it was a night *gast*, a thing of sly ambushings, a bloodthief. It reminded the wulf of the bloodsuckers that sometimes infested the fur and skin of an unhealthy animal. This one just happened to have the gift of conscious thought and a face that resembled a human's. Fenrir neither trusted it nor respected it. And he would keep a watchful eye, for if Tsep attempted trickery then Fenrir would kill it in an instant.

Sebalrai also was worried. There was cunning in Tsep's

manner that reminded her of the plunderer Chertan. And while she had the art of camouflage, the little-wing's disguises were altogether cleverer and more wilful. It was a deceiver through words and glances, and nothing it had said or done yet had persuaded her otherwise.

As for Skjebne, he took Tsep on trust because of Kell's opinion, but also of course because the labyrinth of the orb would now be opened.

The leave-takings from Uthgaroar were brief. Thorbyorg had nominated six men to assist the expedition however they could. All agreed there was little point in mustering a larger force: the Tarazad were many in number and Skjebne believed that stealth would be a more successful road to Thule.

So it was that Hora and Zauraq, Fwthark and three others − Alef, Thoba and Myrgen − boarded the Skymaster shortly after noon that day. Verres and Heorrenda were left in the care of comrades. They were beasts of open battle and would not appreciate sneaking about in the shadows. Magula agreed to allow Fenrir and the mighty Wyldewulf to accompany the band, while Sebalrai insisted on going too.

And so the company went aboard the Skymaster. After the portal had closed, the attendant orb rose smoothly upward into the hazy sky until it could no longer be seen. Then Skymaster itself began its journey: the tension changed in the air and some small stones beneath the huge vessel rattled and scampered away like leaves in a tiny whirl of wind.

Thorbyorg and most of the crowd lifted their hands in goodbye, not knowing if the travellers could see them . . .

But Skjebne, standing alone in the crystal room, was able to watch the hope in their eyes until Skymaster passed over the encircling mountains and moved away beyond them.

Distance was no longer a consideration, and the sphere offered the best of safe havens. After a short meeting of all twelve travellers, Sebalrai's suggestion that they should search out Alderamin and his scattered people found favour. Earlier, the wisest plan had been for the families of Edgetown to disperse. Now, with circumstances so drastically changed, it made better sense to gather them up and transport them to greater safety.

'The problem will be finding them,' Hora said. 'The valleys around Edgetown are densely forested.'

'We have the use of the Skymaster's eyes. Thanks to Tsep,' Skjebne added. The man-bat had shown them a chamber where a hundred small orbs nested in niches in the wall. A brief spell in the room of screens had taught Skjebne how to mobilise them.

Perched nearby, the man-bat sat up straighter and preened and smiled at the company with a childlike pleasure.

'So we can look in many places at once,' Kell said. 'And we have the wulfensong – Fenrir and Wyldewulf can draw lost souls towards us.'

The trees and the rocks and the earth itself will guide us, Fenrir said. *If Alderamin's people are there, we will find them.*

The orb knew its own way, and before sunset arrived at Alderamin's Land. The hills cupped low cloud and the air was raw and laced with sleet. Skymaster sank to within a few spans of the treetops – and the lights in the room of controls became hooded, and the eye-windows glowed into life. A battery of small orbs had been deployed, and now a score of misty viewpoints began moving across the screens . . .

'Skymaster is learning from us!' Skjebne said delightedly. 'I have not issued any instructions!'

'Then be careful what you wish for,' Hora advised with a mischievous smile. 'The orb seems attuned to our minds, more so as each hour passes.'

As patiently as they could the travellers studied the screens' moving pictures and grew weary of the drifting mists and the endlessness of trees and the slow brutality of the sleet.

The eye-orbs were working in a pattern of widening spirals, and night had come before they detected any movement. Unexpectedly, something as grey as the fog itself crossed one of the screens and disappeared swiftly into the forest deeps.

Wulf, Fenrir said without doubt. His eyes had been the only ones fast enough to notice. *Another pack has moved into the valley now.*

If wulfen are there, there must be good meat nearby, said Wyldewulf.

He's right, Fenrir agreed. *The hunting must be rich in the forest. How could that be unless some of Alderamin's people are still here?*

Kell conveyed this to the others.

Set the orb down and let us out. We will know better than the Skymaster's eyes what to look for, and where it will be found . . .

It was done. By the time Fenrir and Wyldewulf had raced to the portal, the orb had settled as low as it could and the hatchway was down. Kell, Hora and Zauraq had planned to come with them, but the drop to the ground was too great.

Hora judged his chances and shook his head warily. 'It would be a bone-breaking step!'

'Nevertheless it must be made,' Kell said quietly. It was almost as though the Skymaster was talking to him, urging him on.

And without thinking of the consequences, Kell walked out of the orb. He heard a shout of alarm behind him – Hora panicking. There was a moment's dizziness and then he was earthbound. Around him the air rippled like heat-haze as the others joined him – including Tsep who relished the night breeze and the prospect of a meal.

Then Skymaster's influence withdrew and dank sleet closed around them. The explorers' breath suddenly appeared in front of their faces.

They gazed up at the vast shadow of the orb floating just above. It was completely dark, with not a single light showing.

'It knows we must not give ourselves away,' Kell said

softly. Then he was diverted by a flurry of thoughts from Fenrir and Wyldewulf.

Wulfen not far away . . . there has been violence here . . . terrible killings . . . Alderamin – 'He's dead?'

His kin . . . this way. Follow us!

Fenrir set off like a streak of quicksilver and was gone in a moment. Wyldewulf walked with the slow-eyes and guided them over the unlighted ground.

Within a short span Kell realised that Fenrir had found what he was looking for: his thoughts grew complex and deep, and became alien to Kell's understanding. The wulf's blood was singing to him now and the melody was of his disgust and horror of humankin and all that it had spawned.

Following close behind, the others came first upon the carcass of a mox, a wain-hauler that had been slaughtered by some unknown weapon that burned and sliced. Zauraq lit a ligetu lamp and the kill was revealed in raw light and stark shadow.

The mox's left flank was split and broken ribs poked through like the splintered struts of a storm-beached boat. Frost had covered the animal with a coat of white crystals. One of its eyes was open, uncaring of the cold.

'This is Tarazad work,' Hora said grimly. 'The drengs must have swept through the forests, killing whatever they found.'

'We don't know that!' Kell shouted, and Hora looked on him impassively, solid in his opinion.

Fenrir had not stayed. Immediately he'd set off again, following the bloodscent.

'There are no shackles on this beast.' Hora felt in the thick shaggy fur at the back of the mox's neck, then peered closely at the small red lights that were glowing faintly there, telling their simple story. 'He was disconnected from the wain . . . perhaps it was abandoned. But he would have followed his masters instinctively though . . .'

'Leading the drengs towards them,' Zauraq added. Hora shrugged.

'Perhaps. What does your wulfen friend say to you, Kell?'

The boy had gone very quiet and his eyes looked down into invisible distance. Hora had to repeat his question before attracting Kell's attention.

'He has found a body. He thinks it is one of Alderamin's family.'

They moved on, allowing Kell to lead now. And in the glow of Zauraq's lamp the dark swung and swayed about them, and stray flakes of wet sleet fluttered down.

Shortly they came to the place where Fenrir had stopped. There was a woman's body lying prone and her face was hidden. She had dark hair streaked grey with age and ice.

I recognise her Kell, Fenrir said. *She was nurse to Alderamin's children. She died less than one day ago. That is all I can discover . . .*

Tsep fluttered its wings and made a hissing sound that was clearly one of contempt for the wulf. It hopped like a raven bird on to the woman's back and bent its head close to hers.

Hora shouted an exclamation of outrage, and made to sweep the hreaomus aside. Tsep turned on him with a fierce face.

Don't dare compound your ignorance by harming me, wanderer! You think I want to sup from her. You fool! The words spat into Hora's mind. *Do you suppose that when the heart stops and the blood cools then all of life is ended? She died but a short while ago, and thoughts still echo in her head like mournful gusts among the ruins. The soul of this woman is not yet ready to leave its earthly home. Some threads of her have gone, but others remain . . .*

Is this your power then, Tsep? To draw out the spirits of the dead?

I count it as one of my skills, Tsep replied loftily to Kell. *You know that the Hreaomus are creatures of the Lowerworld, both in a physical sense and at a subtler level. We do not let your narrow idea of life limit our thinking . . . now, if you would like me to find out more . . . ?*

And no one there moved against him as Tsep spread his

185

arms to their full reach and winged the woman's head round in their span, cradling her like someone he loved.

She is called Mirach.

The friend of Shaula, the daughter of Jadhma and Alderamin, Kell said.

Ah, she feels such agony of loss to have them torn from her!

Are they dead too?

Wait, wait! . . . the merchant sent the women away on their own . . . the Tarazad were coming through this valley . . . Alderamin set the mox loose and took weapons . . . Mirach remembers the sound of battle . . . there were huge insects among the trees — the drengs — men wrought with metal to give them height and speed and strength . . .

We have fought them and beaten them.

There were too many this time and they were relentless. Through their steel mouths they thundered news of their victories throughout the valley . . . the slaughter of families . . . the taking of Alderamin the merchant — they have him, Kell! They have him alive!

What else, Tsep? Tell me please!

The little creature was silent for some time.

Tsep. Please.

I do not need to speak the truth for you to know it.

But Kell demanded and Tsep revealed what the spirit of Mirach had revealed to him.

'They killed them!' Kell wailed. 'Hora, they slit the throats of the women! And they brought Alderamin there to watch . . . then they took him back to Thule — I will wipe them out! I will destroy every last one of them!'

Kell's face twisted and he shook, raising a cry of such terrible torment that even Fenrir crouched down and could not bear to look. Nor did anyone move to ease the boy's torture; the agony of his childhood's end.

'We will tell the wyrda at Uthgaroar what we have discovered. And we will assemble the wulfen pack to search for any survivors of the Tarazad's atrocities — the forests are vast and the drengs' main purpose was to capture Alderamin, probably to lure us to Thule on Helcyrian's instructions. And there we will go and put an end to her evil.'

Skjebne spoke quietly, holding back his tears at the look on Sebalrai's face. After they had returned from the forest, Kell had insisted on speaking with Sebalrai alone. They had spent a long time together, and when they rejoined the main group the girl's expression had been hard and unyielding. So it was with Kell, who believed only vengeance could save them.

All that Skjebne said had been agreed with Hora and the other wyrda men, and with Fenrir who decided on Magula's behalf.

Through the power of the orb Skjebne acted, and by nightfall of the next day he had realised his intentions and Skymaster was sailing to Thule. It was a quiet and joyless journey. Skjebne spent much of the time in the crystal room gazing out at the stars and the broad dark lands with their rare specklings of light that marked a few scattered settlements.

Before first light, Thule, the Broken Place, came into view. Skjebne sent out a handful of small orbs and they watched as the enclave was revealed to them.

'Nothing seems to have changed. The Tarazad are not massing in their thousands to defend against us,' Hora said with a bleak cynicism.

Skjebne smiled mirthlessly. 'Perhaps Helcyrian plays a clever game. Or perhaps the Shahini simply have no fear of us.'

The orb floated down to settle above the bleak shore of a muddy lake, shielded by hills from the city. The deep waters were tainted by the dirt of much mining. The closest settlement, a small village of earthworkers and their families, lay beyond an untidy wilderness of spoil heaps some distance away.

We can get there by going through the hills, Wyldewulf said.

And Kell recalled his earlier escape from the Broken Place, and how the wulfen had so effortlessly known the tunnels that mazed within the rock.

'I am worried about you, Skjebne,' Hora looked at his friend. 'How can you possibly negotiate the tunnels with that injury to your hip?'

'Oh, I have thought about that, my friend, and the answer is simple.' With a showy flourish Skjebne snapped his fingers and held up his hand. An instant later one of the little orbs drifted into the room and settled weightlessly upon his fingertips. 'Where this eye goes, so goes my assistance.'

'It is settled then.' Hora picked up his axe that was leaning nearby. 'Let us be on our way.'

The company watched the Skymaster sink almost without a ripple into the wine-dark waters of the lake. Skjebne alone was aboard. Then, as the dawn light began to strengthen in a clear sky eastward, Wyldewulf took them among the chaos of stones and the mounds of grey tailings, until they came to a ragged slit of shadow. That shadow was the entrance the wulf had been looking for, and the portal to the start of their quest.

They made good time, since the route was clear in Wyldewulf's mind. Above them the morning was brightening and the business of the *eardstapa*, the wandering merchants who came this way, had begun.

That is the circle of trade, Wyldewulf said as they paused for rest, and to discuss their plans. *Then, an inner circle where the Tarazad live and train. You have seen it Kell – it is covered over by the ruined shell that was the sky of the old enclave.*

'I recall it,' Kell answered.

The eardstapa and earthworkers do not go there. It is a tainted zone where the illusions of weorthan can twist the mind beyond its breaking point. And past it lies the rotten heart of Thule, the sanctum of Helcyrian. Here she presides over the Dreamhoard, which legend says is the repository of weorthan crystal that has been mined from the ground over many generations . . .

'Was it lost then?' Hora wondered. Wyldewulf's gaze grew distant.

Wulfensong tells of a time long past when the Ice pressed down on the land with unimaginable weight. The very rocks groaned and then sheared as their stresses grew too great. The centre of Thule collapsed and was swallowed into the ground, taking with it the wisdom of the gods that was said to be locked within lucite glass. The same cataclysm caused half the sky to fall, and the world burst in. The Shahini Tarazad were free in the land, but since the coming of the cold they had changed. They had given up their minds to the Uniarch Helcyrian, who controlled them absolutely.

'The same thing was happening in Perth,' Kell said with a shudder. 'So is it the same Helcyrian who is alive today?'

'Hardly,' came Skjebne's voice from the orb that floated close by. 'The name must be handed down through the bloodline.'

They continued on their way. Tsep went skittering ahead and sent back fragmentary thoughts as this pretty stone or that, or the sight of a cave bat attracted him. Wyldewulf and Fenrir led the party; Kell and Sebalrai followed Hora, Zauraq and Fwthark; Alef, Thoba and Myrgen brought up the rear. Skjebne's orb floated above and provided what light they needed.

'We must be under the innermost domains by now,' Sebalrai spoke up as they walked. 'I can feel it.' Kell nodded and smiled thinly, the others said nothing. Nobody doubted her instinct.

Gradually the nature of the darkness beyond the orb's small light began to change. The travellers grew aware of a sense of huge spaces; and a thin and steady wind, chilled and sterile, began to blow in their faces.

Somewhere ahead Tsep set up a chittering call.

'He is nervous,' Kell said. Ahead and behind came the clink of wyrda weaponry being brought to bear.

Movement. Fenrir's impression arrived with the clarity of icy water.

'We need more light.' Kell strained to see ahead. 'Skjebne, can the orb –'

And light came in a blazing flood and the group stood like insects before the awesome bulk of the Ice Demon.

12

Helcyrian

But the Ice Demon was dead! Kell had felled it on that terrible night when Shamra had been lost to him! And Kano had given his life by destroying it utterly through fire. That was no trick of memory – it was dead. It was dead . . .

The phantoms of the old ordeal swept through him and were gone, leaving lingering echoes of the fear. Then he saw that the 'demon' was nothing but a mechanism; roughly man-shaped, but six spans high and wrought of age-blackened steel. It was a giant skeletal thing, part vessel and part weapon.

'The cunning of it!' Skjebne stared in open admiration as Tsep alighted on the tarnished head of the colossus. Kell's first dread had turned to anger, and at the core of the anger lay hatred.

'I'd have no problem with my hip if I rode in that! So, that is what you and Kano fought last time we were here. Your achievement is not diminished just because it is a machine.'

'But it was so real –'

'As Perth was real Kell – as real as the All Mother wanted it to be. There is no mystery here, just ancient deceit.'

I have seen these things a few times before, came Wyldewulf's quiet thought. *Striding through the inner regions of Thule. They are protective devices, patrollers. They frighten the peasants away.*

'Guard dogs,' Hora added with a note of contempt. 'This one seems to be inert. Perhaps it is damaged . . .'

'We should take no chances,' Skjebne advised. 'The chamber is receptive to our wishes – the light appeared as we framed the idea. This is no dead place. Helcyrian might already be alerted to our presence. We should go.'

Kell put out his will and darkness returned again, save for the small comfort of the ligetu lamp. Out of daring, he brought back the memory of the Ice Demon and knew it had been born of the power of weorthan working in him, and by the terrors he had believed as a little child. His teachers had a great deal to answer for.

And daring further, he imagined the skeleton giant moving again – just fractionally. But there came no creaking of iron or the hum of ligetu energy from the metal patroller behind him, and presently he forgot about it as they continued on their way.

By and by a breeze began to stir along the passages and the atmosphere grew dank, and then they could hear the splash and plink of water in other nearby tunnels. The air also became laden with the foul smells of waste and decay.

We are coming near to the surface, Wyldewulf told the others. *Soon we will be above ground, and close to the centre of the enclave.*

They proceeded cautiously. The wyrda men unbuckled helmets from their belts and pulled them on and drew down their slitted visors. Kell unslung his multiblade. His practised fingers brushed the controls and the shaft doubled its length and sprouted a lean blade, sharp as a spike of ice. Beside him, Sebalrai sighed and faded from view: even Fenrir startled as she vanished, leading him to realise the depth and power of her gift.

'Daylight,' Hora whispered – *if the dreary greyness ahead of them could ever be called such*, came Kell's unspoken response.

They followed Wyldewulf's loping form and soon caught sight of the broken curve of carven stone that had once been the sky over Thule. Above it the true sky was piled with cloud, dropping a steady snowfall. The huge gloom echoed with distant sounds, though the scape into which the explorers emerged was empty and still. The ruins of once-magnificent buildings lay all about them: walls had tumbled; stout columns supported a nothingness of air, or else leaned unstably against one another, or had toppled entirely and crumbled. Broad expanses of marble floor were badly fractured: out of some of the pits a rank smoke rose. Here and there, seemingly patternless, foton lamps threw a moon-pale glow into the dimness. Some of them – large glassy globes, opaque as pearls – flared and guttered as though a life inside was faltering. The lamps dwindled away into the dark recesses of the enclave and were finally lost to sight.

The group kept to the walls, using the darkness with instinctive ease. Once they stopped through caution as a cacophony of sound started up. A clutch of creatures hurried by in the distance; child-sized, armoured, their backs irides-cently alight like a beetle's hard carapace.

'Dreng variants,' whispered Skjebne from his advantage point of the little orb. It lifted like a bubble to see better and dropped again lightly to the level of Kell's shoulder. 'And in the direction they have come from is a wall –'

The Bismerian Wall, Wyldewulf said. *The Wall of Shame. It is where we will find Alderamin, if we are to find him at all.*

At first sight the wall seemed unimposing, a long crescent of stone built within an amphitheatre and decorated with hundreds of dark bosses of grey iron. Only as the party drew closer did they realise the scale of the structure; for the ramparts stood fifteen or more spans high and the 'bosses' were cages containing people, or the remains of people. And coming closer still, they saw that the ground at the base was littered with filth, and that among it crawled scores of black carrion rats.

Kell felt a clutching at his sleeve and Sebalrai's weight against him.

'This is worse than anything I ever saw with Chertan. He was a brigand, but he killed cleanly.'

Helcyrian puts no value on life, Fenrir said. *If she can do this – what kind of monster must she be?*

It was a question that none of them could answer, besides which their immediate concern was finding Alderamin.

'There are hundreds of cages here.' Kell swept his eyes across them hopelessly. 'And we will be in plain sight as we search . . .'

'It could be a trap.'

'If it is a trap, Hora,' Skjebne replied, 'then we are already inside it . . . stay hidden, and I will look for the merchant.'

And give me his image. Tsep's voice lit like a spark in Kell's head. *I will look for him too.*

They watched Tsep and the little orb streaking away, becoming like two flecks of ash from a hearthfire. The orb had no power to reach the onlookers' minds; but Tsep's all-too-vivid impressions sickened them. Men and women had seemingly been locked in their cages and left. And the cages had been deviously built, so that no adult could stand upright or sit with any comfort. Someone of Alderamin's bulk would have found his knees pressed against the bars at the front, and his arms pinioned against the sides. Many of the prisoners had obviously died in torment, bereft of farewells.

The hreaomus, fleet and intelligent, did not take long to complete his task. He settled upon one particular cage and mentally Kell found himself looking down upon the bowed head of Alderamin. The merchant's hands, still clenched in suffering, rested on his knees, and the skin was lifeless and grey.

'No . . . no!'

'Keep your voice low, Kell!' Hora hissed. Kell covered his face with his hands and wept, for Sebalrai's grief was rising in him too and it was almost more than he could bear.

'He can't be dead. He can't be dead!'

He is dead, Kell, Tsep said. He struggled to squeeze between the bars but found a barrier there. *I can't get through. But I have no doubt life has left him.*

'I must make sure.' As though entranced Kell moved from cover and hurried down the terraces of stone into the well of the amphitheatre.

'You're a fool Kell, come back!' But Hora too left his place of safety out of concern for the boy and hurried after him. All followed, realising that Kell was right and they had to know with certainty.

The orb had swept up to where Tsep was perched. Skjebne angled the device but was unable to see Alderamin's face; his head hung down so that his chin touched his breastbone, and his shaggy hair cauled his eyes. But there was no sign of movement; no impression of the huge and radiant life that had been Alderamin.

'You will not die until all the lives that touched you are gone,' Skjebne said softly, then was distracted by a commotion at the base of the Bismerian Wall.

Kell was climbing with a hard and unyielding determination, using the regularly spaced cages and bars to haul himself up; five spans above the ground – ten – twelve. Then Skjebne was with him as the boy stared into the cage . . .

Alderamin looked up and his eyes were glazed with pain and the memory of horrors.

'Kell . . . I never doubted you would come . . .'

'It's a lie Kell!' Skjebne warned. 'Deny him – deny him!' And Tsep fluttered down and worried around Kell's head as he tried to reach into the cage . . .

'She will release me if you tell her, Kell . . . tell her what you have learned of weorthan. Tell her of Skjebne's discoveries, and of your bond with the wulfen . . . how you bathe in their thoughts like a running river . . . tell her, and she will let us all go free.'

He does not move, Kell. Your friend is dead. I cannot even smell the ghosts in him . . . You are being deceived.

And in proof of his point, the hreaomus flung itself at the bars and between them, and clattered against the rare membrane that separated the truth from the lie.

'It's weorthan crystal!' Skjebne declared 'Destroy it, Kell. Do it now!'

'You have betrayed us, Alderamin . . .'

You friend is not here, only the vessel he has abandoned at the end of his voyage. Break the spell. Shatter the glass —

Alderamin lifted trembling hands in a final plea, but Kell knew that his companions were right. There was nothing left but the man's body: there was only the memory in Kell's mind of a life that had once been.

Slowly and deliberately Kell reached behind his back and drew the multiblade from its sheath. The words of the Seetus, the last great whale, came back to give final purpose to his act.

If you meet the Goddess on the road – kill her! It's the only way.

He drove the spike forward and the illusion shattered, thin shards of glass like the last ice on a warm day falling down to disintegrate upon hitting the floor.

And inside the cage Alderamin's corpse was unmoving.

'Hwaet! The hordes come!'

Hora's yell alerted them all. Kell swung round and kept his grip firm on the bars. Out of the darkness and across the vast floor of the amphitheatre the Tarazad drengs appeared – a chaos of forms; men and women and children welded into their armour as Helcyrian's slaves. The noise of their arrival, of claws and steel boots and the clinking of blades became deafening.

Wisely, both Skjebne's orb and Tsep soared upwards into the shadows and vanished. Kell's mind spun in search of a plan, but deep down he knew there was nothing worthwhile to be done.

The drengs swarmed around the hopelessly small force of wyrda men. Fenrir and Wyldewulf stood proud with their fur bristling and their eyes lit with fire. Sebalrai, close by Hora's side, was a faint mist, but even so she was unable to escape. They were soon overpowered.

Presently, inevitably, two drengs climbed up to catch Kell. He waited for them, sheathing the multiblade, knowing that his moment was not yet; watching in a kind of amazed revulsion as the creatures came towards him. The larger

196

dreng was solidly armoured and its face was hidden behind a featureless mask of black porcelain – Kell was reminded of Feoh's mask, and his unease at what it might conceal.

The other dreng, smaller and faster, got to him first. It had the body of a dwarf wrapped round in silver bands, the limbs extended and strengthened by steel. Its hair was fair as wheat, and it had a child's face – but its eyes were empty of innocence – empty of everything, as cold and dead as Alderamin's eyes.

To fight would be to die. Fenrir's call rang clearly across the mental field that increasingly united the group. *To fight would be to die.* It made good sense to the wyrda, whose purpose had never been in fighting for itself, but only in search of the Sun's Way. Even so, as the drengs snatched their weapons and tore their protections away, Hora's desire was to reach out and break necks with the raw strength of his hands . . .

Wyldewulf too restrained himself with an effort, for the old hatred of the Tarazad and their pillaging of the earth was rooted deep in his ancestry. And when one careless dreng soldier moved too close, Wyldewulf lashed out with a snarling bite that left crush marks in the metal around the man's calf.

A dozen soldiers turned upon the wulf and would have finished him then.

'He is the one who sings to our minds,' Kell said stridently. 'He joins us in thought. If you kill him his secret also dies. Helcyrian will rip out your hearts.'

The warriors held back, and one by one withdrew and let Wyldewulf be. A few looked curiously on the boy, the slightest of the males, but somehow the one who held the greatest authority.

One dreng, a tall thin man whose body had been ravaged some time in the past by fire or disease, strode forward and spoke the words that had been put into his mouth.

'There are more of you than this, I know there are. Such a meagre force would not come to attack Thule.'

197

'We came to find the merchant Alderamin. He helped us once. He is our friend.'

'*Was.* He died screaming two days ago.'

'You have been deceived by your own weorthan,' Kell said, taunting. 'He is alive in us . . . and that is important to you, isn't it?' He had noticed the change in the man's expression, the sudden greed and longing to know.

'Isn't it, Helcyrian?'

The dreng smiled and in a flash struck out with a mailed fist that smashed Kell unconscious to the ground.

He woke slowly, spitting blood and curses, roused by the sweet stench of the chamber where he lay. Somewhere far off were his friends – Fenrir's clear presence penetrated the haze of dizziness and pain and counted Wyldewulf and Sebalrai and all six wyrda safe.

Skjebne and Tsep are with us too, Fenrir added with veiled softness, deep as a midnight dream.

Close by the drengs moved with a gentle reverence; acolytes with special dispensation to attend Helcyrian in her temple . . .

Kell sat up awkwardly and his light-headedness increased. The drengs were drifting phantoms in a labyrinth of mirrors, going in and out of view, remembered then forgotten. All around him and above, and perhaps in the ground far below, the weorthan spun its lies and flickered like light through the million fractured fargments of the huge crystal matrix.

'Helcyrian.'

'I am here.'

The air became still and time paused like a held breath. The heaviness of the room's perfume increased and a dreng appeared; a woman clad lightly in sylk, caged within her prison of metals and filigree wire and ceramic shell. Only one arm and half of her face, withered with age, were visible; and a dry straggle of grey hair that had used to be night-black and so fine.

Kell choked back his surprise – not at the crone herself, who probably had little idea of what had been done to her – but at her faded resemblance to Shamra. And suddenly and unexpectedly his pity for Helcyrian was immense.

'How can anything I say be of use to you?' He spoke to the whole room rather than the cadaverous thing before him. 'Why can't you be content where you are? Why can't you use the weorthan to forget all about the world where I live?'

'Forgetting is always denial,' Helcyrian said. 'Some part of me would know the truth, and despair of it.' The crone's mouth barely moved: Kell realised the words were either being artificially generated in a similar way to Skjebne's voice through the roving orb; or they were coming directly into his mind –

Kell rubbed his eyes in a pretence of waking further, but could feel no weorthan there.

Its influence is all around us. That was Fenrir, clear as the moon's reflection in still water, leaving no trace.

She is in the weorthan, Kell! Helcyrian is no more than an apparition . . .

'When you spoke to me on the Bismerian Wall through the mouth of Alderamin, you wanted to know more of weorthan and how I run with wulfen. How is that of use to you?'

'I don't know that it is.' Helcyrian spoke without bitterness or disappointment, but with a weariness that came from her soul. 'Yet you escaped the weorthan's hold.'

'It was never inside me: it never truly possessed me. But you –' Kell looked, not at the chained hag, but all around him at her shimmering web. 'You and the enchanted glass are one and the same.'

'Not always! Once I was free!'

The Uniarch's voice rose to a shriek and the air itself shivered, and beyond the veils of crystal the dreng slaves stirred and lifted up their weapons.

'Once so long ago; before the Ice, before time, I was

199

imprisoned here . . . ahh, it was such a freedom then, to spin the world round with the turn of a thought. I spoke with all peoples, and everyone grew wise from my teachings. I was truly the mother of humanity.'

'The All Mother . . .'

'Oracle, enchantress, seducer. I was a vision with many voices, with a knowledge as deep as the sea.'

The harridan smiled at a memory that was never her own, of days that existed thousands of moons before she was born. Helcyrian's voice was rich in its wistfulness.

'But the Ice grew stronger and became an overwhelming enemy. It was brutal and unthinking. It crushed the eggs where the children slept; it wiped out whole communities; it tore the harmony out of the world. It shattered my mind.'

'So the Ice is *your* nemesis, diviner. Not mine.'

'What I fear makes the hearts of all men tremble.'

'Why have you released the Shahini Tarazad into the world?' Kell wondered, since Helcyrian seemed in the mood for revelations; and since he knew that Fenrir and Tsep would be listening, and probably Skjebne would too.

'The ground twisted under the weight of the Ice and the rocks cracked apart and the enclave was breached. The Shahini had been the most industrious of tribes. They were craftsmen and artisans. Their ability to work metals and ceramics and stones remains unsurpassed. They understand how to confer life through the application of the ligetu force . . .' And here the voice of the sorceress became softer and more intimate in its secrecy. 'They know how to spin fancies in the mind – and beyond the dexterity of spiders, how to unspin them too.'

Kell had been so engrossed by what Helcyrian was saying that he failed to notice two drengs moving up closer behind him. And between them walked a kind-faced man whose bronze-tinted skin shone with health. When he spoke, Kell jolted and the spell of the enchantress was broken.

'How are you today?'

The simple question paralysed his thoughts and froze Kell's blood which was hot with memories, some of which Tsep and Fenrir detected an instant later.

He is the one who beguiled us, when we were trapped before in Thule!

Still it meant nothing to Kell. The technician commanded the drengs to pinion the boy's arms. In one of his hands gleamed a knife with an edge fine as terror.

They stooped down to take him —

And the room flew apart in a thunderous roar and showers of cascading glass.

Something twice the size of a man's head; black, spherical, hurtled through the delicate veils of crystal — the weorthan matrix where the insane Helcyrian lived. Behind the roar came Skjebne's cry of defiance. Using all of the power he could muster, he sent the orb plunging deeper towards the heart of Helcyrian's domain, causing as much damage as possible.

Amidst the awful clamour and the whirling storm of splinters Tsep spun down and plucked at the eyes of one of the Tarazad minions. It yelled with a strangely metallic squeal. Weaponry sprouted from the other's metal hands.

Kell kicked out, offbalancing the dreng. The distress of its controller confused it. Kell scrambled up and lashed out hard with his boots. A blade whistled past a handspan in front of his face.

Then Fenrir appeared, rage wrapped in silver. At five strides he launched himself high in the air and hurled his full weight into the attacking dreng. The soldier tumbled backwards and deep inside him a mechanism failed: ligetu light sparked and platinum wires, fine as hair, snapped and withered. The dreng's very heart muscle clenched and spasmed and relaxed into death.

The wulf drew in the last breath of his enemy — a breath that was always unique in its smell of infinity. And while Tsep dispatched the other guard with his nerve-numbing venom, Fenrir turned upon the bronze-faced man.

His first horrendous bite tore off the technician's lower jaw and half of one side of his skull. Beyond that Kell was unable to watch. He looked away and took the fallen dreng's stabbing sword, detaching it with a few deft twists from the steel-sheathed arm.

Elsewhere in the sanctum other drengs were scurrying in disarray. The orb had driven deep into the crystal curtains of the weorthan matrix and had caused huge destruction – possibly fatal damage – to Helcyrian's mind. But the orb itself was spitting fires and sparks, and all of a sudden it dropped heavily to the ground and rolled to a standstill, smouldering.

Kell realised they had now lost contact with Skjebne, though the sacrifice of the orb had created the opportunity of escape . . . and as he swung his sword this way and that, shattering as much weorthan as he could, a thought came to life in his mind – a thought of such darkness that Kell wondered if he was still being plagued by Helcyrian. But still, he took the thought into himself; took it and owned it and accepted its consequences, and promised to himself that he would never justify his actions to anyone, regardless of the punishments he received . . .

He came upon Hora chained beside Zauraq and the other three wyrda.

'The lock is in that casket,' Hora told him, indicating a box high up on the wall. Inside Kell discovered clusters of jewelled buttons and fine silver strands, set as a conundrum.

'We have to leave quickly!' There was an edge of panic in his voice. 'I don't know how to solve the puzzle!'

'It's only a puzzle when you play by its rules.' Hora grinned and Kell read the intention in his face. He changed his grip on the dreng sword and brought the hilt crashing into the box. There was a brief spitting fire and the warriors' manacles fell free.

Together they searched the rest of the chamber and

quickly came upon Sebalrai – similarly restrained and similarly freed – and then Wyldewulf bound in a mesh, being too dangerous to confine in any other way. Moments later Tsep and Fenrir joined the band and, save for Skjebne, they were complete.

'We must avoid the Tarazad and spread the word to the peasants and the earthworkers, to the eardstapa and all the passing strangers – they must leave the Broken Place and seek the shield of the hills. Quickly now, quickly!'

As Kell made to hurry away, Hora took hold of his arm.

'What are you going to do, *bearn*?'

Kell could see that the man was very frightened.

'It is already done,' Kell said shortly, and with no note of guilt. 'I am going to allow Helcyrian to forget her nightmare.'

They hurried through the mayhem. Kell came to see that Helcyrian's binding of the Shahini Tarazad had been so complete that her derangement was theirs as well. Hundreds of drengs in all their varied armours stumbled by, or ran with manic urgency to destinations that were a mystery to them; some had simply fallen and lay staring at the world they no longer recognised: one dreng, a man of unnatural height and leanness, sang in the middle of an otherwise empty courtyard, his head thrown back, his face transformed by bliss, his melody so beautiful and poignant that it brought tears to the onlookers' eyes. And shortly after, as the group emerged from beneath the jagged edge of the enclave's canopy and into the natural light of the day, they chanced upon the crone who had at some distant time held a special importance for the All Mother.

The woman lay confined in her metal skeleton. She had fallen and her body was moving with a strange mechanical rhythm; unfolding like a flower, curling back into the huddle of a womb-bound child. She saw nothing, she heard nothing, she believed nothing but the babblings that howled in her mind. Again Kell was struck by Shamra's memory, and wondered in that passing moment if the resemblance had been part of Helcyrian's purpose.

Sebalrai knelt to the old woman to give comfort. But Kell drew her away and Hora, asking no leave from any man, took the boy's sword and with a single blow clove the crone's head from her body.

Quickly now they ran towards the outskirts of Thule telling all they met to get away from that place. There was already a sense of alarm among the merchants and travellers and the earthworkers thronging the markets: everyone had seen the inexplicable and frightening change that had come over the patrolling drengs. Now a great number of the traders were bundling up their waggons and mox-panniers and whatever containers they could find and hurrying to be on their way. Here and there, without the drengs to oversee order, fights were breaking out and looting began. Kell saw the bright flare of flames in the distance and was reminded of the last day of Perth, and was sickened by it.

'We haven't much further to go,' Hora called back to the others. He was forging his way ahead at the front of the group, shoving people aside and with the other wyrdas' help clearing a path through the crowd. They had left the centre of Thule behind them now, and a fitful rain swept in from a dismal sky. Far away, beyond the hills that were their destination, a single cutting edge of sunlight struck down through the clouds.

I cannot go towards it, came Tsep's thoughts with a sudden frightened insistence. *The light will destroy me.*

Kell paused and cast round amongst the rubbish on the street, snatched up some sacking and wrapped the creature in its folds.

We can't leave you here, little hero! Your discomfort will only be for a short while.

Meanwhile Hora and his brothers had hurried on, Fwthark turning briefly to check on Kell's position and call him to keep up. The warrior raised his arm to wave him on . . .

Kell saw a dreng who was standing some five paces away — a young man, his face half metal, cruelly handsome in a ribbed chestplate of gleaming chrome, with sheaths of the same protecting his arms and his legs. There was a keen hard intelligence in the dreng's one visible eye: a knowingness; an intent.

Fenrir!

The wulf instantly picked up Kell's suspicion and swung back to search out the danger. But high-backed and swift as he was, Fenrir still only came to a man's hip-height, and the street was aseethe with hurrying people and moxen and other animals unnerved by the clamour.

Which way brooor!

Kell knew clearly that the dreng was self-aware, which meant that either it had remained untouched by Helcyrian's madness, or else the enchantress's mind was intact and recovering.

These ideas were swept up with horror as the dreng pointed at Fwthark. There came a harsh, brief whistling sound and something struck the wyrda with a tremendous impact. Blood splashed on his shoulder and he was smashed sideways and down.

Fenrir came upon Fwthark as the life left him, then leaped at the dreng an instant later, with Wyldewulf close on his heels. Together the two wulfen slew the guardian with a swift and savage precision.

Something has changed, Fenrir said. And Kell knew with certainty what he meant.

All of this had happened in a few heartbeats. Only now were Hora, Zauraq and the other wyrda becoming aware of the new danger and returning too late to help.

'Helcyrian is rising from her delirium.' Kell ran to Hora and began dragging him away from the spot where Fwthark had fallen. He hated the look of stunned grief on his friend's face. 'The Tarazad are coming back to themselves. Quickly Hora, quickly! We must get ourselves away!'

Close by, Sebalrai stood pale-faced and drenched by the rain. Kell went to her and put his arm about her shoulder, turning her aside from the sight of Fwthark's body.

'Come on, we must leave. There is nothing else to be done.'

He urged her on, while Fenrir and Wyldewulf appeared at their side and in silence. Kell knew there would be no reasoning with Hora now, no leading him to safety as easily. He looked back once and saw his friend barging through the people with Zauraq beside him and Alef, Thoba and Myrgen closely following. A dreng soldier saw them, but now the advantage lay with the wyrda. The dreng went down like a trampled doll. Kell saw Hora's arm rise and fall, rise and fall, and even above the cacophony of the crowd he heard the warrior's howl of blood-vengeance.

People were streaming out of Thule in their hundreds. Kell grew numb to the shouts and cries, to the terrified faces and the look of lost isolation in people's eyes. Once a woman fell in the thick black mud of the track. Once a man was set upon and robbed for his goods and his money. Once a child stumbled past calling for its mother . . . Kell passed them by, for whatever their ordeals may be they were nothing compared to the greater doom that he was bringing down upon the city.

On and on, step after step until the steps became mindless, Kell trudged heavily towards the hills. Sebalrai kept up but her face was grey with exhaustion. Wyldewulf and Fenrir flanked them, loping tirelessly, their minds relaxed but alert, their eyes settled with the contentment of those who follow their Wierd and accept it utterly.

A little later the road forked and they took the right-hand way. The other track wound up to the outskirt settlements. Many of the earthworkers would be going there to shelter in their homes, or to collect up their possessions and move on. Kell's path brought them to a wood of silver birch, and on Fenrir's advice they struck out into the trees to quieter places where the wulfen could map the air and gather back strength from the land.

We can simply keep climbing. The woods are quite thin and the way is not hard. Once we have crested this hill we will see the mere where the Skymaster waits.

They rested for a short while and then continued the journey. As Fenrir said, the birch wood was spacious and they could easily pass through. It did not take long to reach the top, and through the spread of branches on the downslope and the dull grey rain they soon saw the muted glitter of the lake.

Can we contact Skjebne? Wyldewulf wanted to know. *There are drengs coming fast through the woods. And without the wyrda's help . . .*

The thought faded like an echo as the wulf's attention was drawn elsewhere. Or perhaps he did not want Kell to recognise his dark anticipation.

The little orb did not destroy the weorthan matrix completely —

Who knows how far the crystal's roots sink into the earth? Fenrir said, and Kell wondered if a similar structure existed in Perth, housing the All Mother there . . .

Whatever the answer, she has recovered enough to come after us. I'll go down to the lake to seek Skjebne —

But there was no need. Wyldewulf's senses had detected the little orb many seconds before as it swished through the trees; a pattern of tiny sounds, a fleeting shadow and flicker of light, the smell of strange metal and the faintest tingling of the energies that gave a false life to the machine.

Now Fenrir was alerted to it too, and then Kell and Sebalrai.

'Ho! Skjebne!'

But it's here, Kell. Fenrir pointed his muzzle westward, to a second and more distant device.

There are many of them! Skjebne must be searching all over the hillsides. Wyldewulf hunkered down, sweeping the scape for information before judging his further actions.

Then one of the orbs caught sight of the group and hurtled towards them.

'Ha! So my plan worked and you escaped from Helcyrian.' Skjebne's cheerful easy arrogance caused Kell to smile. 'I have dispatched orbs to keep track of the dreng forces following you . . . if you hurry now you can reach the shore before they do.'

'We don't know about Hora. He stayed behind with the other wyrda . . . Fwthark was killed, and Hora's anger was boundless . . . if he remains in the city . . .'

'Events have tears, little ploughboy. A while ago there were changes in Skymaster. The room of screens grew dim and the life of the vessel itself seemed to recede. I could not find out what had happened at first. But the voice of the orb spoke to me Kell – it spoke to me directly for the first time! And it told me your secret.'

Kell listened for condemnation and found none. The sphere hung in its lattice of forces just an armspan from Kell and at head height. It was immensely comforting to hear Skjebne's voice and to have the advantage of his view once again. But how Kell wished he could look into his friend's eyes to judge the truth of his words.

'The Skymaster has not challenged my instruction?'

'Not as far as I can tell.'

'Then you know we must find Hora and –'

'Finding him is not enough, Kell. You understand that. What is done is done and you cannot call back the sped arrow or the spoken word, or a wish cast into the river of Wierd. Let's have you safe now, and then we'll decide what to do.'

All this time the two wulfen had stood silent while Kell and Skjebne conversed. Now Fenrir nudged him gently, having understood the great and terrible thing he had dared to imagine and conjure to life.

Helcyrian's desire to kill us can still be satisfied, brooor. The smell of the Tarazad grows stronger.

Then we'll be guided by you. Kell turned to Sebalrai. 'We're

208

going down to the lake side now. Once aboard the vessel we'll be secure.' *Are you quite comfortable in there Tsep?*

Never more so, came the waspish reply from the bundle of sacking under Kell's arm. Kell smiled at the strength of trust in the little hreaomus. He tied the cloth more tightly and bound it to a ring in his belt.

'Then let us be on our way.'

They followed the natural order. Fenrir moved ahead while Wyldewulf wove across their path into the depths of the wood. The eye orb stayed with them, and Kell could clearly imagine the many others scattering across the hills and through the settlements of the earthworkers and even beyond the outer regions of Thule, searching for Hora and his companions.

By now the rain had soaked them all through. Kell took Sebalrai's hand and found it cold as clay, and she was shivering. He slowed as they approached the line where the trees ended and the scrub-covered slope down to the water's edge began.

Look there. Fenrir's thought directed Kell's attention.

The mere's surface was bulging as the great bulk of the Skymaster rose, lifting clear, sloughing off cascades of foaming water. The sight encouraged them on. Fenrir reached the treeline and read the book of the wind. He said nothing, but Kell still detected the bright note of danger in the song of his mind.

Fenrir broke cover and the others followed. But Wyldewulf was suddenly running away from them, moving at full speed towards a dark spread of woodland – from which a cadre of drengs now emerged; a half-dozen of them, lank and frightening figures clad in grey armour, weaponed with spikes and blades, driven on powerful machine legs. The sound of their engines was a grinding roar, and above it the shrieking ululation of their alarms called to the skies.

'Wyldewulf! Wyldewulf come back!'

The helplessness in Kell's voice made it weak. Through the

rain and the rising wind his words had no force. But Wyldewulf's intention was clear – to trade his life for a handful of seconds for his friends.

Run on! Run on!

Fenrir understood his wulfkin's intention and would not have it wasted. But Kell could not take his eyes from the sight of Wyldewulf's last and finest gift. He swept like a breath of light over the land, like the merest sunbeam released by the swift passing of clouds.

The foremost drengs sensed him and stopped, swivelling on their pivoted limbs, angling their weapons towards him.

A red flash lit the rain veils; then several more like flickering spatters of blood. Bushes burst into fire, grass scorched and the air itself hissed and stank like burned iron.

Run on! Fenrir urged, for every heartbeat was precious and delay held nothing but death.

Two drengs fired together and their aim was true, because that was Wyldewulf's Wierd. The crossbeams caught him and he blazed like the morning and then was gone in a whirling flurry of flames.

But now the Skymaster was a mountainous presence, and a number of the smaller orbs swung round it like fry round a dark ocean whale. Kell could feel the cold air pouring from it and the smell of lake bed mud was cloyingly strong.

Fenrir reached the great orb as the portal opened. He leaped a man-height up to the lip of the ramp.

A dreng fire-arrow shrieked and sizzled into the metal close by him. Now the whole Tarazad group was advancing.

Kell clenched his teeth against the pain of effort and the pain of cold, and the deeper torture of anticipation. He came within the shadow of the orb, plucked Tsep from his sacking and flung him into the vessel.

'Be quick Kell!'

Skjebne's voice crackled nearby. An eye orb swung past and streaked away, crashing at great velocity into the closest of the dreng warrior-machines.

Kell came to the spot below the Skymaster's hatchway. He paused and grasped Sebalrai by the waist and lifted her so she could take hold of Fenrir's fur.

Then her weight was lifted from him, and there was a thunder in the air, a storm coming.

Light was everywhere. A fireflash burst close to Kell's right side and seared his body and face. He cried out, twisting reflexively around the agony of the heat.

The drengs were much closer now, speeding over the scrubland with great striding steps. Through the drifting rain he could even see the strangely doll-like faces of the men inside the machines; soulless as stone, alive with Helcyrian's passion.

Hope fell away like a shed skin. The dreng at the vanguard fired again and the world burned . . .

But the thunder now was inexorable and a shadow was darkening the sky. Something huge was imminent, and Kell for all his fear felt glad to be alive to see this stone cast in history's river –

The Skymaster's twin came drilling down through the clouds in a chaos of hurricanes. It was visible for a moment before it dropped below the rain-vague line of the hills.

There was a moment's hesitation, as though Wierd itself was reluctant to decide.

Then a vast explosion rolled out towards the horizons, destroying the centre of Thule.

The blast-wave arrived seconds later like a tide over-whelming the woodland. Kell saw the trees lashed about like reeds, and the drengs and his thoughts and all that existed were blown away like leaves on a welcoming wind.

The World Of The Wintering

GLOSSARY

Aethgar – One of Alderamin's soldiers, killed in the last battle of Edgetown.

Aglaeca – Monster.

Alderamin – Alderamin is the amber merchant Kell and his friends meet in *Ice*.

Alef (and Thoba and Myrgen) – Three Wyrda companions who accompany Kell and his friends to Thule to destroy Helcyrian and the Shahini Tarazad.

All Mother – Aka the Goddess and Little Sister. The All Mother is the controlling force in Perth, an apparently omnipotent presence who maintains the world of the enclave at all levels, from the environment to the spiritual structure of the Community. Kell and his friends finally discover that Little Sister (like Orwell's Big Brother) is an intelligent construction that exists planet-wide – but it is flawed and fragmented, both in terms of its physical interconnectedness and the ghost of the neurotic/paranoid personality that lies at its heart. The All Mother represents the smothering mother archetype, the Earth Mother, and the 'mystification of technology' that afflicts the general populace.

Amber – A fossilised resin which quite often contains the perfectly preserved remains of plants, insects, even small lizards. In the Wintering it represents preservation through imprisonment, a state that exists also in Perth.

Anwealda – Ruler.

Aquizi – One of Kell's tutors, whom Kell despises for his arrogance yet fears because of his cruelly-applied power.

Aurok – A huge bull-like herbivore, sacrificed by the Wulfen so that they can talk with their deity, the Godwulf. An aurok must be defeated in one-to-one battle for this to occur.

Awyrcancoin – Payment for labour.

Bealdor – A leader in war.

Bearn – Child.

Beorc – The leader of one of Kano's escapee groups. His name means birth or regeneration.

Birca – Birca is one of Kano's rebel band. He did not survive the escape from Perth. His name signifies growth, but is used in a darkly ironic way when set within the false paradise of the enclave.

Bismarian Wall – The Wall of Shame in Thule on which Helcyrian's prisoners are caged.

Bord – Table.

Broken Place – Another name for Thule, an enclave which is also broken in a psychological sense, ruled as it is by the psychotic tyrant Helcyrian.

Brooor – Brother.

Ceorl – Peasants.

Chertan – Leader of a bandit pack whom Kell and his friends encounter on their journey East.

Ciepemann – A trader.

Community – The name by which the population of Perth is known. It is used ironically throughout.

Compound words – Appear throughout the story; heart-bonded, honeygrass, lantern-apple, elderman, meltstone and others. Apart from being a stylistic device, such compounded words create links with the linguistic structure of the Anglo-Saxon culture which provided a model for the culture Kell and his friends meet through Alderamin.

Corvus – Wulfen word for crow.

Cristilla – Generally, a crystal or gemstone. In Thaw the word refers to a powerful weapon of radiance which Feoh passes on to Kell, having received it previously as a gift from Alderamin.

Dispossessed – The dispossessed are those members of the populace who, like Kano, have removed the weorthan glass from their eyes (see Weorthan).

Dreamhoard – The mass of weorthan crystal below Thule containing the vast knowledge of the world. But the knowledge, like the 'Hoard itself, is fractured and incomplete.

Drengs – Biomechanical minions of Helcyrian. Drengs are once-human beings shackled more or less completely to artificial components.

Drycraeft – Magic or enchantment (or, from our perspective, sophisticated technological processes or effects).

Drycraeftig – Magically skilled.

Dweorg – A dwarf, one of the Brising or Shining Ones. The Brising traditionally reside in Kairos: they are metal workers of great skill.

Ealdbeorn – An older brother in terms of friendship and wisdom rather than blood links.

Ealdmodor – 'Old Mother', ususually used as an insult. Pl: ealdmodoren.

Eardstapa – Travelling merchants.

Eargnewulf – A Tarazad word meaning 'the miserable (wulf)'.

Edgetown – The trader settlement ruled by Alderamin. Edgetown represents a frontier; it is a fledgling community eventually wiped out by the Shahini Tarazad who come from Thule in the Barbaric Lands.

Elhaz – A Wyrda warrior killed in Thule.

Enclave – An enclosed environment within which communities live in isolation protected from the global ice. The enclave of Perth is a hollowed-out mountain.

Enjeck – Husband of Munin. They were Kell's last temporary family before he left Perth.

Eodor – A young wulf in Magula's pack. Also a word meaning 'protector'.

Eofor – Boar.

Eoldermen – The elders of a group.

Erulian – An esoteric group (some believe they are a distinct breed) of Thrall Makers or enchanters. From what can be gleaned of their powers, it appears that the Erulian use a combination of innate mental abilities and technological devices to affect the fabric of reality. It is said that they among few mortal creatures can change the way that Wierd is woven.

Eye Of The Rad – A mysterious room near Uthgaroar. Made of a strange translucent substance, the room creates the viewpoint of one standing in the centre of the heavens. This signifies the purpose of the Sigel Rad and the destiny of the Wyrda Craeftum.

Faeder – Father.

Faedera – The pack leader before Magula.

Faellanstan – The Tumblestones, a high pass lying to the north-east of Edgetown.

Faest – Secretly.

Fenrir – One of Magula's pack and a young wulf touched by Wierd. Fenrir or his offspring are fated to drive humankin from the world and fill the sky with blood. The symbolism of this prophecy is unclear.

Feoh – Feoh is a powerful telepath and healer. She is one of Kano's rebel group and is heartbonded to him. After Kano's death and Shamra's mysterious capture, Feoh goes in search of her and becomes initiated into the Sustren. Feoh's name is linked with fulfilment, well being and nourishment.

Ferhocraeft – 'Mind craft'; the process of creative thought and the products of that thought which in the past has been called Teknology.

Forraedan – One of the Thrall Makers of Kairos, and a lyblaeca or master mage.

Frea – Master, as in 'sir'.

Frio – Friend.

Furhwudu – Fir trees.

Furrow – A furrow is one symbol of Kell's life. It implies predetermination and the illusion of choice. See Wierd.

Fwthark – Hora's friend and a fellow Wyrda warrior. Fwthark dies during the fall of Thule. His name means unity.

Gaeleran – A teacher.

Gaest – The soul or spirit of an object or place.

Garulf – Genera (pl: generan), or assistant, to Thorbyorg.

Gast – A night spirit, any ghostly thing.

Gat – A mountain goat.

Gauda – A wulf in Magula's pack.

Gebedraedan – A dangerous and powerful ritual performed by the Lyblaeca in which bio-formative fields are activated and modified to create subgenetic changes in individuals or an entire species. The Seetus, Wulfen and Hreaomus were all created in this way. Latterly the ceremony has been corrupted to produce the Slean.

Gebrooor – True Brother. This is a term of great affection and respect.

Gedrhyt – Band or company of people.

Gefera – A wulfen word for companion.

Gegilda – A guild member.

Gesittan – A command to be still and calm.

Gifu – Gifu is the landsman who trained Kell in his craft. He represents 'ignorance is bliss', perfect Zen. Gifu never questions what's around him. He observes the rhythms of the world and draws a deep pleasure from nature. He has lived and will die like an ear of the wheat that he cultivates. The name Gifu (also Gyfu) is a runic word meaning a gift.

Glass – Glass has a special significance in Kell's world. The glass of Skjebne's farscope opens up the horizons, but usually glass has a sinister aspect linked with the controlling influence of the All Mother. Every child of Perth is given an oyster-shaped chunk of glass in infancy. It is tuned to the innocent's mind. It whispers to him, reinforces the Mythologies, and allows the Goddess to know his actions, words, and even perhaps his thoughts. Kell and Shamra's destruction of their oyster glass after meeting Kano is a profoundly symbolic and empowering act. Glass is also crafted into subtle lenses or pellicles which are placed over the eyes of babies to filter their reality. Kano allowed Kell to see the truth of things by plucking out his lenses.

Godwulf – The one deity of the Wulfen. The Godwulf is composed of the souls of all dead Wulfen, and is a day-to-day part of the existence of all that are alive. The Godwulf is the past and the destiny of the species, expressing itself most powerfully in the here-and-now.

Guardian helmet – Headgear which allows the wearer simultaneous control of all the Orbs of the Wyrda Craeftum.

Hacele – A cloak.

Hagen – One of Alderamin's kinsmen.

Healm – A mat.

Heartbonding – Couples are predestined to live together in adulthood and produce offspring. It is of course the All Mother who decides which boy and girl shall be introduced as children. From that point on they are required to meet socially until the time comes when they are officially bonded. Their children are soon taken away from them, however, to have their minds moulded at the Tutorium. From there they live with a succession of temporary families until they are old enough to be independent.

Helcyrian – Dictatorial ruler of Thule. One of the Sustren, she maintains an iron control over the drengs of the Shahini Tarazad.

Heoden – A wulf in Magula's pack.

Heorot – A wulfen word for deer.

Heorrenda – An armoured boar of the Wyrda Craeftum. He is put under Hora's care.

Hora – One of Kano's rebel group. Hora was a fisherman who later joins a mercenary warrior band known as the Wyrda Craeftum. It is through Hora's contacts with the Wyrda that Kell and his friends find the means to explore the outer world.

Hreaomus – A species of man–bat that Kell and his friends encounter at the plateau of the orbs.

Hrothwulf – The oldest wulf in Magula's pack.

Hugauga – A large settlement on the Plain of Thurisaz (Gateway) where Kell and his friends meet with the Thrall Maker Wrynn.

Hwaet! – Meaning 'Greetings' or 'Listen!'

Hyld – A wulf in Magula's pack.

Hyrdefolk – Tenders of cattle and sheep.

Hyrnetu – Literally 'hornets' or insects. The hyrnetu are mechanical servo-devices which have evolved into the slave-weapons of the Slean, who in turn serve the Lyblaeca – indeed, some of the Thrall Makers themselves have undergone the process of becoming Slean.

Ice Demon – The Ice Demon symbolises the harshness and destructiveness of the world beyond the enclave. It is the bogeyman invoked to frighten children and adults alike. Kell's encounter with the Demon at the conclusion of *Ice* marks an important step in his rite of passage to adulthood and independence.

Jadhma – One of Alderamin's wives, and birth-mother of Shaula.

Kairos – Kairos has been called the City Out Of Time. It is a strange and enigmatic place, as though built on a gateway between worlds, curiously unaffected by climate or circumstances. It is the home of the Erulian, the Thrall Makers whom the Sustren believe can make the dreams of weorthan a living reality.

Kano – Leader of the rebel movement in Perth. Kano's power lies in his ability to see things as they are in the enclave (and there is a technological explanation behind this), coupled with his vast anger that the people should be made to live under an illusion. It is that anger which makes Kano's life burn briefly but bright as the sun. He dies in battle with the Ice Demon at Thule. His name is a runic word signifying an opening up, renewed clarity and a dispelling of the darkness.

Kell – Kell is the archetypal adolescent caught between innocence and experience. His world is uncomplicated in itself (so he thinks), and his life as a ploughboy is simple but for the questions that trouble him greatly and which eventually lead to his escape from Perth. Like all of the inhabitants of the enclave, Kell has no family name.

Lesath – An old friend of Alderamin's, slaughtered horribly years before in the Dawn Mountains.

Ligetu – A mysterious flameless energy used for light and heat.

Loefsonu – One of the eoldermen of Uthgaroar. Leofsonu represents the wish to maintain the status quo, and is very resistant to Kell's ideas for change.

Luparo – The Wulf Slaughterer, a mythical being personifying the nemesis of the Wulfen.

Lyblaeca – The most experienced members of the guild of the Thrall Makers, seduced by the Sustren in Thaw into furthering the All Mother's plans.

Maegenwulf – The strength of the pack, in all senses of the word.

Magula – The leader of the wulfen pack Kell encounters at the end of his imprisonment in Thule.

Meodu – Honeyed liquor.

Mirach – Nurse to Alderamin's children. She is slain in the forest by Tarazad drengs.

Modor – Mother.

Mox – 'Mechanical ox'. The mox represents the blending of biology and technology which reached its peak just before the onset of the Ice. The early mention of the mox is a precursor to Kell's realisation that electronic implantation has gone way beyond the control of beasts.

Munin – Wife of Enjeck. They were Kell's last temporary family before he left Perth.

Mwl – A strong horse-like pack animal.

Myrgen – See Alef.

Mythologies – The body of knowledge that every member of the Community is taught as gospel. The Mythologies serve to perpetuate the influence of the All Mother by creating a deep dread of all that supposedly lies outside the enclave. By doubting the truth of the Mythologies, Kell suffers increasingly severe punishments inflicted by the All Mother and the educational system she maintains.

Odal – The main city which lies at the centre of Perth, close to the Central Lake. Odal is the commercial and, so the population supposes, the industrial centre of Perth. No-one bothers to question where new moxen and other animals come from, nor the vehicles which always seem to be in plentiful supply. Kell discovers that a huge industrial complex seems to run automatically behind the façade of the enclave. The word Odal means 'home'.

Onweardnes – The spirit or essence of a thing.

Opticus – See Sky gleams.

Orbs – Faceted metal orbs of various sizes are inextricably linked to the tribe of the Wyrda Craeftum and their destiny known as the Sigel Rad. Small orbs (somewhat larger than a human head) are free-floating and can transmit distant images to the Wyrda. Kell and his friends eventually discover huge globes of similar construction. These are vehicles capable of astonishingly swift travel. All of the orbs are somehow connected to the largely unknown workings of the Universal Wheel.

Othila – This is the village where Kell lives and was raised. The name comes from a rune signifying separation.

Perth – The enclave in which Kell lives. It is an enclosed and totalitarian world, controlled completely (we assume at first) by the All Mother. Perth or Peorth is also one of the 'basic runes' signifying a pot, a container, the womb.

Praeceptor – The head tutor at the Tutorium. His word is traditionally accepted and followed unquestioningly.

Rad – The leader of one of Kano's escapee groups. His name means movement and direction.

Rof – A wulf in Magula's pack.

Saeferth – One of Alderamin's kinsmen.

Sceatt – A gold coin of relatively little value.

Sealt – A savoury nut.

Sebalrai – A young girl whom Feoh rescued from Chertan and his crew of bandits. Sebalrai's rare mental gift acts upon the mind to make her imperceptible. As she develops this power she is able to include others within her area of influence. Although Shamra is Kell's heartbonded, Sebalrai comes to have a special place in his affections.

Seetus – The 'Zen whale', the last great whale of the oceans. Seetus is a semi-mystical being who understands very clearly the relationship between mind and matter and the illusion of the perceived world. Seetus seems able to manipulate matter itself by changing the matrix of space-and-time within which physical objects have their existence.

Setl – A couch.

Shahini Tarazad – The swarm-like tribe of soldier minions ruled absolutely by Helcyrian.

Shamra – Shamra is Kell's 'heartbonded', his chosen mate. She has to undergo a special teaching to develop her outstanding telepathic abilities. Before she escapes from Perth with Kell, Shamra's destiny was to have been an academic at the Tutorium. Subsequently she is captured and initiated into the Sustren, a mystical group consisting only of women. Their purpose is connected intimately with the enhanced mental powers that some people possess, and the occult technology of which Little Sister is a part.

Shaula – Youngest daughter of Alderamin the trader. Years before, Shaula was traumatised by a creature that attacked her camp and slaughtered her father's old friend Lesath.

Shore People – A community led by Faras, whom Kell and his friends encounter after escaping from Perth. The shore people display onemindedness to a high degree: they act as one individual. Furthermore, their genetic structure is changing generation by generation. Soon they will have evolved into ocean-dwelling creatures and will leave the land forever. Their deity, or at least their guide, is Seetus the last great whale.

Sigel Rad – The Sun's Way. It is the ancient Wierd of the Wyrda Craeftum to journey to the sky along this sacred path.

Skjebne – One of Kano's fellow rebels and, eventually, a mentor and close friend to Kell, who delights in and respects the man's boundless curiosity and vast fund of knowledge.

Sky gleams – These are the mysterious lights which drift and swarm across the sky every night in Perth, after the sun has 'ungathered'. Virtually all inhabitants of the Community fear the dark and so very few of them ever witness the spectacle of the sky gleams. Kell goes out of his way to watch them. At first he carries the general belief that they are mysterious elemental beings, or maybe the thoughts of the All Mother herself. Only gradually does he realise that the gleams form part of a sophisticated surveillance system, which Kano calls the opticus.

Skymaster – The first of the Great Orbs of the Wyrda Craeftum to be discovered by Kell and his friends. Others include Cloudfarer, Heavenwalker and Windhover. The human race has a long history of naming important vehicles!

Slean – Literally 'Shadow-Slayers', referring to the notion that a man gives up his humanity (his shadow) to become immortal through the process and ritual of Gebedraedan. Slean flesh is greyish and does not bleed, though it can be damaged beyond the point at which a creature can sustain its quasi-life.

Snaka – Snakes or serpents.

Spedigfeolc – 'Wealthy ones'.

Straetfolc – 'Street folk', the common people.

Sustren – A mystical female group also known as the Sisterhood. Their allegiance lies with the entity expressed through the All Mother in Perth (and in various other guises across the world). The Sustren train their initiates in diverse mental arts of an occult nature. Their purpose seemingly is to incarnate their goddess on Earth.

Sweorian – Be calm.

Swoestor – Sister; a term of endearment.

Synerthy – Thinking-together-all-as-one. This ability, inherent in the Shore Folk and some wulfen packs, confers great power upon the group in whatever they do, from communicating to hunting to prayer.

Thoba – See Alef.

Thorbyorg – The First Eolder of Uthgaroar and leader of the Wyrda Craeftum.

Thrall Makers – Another name for the Erulian, a breed of enchanters who supposedly possess the ability to affect the weave of fate and realise the heart's deepest dreams.

Thule – A dark and mysterious enclave east of Edgetown. It is ruled by Helcyrian, an insane and corrupted dictator.

Tir – An elder wulf in Magula's pack.

Traveller – A semi-sentient vehicle that Kano and his group use to escape from Perth. Alderamin and the people Outside also call them ice-wains.

Tsep – One of the Hreaomus horde who stows aboard Skymaster and befriends Kell and his companions.

Tyr – A young girl terrified by the darkening of Perth. Her name represents the female quality.

Universal Wheel – The central symbol of the Wyrda Craeftum. The actual Universal Wheel is a device which is in contact with and somehow controls all of the orbs possessed by the Wyrda or spoken about in their legends. The Wheel seems to act beyond the boundaries of time and space that mark out the human world.

Unsynnig – Untainted, innocent.

Utewulfen – The 'out wulves', the outrunners of a pack on the move.

Uthgaroar – The ancient mountain home of the Wyrda Craeftum, sacred because of the presence of the Eye of the Rad on a nearby mountaintop.

Verres – A genetically modified armoured boar owned by Zauraq of the Wyrda Craeftum.

Waere – A guard at Edgetown.

Wayd – One of Alderamin's soldiers, killed in the last battle of Edgetown.

Weorthan – This word, from the language of the Wyrda Craeftum and other peoples of the outer world, means 'to be' or 'to become'. It is linked with the notion of destiny or Wierd.

Wierd – This word is of central importance to Kell's life and the world of the Wintering. Its subtle aspects include destiny, 'what will be will be', yet also 'that which is to happen', Wierd (nothing to do with weird) implies the flexibility to act within a framework constructed by higher powers. As Hora might say, Wierd is like a game of cards. The hand you are dealt is your predestiny, but how you play those cards is your free will in life. Wierd is linked with weorthan and with Wyrda, 'the fates'.

Wildedeor – A wulfen word meaning wild and led only by instinct. Used often to describe wulfen packs who lack reflective thought and the gift of onemindedness.

Winsael – A wine drinking hall or tavern.

Wintering – The period, measuring some tens of thousands of years, during which the peoples of the Earth outwaited the terrible cold of a global ice age. The word comes from the first line of Ted Hughes's poem *Snowdrop*: 'Now is the world shrunk tight/Round the mouse's dulled wintering heart.'

Wisp – Feathery seeds that move with apparent purpose through the airs of Perth.

Wraith – Wraiths or phantoms are occasionally seen drifting along the roadways of Perth. The folklore of the enclave remains ambiguous as to their nature. Perhaps they are ghosts of the dead, or illusions created by the All Mother. They seem to be sentient because they react to whoever encounters them. The wraiths that Kell meets always remind him of Shamra.

Wrynn – A Thrall Maker but also something of a maverick influence among his kind. He embodies aspects of the Trickster archetype, as does Kell, ensuring his kin do not become too set or complacent in their ways.

Wulfen – A species of the outer world modified from preglacial wolves to survive the ice. Some wulfen packs rely almost solely on their base instincts, while in others intelligence has flourished. This ability to reason has been enhanced by the evolution of a form of telepathy called onemindedness, which allows the individuals in a pack to hunt with the co-ordination of a single animal.

Wulfenhoard – The accumulated wisdom of the wulfen, whose wealth lies in their songs and sagas.

Wulfensweor – Wulf cousin, also used as a term of great respect and affection.

Wulfmaer – A wulf in Magula's pack.

Wyldewulf – 'The one who roams in wild places' and an elder wulf in Magula's pack. Wyldewulf sacrifices himself at the conclusion of *Storm* to save his friends.

Wyrda Craeftum – A tribe of mercenaries united by their unique and startling appearance and their commitment to the Sigel Rad. This translates as 'the sun's way' and represents long-lost knowledge of Man's exploration of space before the Wintering began. The name Wyrda Craeftum means 'with skill given by the Wierds'. This is a reference to the 'loom of fate', a woven predestiny in which the Wyrda and other peoples believe.

Wyrtegemang – A spicy tobacco-like leaf much favoured by the Wyrda Craeftum.

Zauraq – The first warrior of the Wyrda Craeftum whom Alderamin's party meet on the outskirts of Thule. Zauraq, like a number of the Craeftum, earns his keep as a mercenary. Whatever these people do, however, it is only to fulfil their tribe's destiny – a fated path to the stars known as the Sigel Rad or Sun's Way.

A note on the language:
Many of the names, terms and mystical concepts used in The Wintering derive from Anglo-Saxon, Norse and Celtic traditions, although I have adapted them freely to suit my own purposes. I love the ring and rhythm of these words and wanted to include them to give added texture to the writing. I also wanted to sprinkle the story with words and phrases that at first sight would seem strange, but which might become oddly familiar in the end because they go back to the roots of our language. Logically, the language of people existing thousands of years hence would likely be completely alien to us – much more so than Chaucer's English sounds to the modern ear – but I wanted to create some sense of it having evolved, while (obviously) allowing readers to understand what was being said.

Two books I found especially useful in my 'word weaving' were *The Earliest English Poems*, translated by Michael Alexander, Penguin Classics (1970) and *Wordcraft*, a dictionary and thesaurus of Old English by Stephen Pollington, Anglo Saxon Books (1999).

It may also be of a little interest to you to know that some of the character names and a couple of the place names in The Wintering are based on runes and runic terms. For instance, *Feoh* is a rune signifying ambition satisfied and love fulfilled (according to the writer Ralph Blum): it is used ironically in the story. By contrast, *Kell* comes simply from 'Celtic' because he embodies a number of important beliefs about the cosmos which derive from that culture.

S.B.